UNDERWORLD
EVOLUTION

UNDERWORLD
E V O L U T I O N

A Novelization by Greg Cox

Based on Characters Created by
Kevin Grevioux and Len Wiseman & Danny McBride

Story by Len Wiseman & Danny McBride

Screenplay by Danny McBride

POCKET **STAR** BOOKS

New York   London   Toronto   Sydney

An *Original* Publication of POCKET BOOKS

A Pocket Star Book published by
POCKET BOOKS, a division of Simon & Schuster, Inc.
1230 Avenue of the Americas, New York, NY 10020

ISBN-13:   978-0-7434-8073-4
ISBN-10:   0-7434-8073-2

This Pocket Star Books paperback edition January 2006

10 9 8 7 6 5 4 3 2 1

POCKET STAR BOOKS and colophon are registered trademarks of Simon & Schuster, Inc.

Manufactured in the United States of America

For information regarding special discounts for bulk purchases, please contact Simon & Schuster Special Sales at 1-800-456-6798 or business@simonandschuster.com.

UNDERWORLD
EVOLUTION

Prologue

*T*he very memory of that night was like a recurring nightmare. . . .

The fog was cold and damp, and an icy wind blew through the shadow-cloaked forest, but Selene barely noticed the chill. Autumn trees, bare and skeletal, clawed at her as she ran frantically through the woods outside her home. Her heart pounded so loudly she felt certain it would burst. Glancing back over her shoulder, she glimpsed vague, indistinct figures moving through the mist behind her. A full moon shone through the barren tree branches overhead. Storm clouds drifted across the moon like a veil.

They were chasing her. Whatever they were.

Only nineteen years old, Selene knew she was soon to die.

Heartrending screams ripped through the night, sending fresh jolts of fear and anguish through the young woman's soul. Her dark brown hair streamed wildly behind her. Panic filled her wide chestnut eyes. Undried tears streaked her cheeks. A thin linen nightgown provided scant protection from the cold. Spilled blood streaked her gown, glistening wetly in the moonlight. The sticky red fluid had soaked

1

through the fabric, causing the linen to cling to her skin. Bare feet raced over a carpet of fallen leaves.

Thunder boomed above her. A jagged bolt of lightning sliced the sky in twain. Rain poured down in sheets, drenching Selene. The forest floor turned to mud beneath her feet. Muck oozed between her toes and she had to fight to keep her balance on the slippery leaves. If she fell, her pursuers would be on her in an instant. Chances were, she would never rise again.

Who are they? she wondered. *What are they?*

More screams penetrated the darkness. The blood-chilling ululations came not from human throats. *Something is in the stables,* she realized. The horses sounded as though they were being torn to pieces, which might well be the case. Selene had already witnessed far worse this evening.

The blood upon her gown was not her own, but it could not have been any more precious to her before it had gushed from the severed throats of her mother, sister, and baby nieces. She had left the butchered bodies of her nearest and dearest strewn upon the wooden floor of their violated home when she had fled madly into the night, seeking out the only family left to her.

Father! she thought desperately. He had gone out to calm the horses only moments before the mysterious invaders had attacked their home. *Please, God, let him live still. Do not leave me alone with these . . . creatures!*

The stables loomed before her, barely visible in the mist and gloom. As she drew nearer the large wooden structure, she saw that the barn door was open wide. Had her father drawn back the door while checking on the horses, or had the monsters already invaded the stables as well? Utter blackness shrouded the interior of the stable, offering no clue as to what might lurk within, but she could hear the frightened horses whinnying in alarm. The poor animals sounded absolutely terrified.

Dare she enter the stables alone? Glancing once more over her shoulder at the hellish shapes surging through the fog, she realized she had no other choice. The sturdy building was her only hope for sanctuary, no matter how meager.

Trusting her life to fate, she dashed through the doorway into the stables. A timber roof provided welcome relief from the pouring rain. Flashes of lightning and sporadic moonbeams filtered through the roof to provide some slight degree of illumination. Crazed horses bucked violently in their stalls, terrified by the storm and God only knew what else. Their hooves pounded against the solid oak doors trapping them in their stalls. They had worked themselves into a lather, the sweat gleaming on their quivering bodies.

Selene could not spare a second to see to the horses. Before her pursuers could catch up with her, she slammed the door shut and bolted it in place. She prayed that the heavy oaken barrier would keep out the bloodthirsty monsters behind her, but feared that no power on earth could truly save her. It was as though Death itself had come lunging out of the fog this night, to strike down her loved ones one by one.

Breathing hard, she turned away from the door. Water streamed from her hair and gown. The dank air reeked of wet hay, dung, horse sweat, and blood. It took a moment for her eyes to adjust to the darker gloom of the sealed barn, and she staggered forward uncertainly. Another flash of lightning pierced the darkness, revealing a supine figure lying motionless upon the hay-strewn floor between the stalls. The sprawled body was as still and silent as the grave.

3

No! Selene thought. An icy certainty spread through her veins, and she felt her last vestige of hope succumb to despair. She stumbled toward the lifeless form, already knowing what she would find. Her brown eyes brimmed with tears.

"Father . . ."

The face of the corpse was contorted with fear, but Selene could not fail to recognize the kindly, bearded visage that had so often looked upon her with warmth and affection. Her father's throat had been torn open, as though by a rabid animal. Bright red blood was splattered all over him, just as it had been on the savaged bodies back at their house. His limbs were twisted and askew. Broken shards of bone jutted from his fractured arms and legs. Glassy eyes stared blankly into oblivion.

Her father was dead—just like the rest of her family.

She was alone.

Why us? she thought in agony. *What did we ever do to deserve this?* She dropped to her knees beside the body, heedless of the blood spreading out from beneath her father's gory remains. *My father was a good man. A decent man.* Violent sobs rocked her body. Tears fell upon the dead metalsmith's face.

A deafening crash jolted her from her grief. She spun around toward the barn door, which shivered beneath the force of powerful blows. *A battering ram?* she thought in confusion as the oak door was smashed to splinters. It crashed to the floor with a resounding thud that echoed loudly throughout the stables.

Selene turned away from the door, back toward her father. She squeezed her eyes tightly shut. Although Death had surely come for her, she had no desire to look it in the face. Trembling, she awaited the fatal blow that would sever

4

her soul from her body. She could only pray that her end would be swift.

Soon, she promised herself, *I will be reunited with my family in paradise.*

Footsteps trod heavily on the blood-soaked floor of the stables. The horses reared up within their stalls, positively maddened with fear. Selene heard the footsteps approach her at a measured pace. She braced herself for the searing pain of razor-sharp fangs or claws sinking into her flesh. She imagined her own blood spouting from her throat.

Instead a steady hand fell firmly yet gently upon her shoulder. She held her breath, expecting the hand to move to her throat, but it remained where it was, as though to comfort her. Puzzled, she opened her eyes and looked behind her.

No monster stood above her. No pillaging berserker. The hand belonged to a regal stranger clad in magnificent black plate armor. An ornate black helmet, of Corinthian design, offered only a glimpse of the man's pale features, but could not conceal the stranger's almost palpable aura of strength and authority. A massive broadsword, so large that it seemed a marvel that any mortal man could lift it, hung at his side. Compassion shone in his luminous blue eyes.

"They've gone," Viktor said.

Can this be true? Selene wondered. *Am I truly saved?* She eyed the armored warrior warily, torn between suspicion and an urgent desire to accept the comfort she so desperately needed. Her entire world had been torn away from her. *What will become of me now?*

Viktor reached down and gently helped her to her feet. Her legs were unsteady, and she would have fallen, save that he took her in his arms the same way her father had. She rested her weight against his, unable to run or fight back any longer. His strong arms held her up and she surrendered to his sheltering embrace. For the first time since this nightmare had begun, she felt safe and protected. "All is well, child," he said. "You need fear no longer. The beasts that slew your family have been driven away."

Praise the saints! Selene thought. An overwhelming sense of relief washed over her.

Closing her eyes once more, Selene failed to see her rescuer slyly wipe the blood from his lips. A stray beam of moonlight caught the gleam of Viktor's pointed fangs.

Nor did Selene see another figure emerge from the murky depths of the barn, not far from her father's body. Soren was likewise clad in black armor. His azure eyes glowed eerily in the darkness. Fresh blood glistened upon his ivory fangs and bushy black beard.

Her father's blood.

A second vampire crept from the blackness. Kraven's handsome face was flushed with stolen blood. A mane of shoulder-length black hair framed a clean-shaven, aristocratic countenance. Cruel blue eyes ravished Selene's trembling form. He leered at her in lustful anticipation.

Moving as silently as shadows, the two predators stalked toward Selene, awaiting only Viktor's command to fall upon the unsuspecting mortal maiden. Her back to them, her tearstained face resting against Viktor's armored shoulder, she had no idea that she was still in mortal danger. Soren thirsted for her blood. Kraven was more interested in her tender young flesh.

But Viktor raised his hand to ward them off. Gently stroking Selene's wet hair, he quietly signaled them to back away. A look of bitter disappointment crossed Kraven's face, but he knew better than to defy his master. With Soren, he furtively receded back into the shadows.

Selene never even knew they were there.

"There, there, child," Viktor cooed in her ear. "You're not alone anymore. You shall never be alone again. . . ."

Thunder pealed in the night.

Chapter One

Six centuries later . . .

The crack of a gunshot broke the stillness of the night. Startled crows scattered from the branches of a bare winter tree. The roar of an enraged beast sent a collective shudder through the nocturnal forest. More shots followed in rapid succession, the blaring noise muffled somewhat by the heavy snow falling from the sky. The fierce roar gave way to the high-pitched howl of a dying animal. A massive body crashed to the earth.

Selene turned away from the fallen beast. Smoke rose from the barrel of her Beretta automatic pistol. She stood atop a jagged cliff face, which overlooked the hilly woodlands northeast of Budapest. The snowstorm, which had arrived unexpectedly only a few hours ago, continued to blanket the wilderness beneath a carpet of fresh white powder. A glossy black trench coat was draped over her shoulders. Lustrous black leather clothed her lithe frame. High black boots sank into the snow beneath her feet. A cold wind rustled her dark brown hair.

She brushed an errant snowflake from her cheek. Her alabaster features betrayed not the slightest hint of emotion.

Killing was nothing new to her. Indeed, it had been all she'd ever known, ever since that fateful night some six-hundred-odd years ago. Selene was a frightened child no more. Now she was a Death Dealer, a vengeance seeker. . . .

Until earlier tonight, when she had discovered that everything she believed she knew was a lie. Her friends were her enemies, her enemies, victims, and everyone she had killed over the centuries, a crime. Once again, her entire world had turned upside down.

It had not been a good night.

She strode away from the fallen beast without a single backward glance. The edge of the cliff dropped away sharply in front of her, but she fearlessly walked straight up to the precipice—and right over the brink.

Gravity seized her and she plunged toward the woodlands one hundred feet below. She coolly ejected a clip from the Beretta as she fell, unconcerned by the snow-covered ground that seemed to be rushing up at her at breakneck speed. Her leather-clad form plummeted gracefully through the branches of the trees, expertly missing the towering tree trunks that threatened to impale her. It was a myth that only wooden stakes could kill a vampire, but that didn't mean the trees posed no danger to her.

Selene knew what she was doing, however.

Her boots touched down at the foot of the cliff and she marched forward, not even breaking her stride. She deftly snapped a loaded clip into the Beretta.

We have to keep moving, she thought. *Dawn will be here too soon.*

A figure awaited her in the woods. She strode past him without missing a beat.

"Let's go," she said.

Michael Corvin hurried after her. The young doctor

was ruggedly handsome, with light brown hair and a face that somehow retained a hint of innocence despite everything he had endured over the last few nights. His brown leather jacket looked hardly adequate for the wintry weather, but he was no longer as vulnerable to the cold as he had once been. Three nights ago, he had been human, subject to the usual mortal frailties. Now he was something else altogether, and not even Selene truly knew what that meant.

She heard him trudging through the snow after her. "Impressive," he said to her back. An American accent betrayed his origins.

Killing that beast? Selene had already put that encounter out of her mind. Exterminating werewolves was just an ordinary night's work to her. It was what she lived for.

Or rather, it used to be.

Now she wasn't sure about anything.

"Who was following us?" Michael asked. Anxiety colored his voice. He still wasn't used to hunting and being hunted, as she was.

"Not us. You."

"Me?"

She paused and turned to face him. *He should know the hard truth,* she thought. *Our lives may depend on it.*

"They were lycan. Like you." She glanced up at the ridge behind them. "They can sense one of their own for miles."

Technically, of course, Michael was no longer just a lycan. He had become a hybrid, blending the traits of both vampires and werewolves. But apparently enough of the wolfen taint remained in his blood to call out to others of that savage breed.

Lucky us, she thought.

She walked on, while Michael struggled to assimilate

11

what she had just told him. "So, on your own, they couldn't track you?"

Selene gave him a knowing look. Not for the first time, she asked herself why she kept putting herself in jeopardy for a stranger she had met only a few nights before.

He saved my life, she recalled. *And exposed the lie that my life had become.*

She left him standing bewildered in the snow, while she trekked on through a stand of tall pine trees. Her mind was already looking ahead to the challenges and dangers to come. A handful of renegade werewolves were the least of her worries.

Viktor had died at her hands, his skull cloven in twain by his own sword. It was a fitting death for one who had lied to her since the moment they had first met, who had kept on deceiving her throughout the long, bloody centuries. It was Viktor, she had discovered, who had been truly responsible for the slaughter of her mortal family, not the feral lycans she had blamed ever since the night Viktor had first transformed her into a vampire. She had been hunting the wrong enemy for her entire undead existence.

Yes, Viktor had deserved his grisly end, but his death was not without consequences. Killing the powerful vampire Elder had turned Selene from the hunter into the hunted. Her own kind would soon be united against her, along with what remained of the lycan horde. Her only hope of survival was to reach the last remaining Elder before her final punishment could be decreed. She could only pray that the truth would spare her life.

Soon, Marcus will take the throne, and the tide of anger and retribution will spill out into the night. A chill that had nothing to do with the inclement weather ran down her spine. *And soon, I will become the hunted.*

Chapter Two

*H*ours had passed in the silent crypt. A trickle of blood pooled atop a polished bronze disk bearing an elegantly engraved letter *M*.

For Marcus.

Crimson rivulets seeped through the edges of the burnished hatch, slithering downward into the buried sarcophagus, where the last surviving Elder hung upside down in his tomb, like a slumbering vampire bat. For over two hundred years he had hung thus, hibernating deep beneath the earth while his fellow Elders took their turns ruling over the coven. One above, two below . . . that had been the way of things ever since he and Viktor and Amelia had agreed to the eternal cycle of the Chain. Undisturbed within his sarcophagus, Marcus had no way of knowing that both Viktor and Amelia had perished this night.

Two centuries of fasting had taken its toll on the Elder's appearance. Dry, blackened skin was stretched tightly over his emaciated frame, so that he resembled a mummy more than a vampire. His once-handsome face had shriveled into a grimacing, skull-like visage. His eyes were squeezed tightly shut at the bottom of sunken, black sockets. Yellowed fangs were locked together in a frozen scowl. Only a few thin strands of hair still clung to his desiccated scalp. His rib cage showed through the papery skin covering his chest. By all indications, the Elder's withered form looked dead beyond all hope of resurrection.

But then the first few drops of blood fell upon his parched lips. More blood trickled down his body into his waiting mouth, bringing renewed life to the skeletal creature. A quiescent heart, shrunken to the size of a walnut, began to pulsate once more, faintly at first, but with increasing strength. Atrophied lungs whistled as they sucked in the dank, stagnant air of the tomb.

What is this? Marcus thought dimly, as his consciousness began to emerge from centuries of darksome slumber. *Has the time come again for my Awakening?*

Perhaps, but this Awakening felt very different from those in the past. A peculiar sensation seemed to spread throughout his body, propelled by the very beating of his heart. Within his veins, lycan blood mixed with his own, merging in an unexpected alchemical reaction. He felt a change come over him, a fundamental transformation in his very nature. Power such as he had never known surged through his veins.

His eyes snapped open, revealing a pair of jet-black orbs.

Hybrid eyes.

A.D. 1202

The village lay in ruins. Flames licked the thatch roofs of peasant hovels. Smoke rose from the charred remains of shops and wagons. Prodigious amounts of blood had been splashed upon the snow-covered streets and market square. The wasted blood glistened beneath the light of a full moon,

14

turning the once-white snow into gory slush. The tantalizing smell of so much blood made the vampire's mouth water, despite the dire matters weighing on his mind.

Oh, my brother, Marcus Corvinus thought mournfully. *What have you done?*

Bodies were strewn everywhere. Men, women, children . . . their throats ripped out as though by a savage beast. Entrails spilled from corpses that had been sliced open by powerful claws. Many of the villagers were still in their nightclothes, death having come for them while the tiny hamlet slept. Their lifeless faces were frozen in expressions of utter shock and horror. Despite abundant evidence of an animal attack, too much flesh remained upon their bones for the townspeople to have been killed for food. Instead they had been slaughtered for sport.

The isolated village was located in a shallow valley surrounded by dense woodlands. Snowcapped pines and firs bore mute witness to the grisly scene, while an eerie silence reigned over the valley. There were no whimpers of pain, no desperate cries for succor. No sobbing kinsmen mourned their dead. Marcus heard only the crackling of the flames and the crash of collapsing timbers.

The funereal silence spoke volumes. There were no survivors.

We are too late, Marcus thought.

"Yet again," Viktor said, "we arrive to witness his aftermath. But the onslaught ends tonight."

"We must move quickly," Amelia reminded him. "Or we will be overwhelmed."

The three Elders surveyed the slaughtered village from atop a slope overlooking the valley. They sat astride their armored warhorses, their faces grave behind their crested helmets. Like their steeds, they were clad in fearsome black plate armor. Intricate runes adorned the finely made armor, which gleamed like polished ebony in the moonlight. Conversing atop their coal-black mounts, they resembled three-quarters of the Four Horsemen, arriving belatedly in the wake of the missing horseman: Death himself.

A company of armored Death Dealers accompanied the Elders. Their weapons drawn, the vampire warriors awaited the Elders' commands. Azure eyes glowed beneath the flickering light of their upraised torches. The pungent smell of the blood had the soldiers all on edge. They bared their fangs. They licked their lips.

The vampires had not yet fed tonight. This massacre was not their doing.

Viktor turned to Marcus. "Is he still here?"

Marcus nodded reluctantly. His youthful appearance, evident even through his Corinthian-style helmet, belied his true age and immortality. His reddish brown hair, and neatly trimmed mustache and beard, held not a trace of gray. Indeed, he looked several decades younger than Viktor, even though he was actually the older of the two.

"Viktor, he must not be harmed."

"I gave you my word, did I not?" Viktor turned his horse around to address their troops. He raised his voice. "Burn the bodies. Search the outbuildings."

The Death Dealers rode forward, spreading out into the ruined village. Their torches added to the glow of the burning carts and buildings. Marcus spurred his own horse onward, anxious to join in the search.

"Marcus!" Viktor called out sharply.

What is it? Marcus wondered. He pulled back on the reins. Steam blasted from the nostrils of his impatient steed. He looked back at Viktor.

"Stay with me," his fellow Elder instructed.

For a moment, Marcus considered disregarding Viktor's request. They were equals, after all, even though he and Amelia tended to defer to Viktor on military matters. The other Elder had been an experienced general and warlord even before he'd become immortal. Marcus gazed intently at the burning village before reluctantly turning around his horse and rejoining Viktor and Amelia. He had no wish to provoke Viktor unless it was absolutely necessary.

I may need his goodwill before this terrible night is over, Marcus thought. *For my brother's sake.*

The rustic hamlet reminded Istvan of the small Wallachian village in which he had grown up, before he had been granted the boon of immortality and recruited into the service of the Elders. He seldom thought of his mortal days anymore, but the familiar setting stirred long-dormant memories. A cold rage flared within him. These butchered villagers might well have been his own family and neighbors, a couple of mortal lifetimes ago. Lowly and short-lived as they were, they had deserved better than this.

This atrocity cannot go unpunished, he thought vengefully. *The Beast must pay.*

With his fellow Death Dealers, he dismounted from his horse and stalked the narrow streets. Bloodstained snow muffled the tread of their heavy iron boots. Flaming torches set fire to gutted corpses, creating grisly bonfires throughout the streets and square. The nauseating aroma of burning flesh joined the smoky smell of the doomed buildings. Istvan's gorge rose.

But it was not enough to merely torch the bodies lying outdoors. Istvan knew they could not afford to leave a single

17

ravaged corpse unburned. They had to search the shops and homes as well—or suffer the consequences.

We don't need another disaster like last time. We've lost too many men already. . . .

A peasant cottage caught his eye, and he gestured to one of his comrades, a Death Dealer named Radu. Istvan had lost his own torch in their breakneck ride to the village, but Radu still had a serviceable brand. The other vampire nodded and they approached the cottage together. A wooden door creaked on its hinges as Istvan kicked it open. Leading with their swords, the two men entered the hovel through a haze of smoke and shadow. Vampiric eyes penetrated the murk, seeing the humble furnishings one would expect to see in such a lowly domicile: wooden stools, a low table, a few straw pallets for beds, and a hearth in the center of the hut, safely distant from the crude wattle-and-daub walls. Dying coals glowed within the hearth.

A mauled corpse lay sprawled upon the packed-earth floor. The body belonged to a full-grown man clad in the torn remains of a linen nightshirt. His face and torso had been shredded by gargantuan claws. Exposed ribs jutted from his open chest. Gobbets of bloody meat still clung to the splintered bones, which were scored by deep claw marks. The man's heart and guts were missing, no doubt vanished down the Beast's gullet. Istvan wondered briefly what had become of the man's wife and children. Were their bodies among the corpses burning in the streets?

He turned toward Radu. "Give me the torch."

The sooner this disgusting chore was concluded, the better. Then they could move on to the more important task of tracking down the loathsome animal responsible for the carnage.

He shall not escape us again, the Death Dealer vowed.

18

Radu handed him the burning brand. Istvan turned back toward the corpse.

Before he could ignite the lifeless carcass, however, a bestial roar erupted from the dead man's throat. The "corpse" sprang to its feet, already in the throes of a grotesque transformation. Glassy mortal eyes turned into feral cobalt orbs. A canine snout protruded from the scarred face, which appeared to be healing itself with preternatural speed. Jagged fangs flashed within the creature's open jaws. A new heart began to form within the sundered chest cavity. Fresh entrails, writhing like overgrown worms, blossomed beneath the heart, which beat with unnatural life. A hairy hide swiftly spread over the creature's torso, hiding the pulsating organs from view. Human nails sharpened into vicious-looking talons. Thick, black bristles sprouted from his face and skin.

Hellfire! Istvan cursed silently. He backed away, almost bumping into Radu. *We're too late!*

Still wearing the remnants of his shredded nightshirt, the newborn lycanthrope snarled like a rabid dog. His savage gaze swept the cramped interior of the cottage, searching for a way out. The two Death Dealers stood between him and the front door, so his crazed eyes turned rapidly toward the rear of the chamber. Before the startled vampires could recover from their shock, the man-beast slammed into the back door, knocking it off its hinges with a single lunge. The door hit the ground with a tremendous crash, and the lycan scrambled out of the murky cottage into the moonlight.

Blast it! Istvan thought as the creature escaped. Still holding his useless torch, he knew he had to warn the others. He shouted at the top of his lungs:

"*They're turning!*"

The frantic cry sent a jolt through every vampire within earshot. Amelia sat upright in her saddle and saw her brother Elders do the same. The small complement of Death Dealers who had remained behind to guard the Elders tensed up within their armor. They raised their swords high in readiness for the battle to come. Amelia heard muttered curses among the soldiers.

It's begun, she realized.

Resting her hand upon the stock of her crossbow, she scanned the village for any sign of the enemy. Exquisite blue eyes spotted a misshapen figure racing into a darkened alley between two crude peasant hovels. The creature looked to be half-transformed already.

She was not the only one to spy the wretched beast. "There!" hollered one of her foot soldiers. He pointed one finger of a metal gauntlet at the same alley.

Amelia required no further prompting. In a blur of motion, she drew her crossbow and took aim at the fleeing lycan. A silver-tipped bolt sprang from the loaded weapon, slicing through the smoky air and striking its brutish target in the arm. The lycan howled in pain and glared back at the vampires. Little of humanity remained in his monstrous features. Cobalt eyes peered out from beneath a sloping brow. Tufted ears tapered to a point. A fleshy black muzzle grimaced. Wincing in pain, the creature ducked into the waiting alley. Desperate to escape the Death Dealers, he paid little heed to the smoldering corpse lying in the snow outside the alley.

"After him!" Amelia commanded. Although born female, she had never been one to shrink from battle. To her mind, immortality was too short to waste it cloistered away like some helpless mortal damsel. She spurred her horse down the snowy slope into the nameless village. A pair of mounted Death Dealers rode after her. "Let him not escape!"

In their haste to catch up with their quarry, the vampires also ignored the charred and smoking corpse upon the ground. The armored chargers galloped past the dead peasant, barely missing the body with their hooves. None saw the corpse's eyes peel open, exposing bestial cobalt orbs. No one witnessed the still and lifeless body start to convulse violently. Bones cracked and twisted loudly as the murdered villager came back to life, caught in the grip of an excruciating metamorphosis. A tortured groan escaped the lycan's contorted jaws, but the pain-wracked utterance went unheard.

By now, Amelia and her men had followed the first lycan into the alley. She drew back on the reins, slowing her horse, while she searched the narrow passage for their prey. The stock of her crossbow rested against the burnished metal protecting her cheek. At first, she could discern no trace of the creature, but then she spotted the monster's shadow upon a moonlit wall deeper within the alley. Silhouetted against the crude stone wall, the shadow depicted the final stages of the unfortunate villager's transformation.

The Change was accelerating at a phenomenal rate. The shadow expanded in size as the lycan gained weight and stature by the second. The frenzied lycan tore at his clothing, stripping himself of any last vestige of civilization. His limbs stretched from their sockets, as though he were being tortured upon the rack. A human scream devolved into an anguished howl.

Poor thing, Amelia thought. She felt a moment of pity for the ill-fated villager, who had surely not asked for such a ghastly fate. Compassion would not stay her hand, however. It was too late for the lycan now. Like the rest of his abhorrent kind, he needed to be put down like a rabid dog. *Death is the only mercy I can offer.*

She used the shadow to gauge the lycan's position. Judging from the angle of the moonlight, the creature was directly ahead, farther down the alley. She led the Death Dealers forward—and found herself face-to-face with their brutish prey.

The transformation was complete. A full-fledged werewolf now stood revealed at the far end of the alley. Standing erect upon his hind legs, the towering beast was over seven feet tall. Coarse black fur covered his naked body. Foam dripped from his gaping jaws. Maddened by the Change, he growled at the mounted vampires, exposing a mouthful of serrated fangs. He slashed madly at the air with claws the size of daggers. His hot, fetid breath misted in the cold night air.

A stone wall blocked the end of the alley, leaving the werewolf cornered. His lips peeled back from his incisors as he roared at the hunters defiantly. He lunged at Amelia, his claws outstretched before him.

The beast was fast, but her crossbow was faster still. A speeding bolt struck the werewolf in midair, lodging deep within his shaggy chest. Two more bolts found their marks as Amelia's men fired their own crossbows at the beast. The silver tips pierced the werewolf's heart and he dropped like a stone onto the muddy floor of the alley. Silver was poison to his noxious breed. A vile ichor, infected with the lycan taint, oozed from the werewolf's wounds. This time he would not rise again. His transformed body retained its bestial aspect. Not even death could restore his humanity.

Another pitiful cur disposed of, she thought approvingly. She removed her stifling helmet and savored the invigorating bite of the wind upon her face. Lustrous black hair, now soaked with sweat, was plastered to an elegant visage worthy of a Grecian goddess. *By the dark gods, I grow weary of this butchery.*

Shouts, screams, and fierce howls invaded the alley from all directions. Her charger reared up in alarm. Clearly, the other Death Dealers were engaged in similar confrontations throughout the village. Amelia recalled the multitude of bodies the original beast had left behind and knew that every one of those bodies now represented a potential menace. For all she knew, she and the other vampires were already outnumbered.

Not again, she thought. *Must we fight this same struggle over and over?*

She turned her horse about, intent on joining the battle outside the alley. She thrust another quarrel into her crossbow. The first of her Death Dealers galloped out of the alley ahead of her, while the second rode up behind her. "Make haste!" she urged them both. "Our comrades require our—"

The crash of shattered wood and plaster drowned out her voice as, without warning, another werewolf smashed through the crumbling wall of the hut on her left. The noisome beast slammed into one of the mounted Death Dealers, knocking both man and steed to the ground. Metal armor thudded against the ground and the frightened horse whinnied in panic. Wolfen claws slashed at the charger's exposed underside. Blood sprayed from deep gashes in the quivering horseflesh. The destrier's rider found himself trapped beneath the weight of his own steed. He struggled to extricate himself, shoving at the armored horse with both hands. His crossbow lay uselessly upon the snow, out of his reach. The werewolf snapped at him with hungry jaws.

"Help me!" he cried. "For mercy's sake!"

Amelia's own horse reared up in alarm and she had to

fight to regain control of the terrified animal. She almost dropped her own crossbow, but managed to hold on to the reins and weapon both. The first rider, already gone from the alley, frantically yanked his horse around, but was too far away to do any good.

Drawn by the clamor, a vampire foot soldier came running into the alley. He charged at the werewolf from behind, swinging a silver-edged battle-axe. The axe sank deep into the monster's shaggy back, cleaving its spine. The werewolf died instantly, collapsing against the bleeding body of the downed horse. The trapped Death Dealer let out a gasp of relief. His rescuer wrested his axe from the creature's body.

Well done, Amelia thought. Looking more closely, she recognized the axe-wielding warrior as Drago, a once-mortal soldier who had only recently been initiated into the coven. As far as she was concerned, his courageous actions had proven him more than worthy of the great blessing that had been bestowed upon him. *I must commend him to his superiors later, should he survive this.*

She opened her mouth to praise the soldier, only to be interrupted by a ferocious roar. A hideous figure, engulfed in red-hot flames, rose up behind Drago. Amelia vaguely recognized the blazing corpse that, only minutes ago, had lain outside the alley. The resurrected visitor was still caught in the throes of his dreadful transformation, so that it was hard to say what tormented him most, the awful agonies of the Change or the searing flames racing over his body. His limbs jerked spasmodically as he snarled and gnashed his jagged teeth. The smell of burning flesh and fur assailed Amelia's nostrils.

Time to put this wretched thing out of his misery.

She raised her crossbow, but there was no need; Drago

24

wheeled about and swung his bloody axe at the flaming lycan. The silver edge of the axe sliced cleanly through the werewolf's neck. Trailing a shower of sparks, the monster's head went flying from his shoulders. The werewolf's blazing skull rebounded off a nearby wall, while the headless body dropped to the ground. Blood gushed from its bisected throat. The werewolf's limbs twitched convulsively.

Drago had little time to savor his victory. With a savage roar, a third werewolf pounced from the roof of a smoldering cottage. The beast tackled Drago, knocking the startled Death Dealer to the ground. He landed hard amidst the bloody slush, with the berserk werewolf right on top of him. The impact drove the breath from Drago's lungs. His mighty battle-axe slipped from his fingers.

"Drago!" Amelia cried out. Her finger hesitated upon the trigger of her crossbow. The Death Dealer and his subhuman attacker were so close together that she feared she might hit Drago instead. Her horse backed away from the thrashing figures. She peered anxiously down the stock of the crossbow, waiting for a clear shot.

But the maniacal werewolf never gave her a chance. A voracious maw closed on Drago's face, crushing it between two powerful jaws. Bone crunched loudly. A geyser of cold vampire blood exploded over the werewolf's snout and furry pelt.

No! Amelia thought, shocked by Drago's sudden demise. The death of mortals was bad enough, but the death of yet another immortal . . . ! The valiant young Death Dealer might well have lived for centuries if not for the werewolf's mindless savagery, yet he had been cut down as readily as any short-lived human. *What an appalling waste!*

What pity she had for the transformed villager vanished

in an instant. An icy fury raced through her veins. Her finger squeezed tightly on the trigger.

A silver-tipped bolt avenged Drago's murder.

But there were still many more beasts to slay . . . including the foul originator of this obscene contagion.

One way or another, she vowed, *this plague ends tonight.*

Chapter Three

*E*lsewhere in the village, another corpse lurched to life, well on its way toward joining the pack of freshly created werewolves. The man-beast leapt to his feet. Yellow fangs gleamed between his jaws as he threw back his head to keen at the moon . . . only to have his howl cut short by the bloodstained silver blade that suddenly erupted from his chest. Eyes wide, he looked down to find himself impaled upon a vampire's sword.

Only a death rattle escaped his throat.

One down, Marcus thought. With a grunt of satisfaction, he withdrew his blade from between the dead lycan's shoulder blades. The werewolf dropped onto the snow like a marionette whose strings had been cut. *How many more to go?*

His horse pawed at the bloody slush as Marcus sat astride his steed at the fringe of the conflict. He removed his helmet to better survey the brutal fray unfolding before him. His hair was combed back from his high, pale forehead. Reddish brown tresses fell past his shoulders. Marcus had been called handsome in his time, but vanity was the least of his concerns at the moment. He frowned at the riotous melee greeting his eyes.

Their tardy attempt to cleanse the contaminated village had turned into a debacle. Everywhere he looked, Death Dealers battled reanimated corpses in various stages of transformation. Driven berserk by the moon and the vile taint in their blood, the former inhabitants of the village sought to tear the vampire warriors apart, pitting their untested claws and fangs against the Death Dealers' arms and armor. Fully transformed werewolves towered about their vampiric foes, taking advantage of their superior size and strength. They sprang from the rooftops and from beneath heavy snowdrifts. Packs of werewolves attacked in numbers, converging on the embattled Death Dealers from all directions.

A female werewolf, still wearing the tattered remains of a linen nightgown, jabbed her claws into the eyes of an unlucky Death Dealer whose helmet failed to save him from her attack. Blinded, he swung out wildly with a mace studded with silver spikes. The mace smashed in the left side of the she-wolf's face, knocking her to the ground. Her agonized yelps steered his hand as, blood streaming from the slit in his helmet, he hammered her with his mace again and again, until two more werewolves pounced on him from behind. . . .

It was chaos.

Around the outskirts of the village, a few mutilated bodies remained inert. These, Marcus guessed, had been the last to die, their attacker striking them down as the poor mortals had fled for the dubious shelter of the surrounding woods. He knew it was only a matter of minutes before they, too, rose as werewolves.

This foul contagion spreads like the plague.

Viktor rode up beside Marcus. Behind his helmet, his

face was grim. He shouted to be heard above the fray. *"Retreat to the woods!"*

"No!" Marcus yelled back. "I will stay and fight." He brandished his bloody sword. "You need my help."

Viktor shook his head. "If you die, we all die. Now go!"

For the second time that night, Marcus contemplated defying Viktor's command. It went against his grain to abandon their men in the heat of battle. But Viktor was correct in one respect; larger matters were at stake than the outcome of this single skirmish, no matter how perilous it might be.

William, he thought. *What of William? Where does my greater duty lie?*

Viktor saw the hesitation in his face. "Go!"

Unhappily, Marcus dug his spurs into his horse's side. Torn between competing loyalties, he galloped into the woods.

At his back, the battle raged on without him.

Istvan looked about him warily. With a torch in one hand and a sword in the other, he stood outside a burning cottage. The heat from the fire was such that he found himself baking within his metal armor. The snow beneath his boots melted into a frigid puddle. He stepped away from the blaze, but was grateful for the fire nonetheless. With any luck, the raging conflagration would consume any infected mortals that might have lain within.

We've got enough of these mangy bastards to deal with already.

A headless lycan lay at his feet. Istvan braced himself for the next attack, uncertain whence it would come. Flames, smoke, and drifting snow obscured his view of the bloody tumult going on all around him. Screams, growls, and angry shouting added to the confusion. Shadowy figures contended in the murky haze, stabbing and slashing at each other without mercy. Blood, both lycan and vampiric, splattered the snowy landscape. Istvan could practically taste it in the air. Thatch roofs collapsed as fire devoured the timbers supporting them. The Death Dealer's black armor was liberally bedecked with gore.

He glimpsed an indistinct figure coming toward him. "Radu?" he called out, having lost track of his comrade in the pandemonium. "Is that you?"

A canine roar suggested otherwise. Moving with preternatural speed, an immense werewolf came charging out of the snow. The beast's body struck Istvan like a battering ram and his boots took leave of the ground. He crashed through a wall of burning wattles into the smoky interior of the blazing cottage. The harsh fumes stung his lungs, throat, and nostrils. Burning embers scattered in his wake.

His collision with the floor left his head ringing. Nevertheless, he leaped to his feet, sword in hand. And well it was that he did so, for two more werewolves lunged out of the shadows at him.

Hellfire! he cursed inwardly. The odds were two to one against him, leaving a swift response his only recourse. Thrusting with his arm, he stabbed the first beast so hard that the tip of his silver blade punched out through the monster's back. He hastily tugged on the hilt of the sword, praying that the blade would not get stuck between the creature's ribs. To his relief, the sword came free easily enough, and he swung it around in one smooth, continuous movement. With lethal precision, the blade sliced through the second werewolf's head, cut-ting the monster's skull in half. Lycan brains spilled onto the floor of the hut.

Istvan could not believe his luck. It seemed his immortality would not end this night after all. "Praise the Elders," he murmured.

Holding his sword before him, he groped through the smoke for a way out of the burning cottage. His overheated armor felt like an oven.

Despite Viktor's urgent instructions, Marcus had not gone far. A stand of snow-covered firs and pines concealed him from view as he watched the battle from the edge of the woods. His steed pawed the ground impatiently, eager to leave the blood and chaos behind, but Marcus compelled the horse to stay where it was. He stroked its mane to calm it.

William is nearby, he thought. *I can feel it in my bones.*

Pounding hoofbeats caught his attention. He watched with interest as a lone rider came galloping out of the forest to the north. Marcus recognized the rider as yet another Death Dealer engaged in the hunt. The vampire rode into the village and alongside Viktor. Marcus strained his ears to hear what the man had to report.

"We found him!" the Death Dealer exclaimed.

Viktor instantly gave the rider his full attention. "And?"

"We need more men."

That was all Viktor needed to hear. *"Find Amelia!"*

Marcus looked on in secret as the female Elder withdrew a wet blade from her latest kill. Responding to Viktor's summons, she hurried to confer with the other Elder. They spoke in hushed tones too low for Marcus to make out, but within seconds a decision appeared to have been reached. Rounding up a half dozen Death Dealers to accompany her,

Amelia galloped off into the very woods from which the rider had emerged, leaving Viktor and the remainder of their forces behind to contend with the transformed villagers. Marcus watched as Amelia and her men disappeared into the forest.

He had no doubt as to whom she sought, or why such reinforcements were required.

They have found William . . . at last.

He knew also where he needed to be. Shooting a glance at Viktor, he saw that the undead warlord was fully engaged in the ongoing battle against the newborn werewolves. Astride his armored destrier, Viktor hacked away at his foes with his broadsword, while simultaneously shouting out commands to his beleaguered troops. "Show no mercy!" he cried out imperiously. "Let not a single mongrel escape!"

He's far too busy to look this way, Marcus realized.

Confident that Viktor was preoccupied with other matters, Marcus took off after Amelia and the others. He rode briskly through the nocturnal forest, ducking the branches that threatened to unhorse him. Small animals scurried away as the charger's hooves pounded through the underbrush after the earlier riders. An owl hooted shrilly overhead.

Broken branches and trampled brush testified to the Death Dealers' passage. The trail would have been ridiculously easy to follow even if the fallen snow had not preserved the overlapping hoofprints of numerous riders. Marcus knew he was heading in the right direction.

He only prayed that he could catch up with Amelia and the others before events passed beyond his control. Much was at stake, not the least of which was his brother's ultimate fate.

I'm coming, William, he promised silently. *I'm coming!*

As if in response to his fevered thoughts, a deafening roar shook the forest. The roar bore some kinship to the growls of the werewolves back in the village, but was deeper in timbre and far louder. Compared to this thundering roar, those earlier growls were like the yelps of newborn puppies.

The colossal roar brought Marcus to a momentary halt. Even though he knew full well who—and what—had produced the roar, the blood-chilling sound was enough to daunt even the most determined spirit. He paused to steady his nerves, only to feel the ground tremble beneath his horse's hooves. The tremor shook accumulations of snow from the treetops, causing avalanches of white powder to rain down upon the floor of the forest. He brushed the icy flakes away from his face.

What the devil?

The source of the tremor was revealed as a knot of riderless horses exploded from the brush. They stampeded past Marcus, their eyes wide with panic. He held firmly on to the reins of his own steed, struggling to keep the anxious horse under control, while the other chargers fled for their lives. The saddles upon the horses' backs were ominously empty. Claw marks scarred the thick metal plates protecting the destriers' heads, necks, and chests. Steam jetted from their nostrils. Foam flecked their lips.

Marcus could not help wondering what had become of the horses' riders.

Another fearsome growl echoed through the night, followed by agitated screams and shouts. Heavy chains clattered in the distance.

It was all too much for Marcus's frightened steed. He dug his spurs into the horse's flanks, but the terrified destrier would go no farther. Marcus could hardly blame the animal, knowing what lay ahead.

Very well, he resolved. Dismounting, he tied the horse's reins to a nearby tree trunk, then set off on foot through the wintry woods. His boots sank deep into the fallen snow.

He did not have far to go. Within minutes, he emerged from the brush and bracken into a forest clearing deeply buried in snow. He froze in his tracks, taken aback by the nightmarish spectacle before him.

Under Amelia's command, a complement of Death Dealers vied against a huge albino werewolf, larger and more formidable than any of the misbegotten beasts back at the village. His thick, matted pelt was the color of the pristine snow. Rheumy pink eyes glared out from the creature's wolfen face. Herculean muscles bulged beneath his milky fur. His hot breath steamed the air.

William. Marcus gasped in recognition. *My brother.*

If the werewolf noted his sibling's arrival, he gave no evidence of it. Instead the titanic beast roared defiantly at the Death Dealers seeking to bring him down. The undead soldiers were spread out in a circle around their formidable quarry, blocking his escape in every direction. Taking care to stay out of reach of William's claws, they fired upon the werewolf with iron spears attached to links of heavy chain.

Crossbows, specially crafted for this purpose, launched the spears at William with tremendous force. The silver tips of the spears lodged deep within his flesh. He flailed about wildly as the chains snapped taut against steel spikes anchored to the ground and surrounding tree trunks. William howled in pain and fury.

Another archer took aim at the thrashing werewolf. A

vicious-looking spear sprang from a crossbow, striking William just below his ribs. Dark blood stained the werewolf's pure white fur.

That the Death Dealers seemed intent on capturing William, not slaying him, provided Marcus with scant comfort. The sight of his ill-starred brother being tormented by the soldiers' lances was more than he could bear.

"No!" he cried out. "Leave him be!"

Distracted by the Elder's cry, the archer failed to unhook the chain from his crossbow quickly enough. William grabbed hold of the links and jerked them violently, flinging the hapless Death Dealer into the air. The soldier's body slammed against a massive tree trunk with bone-crushing force. He slid down onto the ground beneath the tree and did not rise up again. Marcus feared that the vampire's neck had been shattered beyond repair.

One more life lost to the madness that had consumed his brother.

William roared in triumph, but his victory was short-lived. Marcus heard the twang of a crossbow being fired and watched in horror as a well-aimed spear pierced William's shoulder, passing all the way through the bleeding meat and gristle. Vicious silver hooks sprang to life at the exposed tip of the spear. The second archer yanked back on the chain and the cruel barbs sank into William's leathery hide. The werewolf could not tug the spear free without tearing his flesh to ribbons.

The crossbow's chain feeder spun rapidly as William reared back on his hind legs and let loose an anguished roar. The second archer hit a switch on his crossbow and the chain came free. Another Death Dealer grabbed hold of the links and hastily secured them to the frozen earth. The chain snapped taut as William tried in vain to tug it loose.

"Stop this!" Marcus shouted. He felt his brother's wounds as though they were his own. *"You're killing him!"*

Standing apart from the battle, Amelia looked at her fellow Elder. She had removed her helmet, which rested on the snow beside her feet. Her elegant face held a cold, inscrutable expression. Snowflakes glistened in her lustrous black hair. Her eyes locked briefly with Marcus's before she turned back toward her troops.

"More!" she commanded.

Ignoring Marcus, the Death Dealers fired spear after spear at their outnumbered prey. More chains were anchored to the ground, trapping the werewolf within the clearing. His brawny shoulders drooped beneath the weight of abundant chains, which hung tangled about him like a spider's web. His breaths grew ragged. He whimpered in pain and exhaustion.

Marcus could stand it no more. Furious, he grabbed one of the archers and hurled him aside with an Elder's strength. The armored soldier landed in a snowdrift over a dozen yards away. Fearful eyes peered from behind the Death Dealer's black helmet as he scrambled toward Amelia, seeking the other Elder's protection. His petrified expression betrayed his terror at being caught between two clashing Elders.

"Enough, Marcus," Amelia said.

Turning his gaze back toward his persecuted brother, Marcus saw that the deed was done. The spears and chains had done their work, overcoming even William's preternatural strength and endurance. Enmeshed in his chains, the werewolf collapsed onto the snow, beaten and bleeding. His chest rose and fell beneath his heavy bonds. Only this labored breathing assured Marcus that his unfortunate brother still lived.

"William," he whispered hoarsely.

Mixed emotions warred within his chest. It could not be denied that his brother had posed a dire threat to them all. His depredations had ravaged the countryside for years now, costing the lives of countless innocent vampires and mortals. Worse yet, his hellish curse had proven damnably contagious, creating an entire breed of subhuman monsters like himself. Before William had succumbed to the primeval infection in his blood, the world had never heard of were-wolves. He had become the progenitor of a loathsome new species.

And yet, William could not be blamed for what he had become. Marcus stared in sorrow at his vanquished brother. If not for a capricious twist of fate, their destinies might have been reversed. *He might have been born a vampire,* Marcus thought, *and I . . . an animal.* He alone understood how hard his brother had fought against the curse.

But what would become of William now?

"Marcus!"

He turned to see Viktor stalking out of the forest, flanked by a complement of additional Death Dealers. The warlord's armor and sword were smeared with lycan blood. His helmet had gone astray somewhere, exposing a craggy, weathered face. Although immortal, Viktor resembled a man in his early fifties—the very age at which he had become a vampire. Pale brown hair, streaked with gray, hung past his shoulders. He appeared enraged to find Marcus present, in defiance of his instructions.

To hell with him! Marcus thought furiously. The red-haired Elder drew his sword from its scabbard. He had his own grounds for anger. His voice rang with betrayal:

"He was not to be harmed! Place him in my charge as we agreed, or you will pay for your deceit!"

A chorus of metallic threats greeted his threat. Looking around, Marcus was surprised to find himself targeted by dozens of loaded crossbows. His jaw dropped as he realized belatedly that the Death Dealers took their orders from one Elder and one Elder alone.

Viktor.

"And you will learn your place," Viktor said sternly. His voice softened as he strove to reason with the other Elder. "Your sympathy for this beast is foolish." He gestured at the captured werewolf. "Your brother is entirely beyond your control." Viktor shook his head. "It will be done my way."

Marcus swept his gaze over the weapons arrayed against him. His face held not a hint of fear. "You know well the consequences if you murder me . . . or William."

"If you so much as speak his name again," Viktor warned, "you will have chosen that future for him yourself."

Was he bluffing? Surely he wouldn't dare . . . ? Marcus's blue eyes were ablaze with fury. He scanned the implacable faces of the Death Dealers, but found no sympathy for his brother's plight, nor any trace of the loyalty to which he, Marcus Corvinus, was entitled. He had no doubt that the warriors would open fire on him if Viktor commanded it. *Turncoats!* he thought venomously. He clenched his fists at his side. *Traitors!*

He looked to Amelia for support, but found none to be had. Her beautiful face could have been made of porcelain for all the emotion it displayed. "There is nothing else to be done, Marcus. In time, you will understand this."

Never! he thought. *Not in a thousand years!* For a moment, he contemplated taking arms against the lot of them, Viktor and Amelia included. After all, he was older and stronger than them both. If he could just manage to liberate William from his bonds, the two of them might stand a chance of escaping Viktor and his treacherous jackals. They could escape into the sheltering wilderness and therein plot their revenge. *I still have my own loyal vassals back at the castle,* he reminded himself. *They will not stand by while I am treated thus. William and I can still reign over the coven as we were always meant to.*

But, no . . . this was only a hopeless fancy. The odds against them were too great. It was two Elders against one, with over a dozen Death Dealers allied with Viktor as well. And, after his ordeal, William lacked the strength to retreat, let alone engage in combat against superior numbers. Although it galled his very soul to admit it, Marcus realized that this was a fight he could not win. At least not tonight.

Scowling, he lowered his sword.

"What is thy will, milord?" he asked, his voice fairly dripping with sarcasm.

Viktor chose to ignore the other Elder's impudent tone. "Imprisonment for all time," he decreed. "Far from you."

He turned and strode away, confident enough in his guards to turn his back to Marcus. He gathered his lieutenants to him and began to make the arrangements for the disposition of the prisoner.

Hatred smoldered in Marcus's eyes. Tearing his irate gaze away from Viktor, he took one last look at his condemned brother. The vanquished werewolf sprawled upon the snow-covered ground, his mighty limbs rendered impotent by the chains wrapped around his furry body. The Fates alone knew when and if Marcus would ever lay eyes on William again.

I shall not forget you, my brother, the Elder vowed. He wiped a bloodred tear from the corner of his eye. *I will bide my time until our moment comes round again. No matter how long we must wait, someday you shall be free once more.*

And the world will tremble before us.

Chapter Four

Present day

*T*he abandoned mine was located in the rocky hills northeast of Budapest. A corrugated-steel door barred the entrance to the mine, which was built into the side of a hill. Rusty metal tracks led up to the sealed doorway. Security cameras monitored the approach to the mine. DANGER! NO TRESPASSING! a sign read in Hungarian. Selene ignored the warning, tramping through the snow up to the locked entrance. A full moon provided the only illumination, but Michael found that he could easily see through the dark.

Another side effect of his new condition?

The young American was still trying to process all the life-altering changes that had been thrown at him over the last few nights. Barely seventy-two hours ago, he hadn't even believed in vampires or werewolves. Now he was some sort of a vampire/werewolf hybrid and caught in the middle of a life-and-death struggle he was only just beginning to comprehend, in the company of a lethal woman he barely knew. He had been shot, bitten, abducted, drugged, and nearly devoured since stumbling into that firefight in the subway station three nights ago.

How did this happen to me? he wondered. *I just want to be a doctor, that's all.*

A pang struck him as he thought longingly of his dinky apartment in the city, and of his residency back at the hospital. Both were less than an hour away by car, but they might as well have been on another planet. His old life was over now. There was no turning back.

It's just me and Selene now.

A high-tech lock protected the mine from intruders. Selene entered the key code, then pressed her thumb against a biometric sensor. The rusty metal door squealed loudly as she threw it open, exposing the interior of the mine. It was pitch-black inside, obscuring Michael's view of what lay beyond. It had been Selene's idea to seek out this so-called safe house, after they'd fled the lycans' underground lair beneath the city. He assumed she knew what she was doing.

I have to trust her, he thought. *She's all I have left in the world.*

A power box was mounted on the wall just inside the mountain. Selene flipped the switch, but nothing happened. The safe house remained as dark as before. She scowled in annoyance.

Power must be out, Michael guessed. He wondered when was the last time anyone had visited this location. From outside, the mine looked as if it had been deserted for years. *Appearances can be deceiving,* he reminded himself, *as I'm starting to learn all too well.*

Take, for instance, the leather-clad woman standing by the power box. Michael recalled the first time he had laid eyes on her, at that subway station downtown. He had been attracted to her immediately, but had thought that she was just another hot-looking European chick. How was he to know that she was really a kick-ass vampire assassin?

I didn't have a clue, he thought.

She drew an automatic pistol from beneath the folds of her voluminous black trench coat. A light mount was attached to the stock of the gun. She pressed a switch and a thin beam of light penetrated the darkness. The searchbeam fell upon . . . the face of an enraged werewolf!

Oh, fuck! Michael thought. His brown eyes turned into molten jet-black orbs as he instinctively started to change into his hybrid form. Sharpened talons extended from his fingertips . . .

But Selene was way ahead of him. She squeezed the trigger of her handgun and fired repeatedly at the monster. Gunshots echoed inside the mine, and the muzzle of the pistol flashed in the darkness as she emptied an entire clip of silver bullets into the creature.

Would that be enough to kill the beast? Michael watched anxiously, waiting for the werewolf to either fall over dead or come charging at them. But the monster seemed to have no reaction to the barrage of silver bullets. Its savage face remained exactly where it was, its open jaws frozen in the same fixed expression. Ivory fangs glinted in the beam of the searchlight. Cobalt eyes stared glassily into space.

Wait a sec, Michael thought. *Something's not right here.*

Selene appeared to have reached the same conclusion. She let up on the trigger and swept the beam over the unmoving creature before them. Michael saw now that the werewolf was hanging lifelessly in a cagelike apparatus at the far end of the chamber. Thick lengths of chain were looped beneath the monster's underarms, suspending the body from the ceiling. A metallic harness was fastened around the werewolf's neck and snout. Old wounds could be glimpsed through its shaggy black pelt. Its jaws were locked in a rictus of agony, not attack.

No blood flowed from the multiple bullet holes Selene had just inflicted on the beast. She lowered her gun and glanced at Michael.

"I may have overreacted," she said, with just a trace of embarrassment in her voice.

No shit, Michael thought. The werewolf was obviously long dead. Michael's talons retracted back into his fingers and his eyes turned human once more. His heartbeat slowed to a less frenetic pace. Obviously, the dead creature posed no threat to them. *Talk about a shock, though!*

He couldn't help noticing how quickly he had started to transform at the sight of a potential enemy. He had changed without thinking, just as he had during that final battle with Viktor back in the underworld. Was his bizarre new existence already becoming second nature to him? The change had felt as natural as breathing, which scared him more than a little.

Get used to it, he told himself harshly. *This is who you are now.*

Easier said than done, another part of his mind answered back.

Tucking her pistol back beneath her coat, Selene located a fuse box on the opposite wall. She opened the box and reset the tripped switches. A generator hummed somewhere deeper inside the mine. Fluorescent lights flickered to life overhead. The sudden illumination hurt Michael's eyes and he blinked against the glare.

The dead werewolf could be seen more easily now. Looking closer, Michael saw that the body had been hooked up to various pieces of sophisticated medical technology, including an electrocardiogram, intracranial-pressure moni-

44

tor, Swan-Ganz catheter, a mobile X-ray unit, and your basic physiologic monitor, all top-of-the-line. Electrodes were connected to shaved portions of the werewolf's anatomy. A crash cart held an emergency defibrillator, just in case the Death Dealers had needed to revive one of their lycan guinea pigs. A metal tray rested on a stainless-steel counter next to the open cage. Scalpels, scissors, forceps, retractors, hemostats, and other surgical tools were scattered atop the tray. He scowled at the obvious bloodstains on the instruments; maintaining a sterile environment was obviously not a priority. Anesthetics were conspicuously absent.

Michael recalled the safe house he and Selene had briefly stayed at in the city, after their escape from the vampires' mansion. Selene had mentioned that lycan prisoners were sometimes interrogated at such locations. From the looks of things here, those prisoners also got turned into guinea pigs on occasion—by vampire scientists looking for newer and better ways to exterminate their ancient foes?

He felt a stab of sympathy for the poor, dead beast. Only a few hours ago, Michael had been strapped to an examination table himself, while Lucian extracted Michael's blood for his own arcane experiments. The lycan leader had intended to use a unique enzyme in Michael's blood to transform himself into an unstoppable werewolf/vampire hybrid, but his master plan had gone awry. In the end, Lucian had perished, and Michael had become the hybrid.

For better or for worse.

Selene lifted a portable hydrocarbon analyzer from the tray and inspected the digital readout. Michael couldn't tell if the numbers meant anything to her. Despite everything they had endured together over the last few nights, he still found her beautifully sculpted face difficult to read. Most of the time, Selene kept her private thoughts and feelings locked up inside her, just as she probably had for hundreds of years. Michael wondered briefly just how old she really was.

In theory, he was now immortal, too. Michael's brain rebelled against the concept, even though he knew for a fact that Viktor and Lucian had been around since at least the Middle Ages. Would he also live for uncounted centuries? Michael couldn't even begin to wrap his head around the idea. *It's hard to think about living forever,* he mused, *when people keep trying to kill you every few hours.*

Selene dropped the analyzer back onto the tray and examined the shaggy corpse hanging nearby. "This thing's been dead for weeks."

"I don't get it," Michael said. He was still trying to learn the rules of this strange new world he was now a part of. "I thought lycans went back to their human form when they die."

"They do," she replied. "This one's been given a serum to stop the regression so that it can be studied in its wolfen form."

Michael remembered the drug Lucian's flunkies had injected him with, to delay his own transformation into a werewolf. He wondered if the serums were related. "How can you tell?"

She flipped the beast's toe tag toward Michael. A notation read, *Subject injected with 850 ml Thasarine to arrest regression.*

"Oh," he said. What the hell was Thasarine? Michael had never heard of the drug before. "Not exactly your department, I guess."

"I just killed them," she said bluntly. "I didn't worry too much about their anatomy."

Now that his eyes had adjusted to the light, Michael was

able to take a better look around. What had once been an empty mine shaft had been converted into a well-stocked bunker and safe house. Weapons lockers, packed with automatic rifles and handguns, lined gray concrete walls, along with file cabinets, workbenches, and numerous crates of ammo. One entire corner of the bunker had been taken over by what looked like a high-tech operations center, complete with computer consoles and plasma screens. A refrigerator hummed against another wall.

The whole place reminded him of that safe house in Pest. Stepping away from the werewolf's cage, he made a mental note not to let Selene handcuff him to a chair the way she had the last time. *We're sticking together this time around, whether she likes it or not.*

He toyed with the scalpels and forceps on the tray. The familiar tools comforted him in a way, providing him with a poignant reminder of his old life. *Do vampires ever need doctors?* he wondered. He remembered treating Selene's injuries after that car crash three nights ago. For all he knew, he might actually have saved her life. *Perhaps I can still have a career of sorts, if and when people stop trying to murder us!*

"How long can we stay here?" he asked.

"Not long," Selene said grimly. She led him over to the control center he had noticed before. Video screens mounted on the wall above the main console offered views of the grounds outside the mine. The night-vision photography glowed an eerie shade of green. A computer monitor resting atop a metal counter ran through a series of maps and status reports. "These safe houses are all linked together on one mainframe, with motion sensors revealing which ones are active. Someone could have picked us up already."

Someone being Selene's fellow vampires, Michael realized. Thanks to him, she was now a fugitive from her own people.

Turning away from the computer station, she started looking over the guns in the nearest weapons rack. She shrugged off her damp leather coat, revealing a lithe figure encased in skintight black leather. Dropping the coat on top of a waist-high metal filing cabinet, she cracked open a crate of ammo and began to reload her guns. Twin holsters were strapped to her thighs. A hunting knife was sheathed on her ankle.

"Now that Viktor is dead," she continued, "the hunt will be on for his killer. It's only a matter of time before I'm found."

"But none of this is your fault," he protested. "We have proof that Viktor lied. Kraven, too." Kraven was a double-crossing vampire slimeball who had plotted to take control of the coven. Michael had only met him once, but was not likely to forget him, considering that Kraven had shot him in the chest with bullets filled with deadly silver nitrate. If not for Selene, Michael would have died there and then. "I have Lucian's genetic memories."

Those memories, transferred to Michael when the lycan commander had bit him, had revealed the true origins of the war between the vampires and the werewolves. It was Viktor who had started the war—by executing his own daughter after she'd fallen in love with a lycan. As far as Michael was concerned, Viktor had fully deserved to have his head sliced in half by Selene.

Surely the other vampires would take that into account?

Selene didn't seem to think so. "All that will be beyond useless if Kraven reaches Marcus first and kills the last remaining Elder." According to Selene, one more vampire Elder was still residing in a tomb underneath the vampires' mansion; she had done her best to fill Michael in on the intricacies of vampire politics on their way to the mine. "Kraven's a coward. He'll want to strike while Marcus is still vulnerable. He knows he's no match for him awake."

Michael had experienced Viktor's awesome power first-hand. He didn't want to think about how strong this "Marcus" might be. *Selene and I barely beat Viktor on our own,* he recalled. *I'm in no hurry to go up against another Elder.*

A thought occurred to him and he glanced at his wrist-watch. Like the clothes on his back, the watch had been salvaged from a dead lycan on their way out of the underworld.

"There's only about an hour until daylight," he said. "Can you make it back to the mansion before the sun comes up?"

Sunlight was fatal to vampires, just as silver was to werewolves. Something the movies got right for once.

"Just," she said grimly.

Michael didn't like the sound of that. Joining Selene by the weapons cabinet, he picked out a couple of pistols more or less randomly. He wasn't about to admit to her that he had never pulled a gun on anyone in his life, let alone shot somebody. He didn't know the first thing about firearms. *Then again,* he thought, *I've never been a hybrid monster before either.*

"Okay," he said. "Let's get what we need and go."

Selene laid a restraining hand upon his arm. "No," she said softly.

Huh? Michael looked at her in confusion. What did she mean by that?

Her eyes avoided his. She hesitated, obviously uncomfortable.

"I'm going alone," she insisted.

Chapter Five

The mansion was known as Ordoghaz in the local tongue, or "Devil's House." Located about an hour north of downtown Budapest, near the sleepy town of Szentendre, the imposing Gothic estate deserved its evil reputation, having served as the vampires' lair since the days when Viktor had ruled over feudal Hungary with an iron hand. Freshly fallen snow blanketed the jagged spires and battlements rising above its looming stone walls. Majestic columns and pointed arches adorned its brooding facade. A cast-iron fence, equipped with spikes and mounted security cameras, guarded the coven's privacy.

To Kraven, Ordoghaz offered sanctuary of a sort, but only if he moved swiftly enough. He limped through the snow toward the forbidding stone gates, drawn by the lights shining from the mansion's narrow lancet windows. *I must reach the crypt before Selene,* he thought desperately. *She cannot be allowed to rouse Marcus and plead her case.* Kraven knew his punishment would be severe if the dreaded Elder ever learned of his alliance with Lucian.

Kraven had seen better nights. Every inch of his fine silk garments and elegant jewelry was coated with blood, muck,

50

and snow. The dark fabric was soaked completely through; had he been human, he would have succumbed to hypothermia by now. His shoulder-length black locks were plastered to his skull. His aristocratic face was taut and drawn. A burning pain in his right leg reminded him of Lucian's dying blow, when the lycan commander had stabbed him with that damned spring-loaded blade of his!

At least that bastard is dead for good, Kraven thought, although that came as scant comfort at the moment. *I should have killed him ages ago.*

Just like I always claimed to have done.

After centuries of plotting and scheming, everything had gone wrong. By now, Kraven had hoped to be the undisputed leader of the coven, having conspired with Lucian to overthrow the Elders and bring an end to the eternal war between their two species. Kraven had expected to be hailed as a hero and peacemaker; instead he had found himself on the run after Selene had exposed his treachery to Viktor. Forced to seek refuge with Lucian in the lycan's squalid underground warren, he had barely survived the final battle between Viktor's Death Dealers and Lucian's lycan army. Only by scurrying away like a rat through the sewers had he been able to escape the underworld in one piece—but not before watching from the shadows as Selene executed Viktor with his own sword!

Bile rose in his throat as he thought of Selene. This was all her fault, she and that freakish hybrid lover of hers! Hidden from sight, he had witnessed the obscene abomination Michael Corvin had become, making Selene's obvious affection for him all the more appalling. Kraven had long lusted after Selene's svelte body, but now he craved only her complete and total annihilation. *She will pay for rejecting me,* he vowed, *and bringing all my plans to ruin!*

To his relief, the limestone gates opened automatically at his approach. Viktor, one hundred years out-of-date at the time of his premature Awakening, had clearly neglected to revoke Kraven's electronic security clearance. *Thank the dark gods for small favors,* he thought. He was in no condition to climb over the spiked fence.

A long, paved driveway led to the mansion's front entrance, beyond a sculpted marble fountain. With the temperature well below freezing, the fountain's water display had been shut off. Plumes of churning white water no longer reached toward the sky.

Kraven staggered up the marble steps in front of the mansion. He pounded loudly on the heavy oaken doors barring his way. "Open up!" he shouted to whoever might be on the other side of the door. With luck, most of the Death Dealers had joined Selene and Viktor on their ill-fated sorties into the underworld. Hopefully, that left his own private security force in control of the mansion. "Let me in, goddammit!"

The huge double doors swung open. A large, stocky vampire peered out at him. Kraven recognized the face of Miklos, one of Soren's thuggish underlings. He stared at Kraven as though he barely recognized his leader through all the blood and gunk. "Regent?"

Kraven was in no mood to explain his filthy appearance. He shoved his way past Miklos into the mansion's sumptuous foyer. Antique tapestries and oil paintings decorated the polished oak-paneled walls. Marble tiles stretched across the floor to where a majestic grand stairway ascended toward the upper stories of Ordoghaz. A spectacular crystal chandelier hung above the foyer. Compared to the lycans' fetid ratholes, the mansion's richly appointed interior struck Kraven as more palatial than ever. He brushed the snow from his head and shoulders, glad to be out of the blizzard at last.

Although it was nearly dawn, the entire mansion was still wide-awake. Undead gentlemen and ladies, stylishly attired in shades of red and black, came pouring out of the adjacent parlor in response to his arrival. More of the mansion's residents rushed down the stairs, having not yet retired for the morning. No Death Dealers these, the milling vampires were instead sophisticates and dilettantes, much like Kraven himself, who preferred to spend their immortality in various hedonistic pursuits, as opposed to never-ending battles against the lycan hordes. Many of them still clutched crystal goblets filled with spiced blood cocktails. Tonight, however, the vampires' habitually jaded faces bore expressions of fear and concern. Desperate for news from the front, they pelted Kraven with anxious questions: Was Lucian still alive? Had the lycans been destroyed? Where were Viktor and the others? Was it true that Amelia had been assassinated by the lycans? What had become of Kahn, and Soren, and Selene . . . ?

As far as Kraven knew, he was the only vampire to emerge from the underworld alive. Not counting Selene, of course. But he had better things to do than waste time answering the questions of these worthless parasites. Glancing over the throng in the foyer, he was grateful to spy no trace of that amorous servant girl Erika. Was she sulking in her room, or had she fled the mansion altogether after he had slammed the car door in her face during his last escape? *No matter,* he thought, *just so long as she is gone.* The last thing he needed right now was that lovesick blond trollop clinging to him.

His mind raced frantically, considering his options. With Viktor and Amelia both deceased, there was still a chance to turn matters to his advantage. *All I need to do is destroy Mar-*

cus, he reasoned, *while the Elder is still asleep and vulnerable. Then the coven will be mine to command.*

That still left Selene to deal with, alas. No doubt she would try to expose his perfidy to the rest of the coven, but it would be her word against his. And who would the other vampires believe, Viktor's chosen regent—or a coldhearted bitch who had willingly chosen to consort with a lycan? Kraven felt certain that he could turn the coven against Selene. Politics was not exactly the female Death Dealer's forte.

Ignoring the sycophants and sybarites flocking around him pleading for reassurance, he nodded at Miklos. "Gather the men," he ordered him curtly. Now that he was back in familiar surroundings, some of his former self-confidence reasserted itself. Not for the first time, he congratulated himself for having had the foresight to assemble his own security team, independent of Selene and the other Death Dealers. "Tell them to meet me outside the crypt at once!"

"Yes, regent!" Miklos replied. He hastened to carry out Kraven's instructions. "As you command!"

Kraven was pleased by the vampire's obedience. Perhaps this Miklos would make a serviceable replacement for Soren, whom Kraven assumed to have perished in the underworld. *I will need a new enforcer,* he thought, *once I have regained control of the coven.*

First things first, however. He still had an Elder to kill.

Kraven took a few minutes to wipe the blood and dirt from his face, then made his way down to the security booth outside the Elders' crypt, in the mansion's lowest subbasement. Closed-circuit television screens monitored the interior of the crypt, as well as the grounds outside the mansion. Thankfully, it had required little effort to persuade the throng of feckless hangers-on to remain upstairs; even at the best of times, few of the mansion's occupants chose to venture this near the Elders' somber resting place.

Miklos had assembled a four-man strike team. Grim-faced, the vampire guards cradled Uzis against the front of their black leather dusters. Kraven gladly accepted an extra rifle from Miklos, having discarded his experimental silver-nitrate gun after running out of ammo during his escape from the underworld. It felt good to be armed once more.

He pressed a button on the control panel and the entrance to the crypt slid open. Despite his newly acquired bodyguards, he hesitated upon the threshold, daunted by the enormity of the task ahead. Killing an Elder, even in his sleep, was no small matter; he still found it hard to accept that Selene had actually defeated Viktor in combat, even though he had witnessed the warlord's death with his own eyes.

If she can do it, so can I.

He reminded himself that Marcus was surely weakened by over two hundred years of hibernation. Even Viktor had required several hours to recover from his recent Awakening, before embarking on his raid into the underworld. If all went well, Marcus would be dead before he even realized what was happening.

Or so Kraven hoped.

Dimly lit and cavernous, the crypt was the slowly beating heart of Ordoghaz. Granite steps led down to the sunken lower level, where three burnished bronze disks were embedded in the stone floor. A concentric pattern of overlapping Celtic runes surrounded the circular hatches, each of which was engraved with a single letter: *A* for Amelia, *V* for Viktor, and *M* for Marcus.

The plaques marked the individual tombs of the Elders, only one of which was still occupied. In theory, Marcus still slumbered in his buried sarcophagus, blissfully ignorant of the cataclysmic events that had rocked the coven over the last few nights. If Kraven had his way, the last of the Elders would never rise again.

A line from *Macbeth* flashed through his brain: *If it were done when 'tis done, then 'twere well it were done quickly.* Kraven had attended the play's premiere in London four hundred years ago and recognized just how apt the quotation was. Macbeth had also murdered a monarch in his sleep, so as to fulfill his vaulting ambition. Kraven could only hope that his own grab for power ended less tragically. *Macbeth was a mere mortal,* he recalled, *and fictional to boot.*

Swallowing hard, he screwed his courage to the sticking place and gestured toward the doorway. "Go on," he ordered the guards impatiently, not about to go first. "Let's get this over with."

Flashlight beams raked through the gloom as the other men preceded him into the crypt. Kraven descended the granite steps behind them, feeling the temperature drop a couple degrees with every step. His nerves were strung so tightly he feared they would snap before he reached the bottom of the steps. A funereal hush enveloped the ancient crypt, broken only by the footsteps of Kraven and his entourage. His undead heart was beating a mile a minute.

Just stick to the plan, he reminded himself. *Everything is under control. . . .*

A lifeless body lay sprawled upon the bottom floor of the crypt, its neck twisted at an unnatural angle. A weathered, middle-aged profile was pressed against the marble tiles. Owlish eyes stared blankly into the void. The man's dingy brown coat was streaked with blood. Dead for hours, the discarded corpse had already begun to stink.

Gagging at the stench, Kraven recognized Singe, a lycan

scientist who had formerly labored in Lucian's service. Selene had captured Singe and "persuaded" him to reveal to Viktor the existence of Kraven's secret alliance with Lucian, forcing Kraven to flee the mansion with all due speed. Singe had still been alive when last Kraven had seen him. He wondered briefly who had actually killed the worthless lycan, Selene or Viktor?

What does it matter? he decided. The loose-lipped scientist had already caused enough trouble. *I only regret that I can't kill the bastard myself.*

A river of blood had flowed from the lycan's crushed skull, pooling and coagulating atop the engraved bronze hatches. Dark, clotted gore defiled the raised letter *M* on Marcus's plaque. The smell of congealed lycan blood turned Kraven's stomach.

He pointed at the hatch. "Open it."

"Yes, regent." Miklos himself knelt beside Marcus's hatch. Heedless of the sticky black goo, he inserted his beefy fingers into the cold metal grooves surrounding the *M*. Ancient gears, untouched for over two centuries, resisted his efforts at first, but then an inner disk rotated beneath his fingers, activating the dormant locking mechanism. Miklos rose and stepped aside as the intricate designs adorning the hatch began to shift of their own accord. Kraven heard the muted rumble of a hidden clockwork apparatus slowly coming back to life. The circular plaque sank into the floor, then split apart into four wedge-shaped segments that retracted from sight, exposing the top of the steel sarcophagus below. Another *M*, illuminated in lapis lazuli, confirmed that Marcus dwelt within.

But not for much longer, Kraven vowed. He fully intended to incinerate the Elder's remains until naught but ashes were left behind. "Ready your weapons!" he informed the guards.

Tonight a new era begins in the history of the coven. The era of Kraven the Supreme . . .

The crypt itself seemed to shudder as a harsh grinding noise suddenly came from below. Kraven's eyes widened in alarm. He had attended numerous Awakenings in his time and they had never produced such a clangor. Instead of operating smoothly, as it had down through the centuries, the ancient apparatus sounded as though it was tearing itself apart. Steel ground loudly against stone, producing a discordant clamor that caused several of Kraven's guards to place their hands over their ears. They looked in confusion to Kraven, who was no less dumbfounded than they. His jaw dropped.

Something's wrong, he realized. *Horribly wrong.*

A look of utter dread washed over his face as the ornate sarcophagus lurched upward from beneath the floor. The empty coffin was torn to shreds, as though Marcus had literally clawed his way out of the metal tomb!

But how? Kraven thought. *Why?* The Elder should have been dreaming in silence, dead to the world. What had roused him from two centuries of unbroken slumber?

An awful suspicion came over him. He shot a worried glance at the body of the dead lycan, lying only a few yards away. His eyes traced the stream of dried blood flowing from Singe's corpse to the empty shaft that had been concealed beneath the bronze M. Crimson stains could be seen within the mangled wreckage of the sarcophagus.

Singe's blood! he realized in horror. Beneath his sodden garments, a cold sweat broke out over his body. *The lycan's blood must have awakened Marcus!*

A dry, raspy sound emerged from the murky shaft. Unseen lungs wheezed noisily.

Marcus?

Kraven backed away from the shaft. Every instinct in his body urged him to bolt for the stairs and leave the accursed crypt behind, but he was hesitant to flee so blatantly in front of his few remaining acolytes. He needed to put on a show of strength if he ever hoped to regain his former position in the coven.

I should have never returned to this goddamn house! he thought bitterly. Eternal exile was sounding more and more appealing. *I had an entire planet to hide in!*

Suddenly, the very floor of the crypt shook beneath him. A tremendous pounding came from below, as though something—or someone—beneath the stone floor was striving to break free. The tremors threw Kraven and the other vampires off-balance. Kraven stumbled and nearly fell. His hand reached out to steady himself, coming to rest against the twisted iron frame of the sarcophagus. One foot landed in the pool of congealed blood around Singe's corpse. The sticky gore clung to the sole of his shoe.

Fear showed on the faces of his men. Like Kraven, they looked about them anxiously, their fingers on the triggers of their automatic rifles. They shifted uneasily on their feet, trying to keep their balance despite the gargantuan blows shaking the floor of the crypt. Naturally pale faces turned even more ashen.

"May the Elders preserve us!" Miklos exclaimed. The other men muttered in agreement.

Not bloody likely, Kraven thought. There was only one Elder left, and he did not appear to be in a benevolent mood. Kraven's confidence deserted him and he opened his mouth to order an immediate retreat. *We have to get out of here . . . now!*

But before he could take another step toward the exit, a shadowy figure erupted from the floor. The force of the explosion threw him backward, onto the floor. Chunks of shattered stone and tile rained down on him like shrapnel. He cried out in pain as the jagged fragments pelted his face and body, slicing through silk and flesh alike. Fresh blood streamed onto the ruptured floor. His Uzi slipped from his fingers.

No! he thought hysterically. *This can't be happening!*

Blood from a scalp wound ran down his face, obscuring his vision. Dazed, he blinked in confusion, trying to make sense of the chaotic scene unfolding around him. Automatic weapons fired wildly, their muzzle flares creating a strobe effect that disoriented Kraven even further. All he caught were fragmentary impressions of a dark figure laying waste to his men.

An inhuman growl echoed throughout the crypt, audible even over the blare of the rifles. The hellish noise sounded like a cross between a wolf's howl and the screech of an enraged vampire bat.

Leathery black skin flashed across his field of vision at preternatural speed. Gleaming black eyes shone like polished obsidian.

Gunfire chipped away at venerable stone walls, but failed to stop the creature loose in the devastated crypt. Dust and pulverized stone went flying. Powdered debris filled the air. The acrid odor of cordite invaded Kraven's nostrils, overpowering the stench from the dead lycan. Smoke rose from the barrels of the unleashed Uzis.

A rifle was snatched right out of a soldier's grip, only seconds before the hapless vampire was catapulted into the nearest wall with enough force to crack the ancient stones. His body slid to the floor, where it collapsed into a heap.

Bloodstained talons raked across another vampire's face.

Blood gushed between his fingers as he clutched his mutilated countenance.

Panicky shouts gave way to bloodcurdling screams. Kraven listened with alarm as, one by one, the guards' rifles clattered to the floor. A peculiar flapping noise reached his ears.

Immortal bones snapped like twigs.

Bright arterial blood sprayed like a fountain from a headless body.

"Heinrich!" another guard shouted in horror, only seconds before a clawed hand exploded from his chest. A bony fist crushed the vampire's still-beating heart within its grip.

Kraven caught another glimpse of an indistinct figure behind the dead guard, but the creature moved too quickly for him to focus on it. Within a split second, the figure retracted its claw and disappeared back into the shadows. Its victim dropped lifelessly onto the shattered floor.

It was a massacre.

A third soldier dashed toward the steps, only to be snatched back by his collar and dragged back into the bloodbath. Smoke and dust concealed what happened next. An agonized shriek was cut off abruptly.

Miklos cried out frantically, momentarily exposed by the flare of his Uzi. A pair of gleaming fangs sank into his neck and his rifle fell silent. The strobing muzzle blinked out, shrouding the guard's fate in darkness. His dying scream trailed off into a pathetic moan before Kraven heard another body drop limply onto the floor.

Suddenly, it was over. The screams and gunfire no longer assailed his ears. Silence descended once more over the abattoir the defiled crypt had become. Kraven trembled uncontrollably as he realized that he was alone in the dark with . . . it.

"Milord?" Kraven had never known an Elder to Awaken in such a bloodthirsty rage, but who else could it be.

He groped desperately for his own rifle, but could not find the weapon amidst the rubble. He choked on the dusty air, coughing loudly. Staggering to his feet, he gazed desperately at the open doorway only a few yards away. His own cold blood continued to trickle down his face.

The nearby exit tantalized him. Escape was so close!

But not close enough.

Something landed on the floor behind him with a meaty smack. He could hear the creature's raspy breathing. It smelled of decaying flesh. Bony talons scraped against the broken tiles.

Kraven whimpered in fright. He wasn't sure what was worse, not seeing whatever was behind him or being forced to face it. His hair stood on end, and he could hear the panicked palpitations of his heart. Marshaling his last ounce of courage, he nervously turned around to confront the mysterious apparition that had just slaughtered his men so effortlessly.

Perhaps he could still talk his way out of this situation?

The smoke, dust, and dim lighting made it hard to see the monster clearly, even though it was now standing only a few feet from him. Kraven strained his eyes to see a hairless, mummified figure wearing black silk trousers. A tarnished gold belt girded the creature's waist. Gilded armbands circled his bony biceps. Molten black eyes, unlike any vampire's, coldly examined Kraven. Fresh blood dripped from its jaws. Its blackened skin was the color of a gangrenous limb.

Shrack! Without warning, a pair of batlike wings snapped out of the creature's shoulder blades. The wings spread out behind him, spanning nearly ten feet from tip to tip. Arched bones and twisted networks of veins were visible throughout the fleshy membranes. Ebony talons crowned the demonic wings.

Kraven's eyes widened in disbelief. Never had he witnessed anything like this. Tales of vampires transforming into bats were foolish mortal myths, nothing more, so how was this possible? What *was* this creature before him?

"Please," he begged.

A sudden flurry of movement cut off his desperate plea. The creature's wings exploded forward, striking Kraven with the force of a wrecking ball. The regent's back slammed against the wall behind him so hard that the impact cracked the dense stonework. Deep fissures spread like cobwebs across the face of the wall. The force of the collision left Kraven stunned and breathless.

He felt a sharp, searing pain in his shoulders. Looking down, he saw with alarm that both shoulders had been impaled by the spearlike tips of the monster's wings. Blood streamed down the front of his black silk shirt. Kraven realized in horror that he had literally been nailed to the wall of the crypt!

The creature leaned toward him. A beam of light from the control room exposed a gaunt, emaciated visage with ebony eyes and an aquiline nose. A mouthful of pointed, sharklike teeth dripped blood onto the figure's bare chest. Tapered ears lay flat against the creature's skull. Purple veins pulsed across the monster's smooth, bald cranium. Its mottled skin was dry as dust.

Kraven barely recognized the transformed Elder. His overwhelmed brain struggled to account for the ancient vampire's bizarre metamorphosis. Marcus's unearthly black eyes jogged Kraven's memory, and he suddenly recalled where he had seen such eyes before: on the face of Michael Corvin during his final battle with Viktor, after Selene's lycan sweetheart had undergone a similar transformation—into an unnatural hybrid of vampire and werewolf.

Just like Singe predicted, Kraven recalled. His gaze darted to the body of the dead lycan scientist. Before his well-earned demise, Singe had explained how a unique component in Corvin's blood, inherited from Alexander Corvinus himself, allowed vampire and lycan blood cells to combine to form a new hybrid species, theoretically more powerful than any other immortal bloodline. According to Singe, Lucian had intended to use Corvin's blood to transform himself into just such a hybrid, but Kraven had killed the scheming lycan before he had the chance to carry out his blasphemous plan. Instead it had been Michael Corvin who had become the hybrid, after Selene added her own bite to the lycan taint already infecting Corvin's blood.

Despite his immediate peril, Kraven could not suppress a flash of jealousy at the memory of Selene bestowing her crimson kiss upon Corvin's unworthy throat. *She could have ruled the coven by my side,* he recalled spitefully. *But instead she chose that ignorant American!*

Marcus's wings dug painfully into Kraven's shoulders, dragging the trapped vampire back into the present. He tried to grasp how the Elder could have become a hybrid as well. Singe had implied that only a pure sample of "the Corvinus strain" could permit the existence of a hybrid, but apparently he had been mistaken. Although separated by generations, Michael Corvin and Marcus Corvinus clearly shared the same singular mutation. Singe's blood had been enough to trigger the transformation in the revived Elder. The gigantic bat-wings, however, suggested that Marcus's vampire side was clearly dominant.

Black eyes glanced at the dead lycan. The Elder's voice when he spoke was hoarse from two hundred years of disuse. "The blood memories of this wretched creature have shown me that your treachery knows no bounds."

Kraven's bloody face turned deathly white. Marcus had obviously absorbed Singe's knowledge of Kraven's secret alliance with Lucian. His heart pounded within his chest. "Milord . . . I can explain—"

"Why should I listen to your lies," Marcus hissed, "when the journey to the truth is so much sweeter?"

The Elder's withered lips curled in a smile of . . . forgiveness? Understanding?

Hardly.

Ivory fangs tore into Kraven's throat. A crimson flood poured down Marcus's throat, and Kraven felt his own memories being sucked out of his body along with his life's blood. Images from the recent past flashed across the minds of both the Elder and his victim:

Kraven sat in the back of a parked limousine, conspiring with Lucian. Pouring rain streaked down the sides of the tinted windows. A crest-shaped pendant dangled from the lycan's neck. The gleaming pendant had once belonged to Sonja, Viktor's daughter—and Lucian's long-dead lover. It had been their forbidden passion that had ignited the centuries-old conflict between the vampires and their former servants.

"Remember," Lucian warned Kraven, "I've bled for you once already." Kraven's false claim to have slain the dreaded lycan commander had led directly to his ascendance within the coven. "Without me, you'd have nothing. You'd be . . . nothing."

Later:

Kraven watched in dismay as Selene sank her fangs into Michael Corvin's throat, triggering his transformation into a hybrid

65

abomination. Lucian lay upon the floor of the underground bunker, his dying body riddled with deadly silver-nitrate bullets. Kraven had shot Lucian repeatedly, but the stubborn lycan had clung to life with the last vestiges of his immortal strength. Distended black veins snaked across his face.

He taunted Kraven with his final breaths. "You may have killed me, cousin, but my will is done regardless."

Kraven opened fire once again, emptying the last of the experimental rounds into the lycan's writhing body. Another dose of silver nitrate raced through Lucian's throbbing veins. Tendrils of yellow smoke rose from his lips and nostrils as his internal organs combusted volcanically.

Lucian, champion of the lycan hordes, died at last.

A few minutes earlier:

Kraven hurled the ugly truth in Selene's face, savoring her shocked expression. "It was Viktor who killed your family, not the lycans. It was he who crept from room to room, dispatching everyone close to your heart!"

He remembered laying eyes on Selene for the first time, in those miserable stables six hundred years ago. The female Death Dealer had been delectably mortal then, a vision of nubile vulnerability in her soaked linen nightgown. If only Viktor had let him ravish her that night, as Kraven had originally intended!

This entire disaster could have been averted if Selene had simply died with the rest of her insignificant, mortal family.

Later:

Hidden away in one of the underworld's many shadowy nooks, Kraven watched as Selene and Michael Corvin battled Viktor in the lowest level of the lycans' subterranean den. Water streamed from broken pipes and rain-filled gutters, flooding the floor of the abandoned bunker. Viktor stood ankle-deep in the turbid water as he throttled Corvin with his bare hands. The American's hybrid strength was not enough to save him from the Elder's murderous grip. Corvin gasped impotently for breath. The iridescent sheen of his gray-blue hybrid flesh began to fade.

Then Selene leaped past Viktor, swinging the Elder's own mighty broadsword. Her sleek black leathers glistened wetly as she landed behind Viktor like a jaguar, still clutching the double-edged sword. The Elder spun around and glared angrily at his former protégée, enraged by her defiance. He drew a pair of silver daggers from his belt.

Unafraid, Selene waved the sword before his eyes. Fresh blood ran down the length of the blade. A stunned expression came over Viktor's face as he realized that Selene had already delivered a killing blow. A thin red line materialized across the Elder's countenance, stretching diagonally from his left ear down to the right side of his collar. A look of profound disbelief filled Viktor's eyes.

Fully half his skull slid away, splashing into the filthy water around his ankles.

Moments later, Selene plucked Sonja's pendant from the rubble. She pressed the gleaming emblem into Michael Corvin's palm.

Marcus withdrew his fangs from Kraven's throat. The victimized vampire gasped in relief, but feared that it was already too late for him. He had never felt so drained before, not even after the most exhausting blood orgy. His entire body had been reduced to a dried husk, stripped of every last drop of vitality. His mouth was as dry as the Kalahari. His eyes were sunk deep into their sockets. Every breath produced a spasm of agony. His bloody clothes felt like sandpaper against his raw, dehydrated skin. An icy chill, infinitely more frigid than the blizzard raging outside, penetrated the very marrow of his bones. Kraven doubted if he could even stand under his own power anymore. Only the Elder's taloned pinions kept him upright.

Centuries of immortality passed before his eyes. Kraven had enjoyed many lifetimes of power and pleasure, but he was not yet ready to die. The prospect of eternal oblivion filled him with mortal dread. *Not now!* he thought pitifully. *Not so soon!*

"Please," he croaked painfully. "I . . . can still assist you."

Bright red blood was smeared all around the Elder's jaws. A hint of a smile lifted the corners of his lips.

"You already have," Marcus said.

His wings snapped outward, tearing Kraven apart.

Chapter Six

Michael couldn't believe Selene planned to leave him behind again.

"If I can plead my case," she insisted, "there's a chance we'll be granted sanctuary." She slipped her black trench coat back over her shoulders as she prepared to depart the safe house. "Right now you'd be killed on sight. I'm not prepared to risk that."

"So what, I'm supposed to just sit here and wait for you?" He laid his guns down on a nearby counter. *No fucking way,* he thought. The last thing he wanted to do was hang around the abandoned mine while Selene endangered her life on their behalf . . . again. "Kraven may still have his men with him. You can't go alone."

She looked him in the eyes. "You're not as strong as you might think."

"What?" he blurted. Wasn't he a superpowerful hybrid now? Hell, he had almost held his own against Viktor in hand-to-hand combat, and the formidable Elder was supposed to be one of the most powerful vampires ever. *What does she mean by that?*

Selene stepped away from the well-stocked weapons

racks. She crossed the floor to the refrigerator on the other side of the bunker. Pulling open a clear glass door, she removed a few packets of frozen cloned blood. The preserved fluid inside the translucent plastic bags was purplish red. Michael had a horrible feeling he knew where this was going.

"You're unique, Michael," she said. "There has never been a hybrid before. However ambivalent you may feel about it, the truth is that your power could be limitless. But you depend on blood. You need to feed. Without it, you'll be growing weaker by the second." She closed the door of the refrigerator. "Use the time for that."

She lobbed the packets of blood at him. He caught them with both hands, then gazed down at the swollen bags. A printed label identified them as products of Ziodex Industries; he recalled Selene telling him that Ziodex was fully owned by her coven. The frozen blood felt cold to the touch, like an ice pack.

As a doctor, he had handled blood bags before, of course, but this was different. The realization dawned on him that Selene was deadly serious. She actually expected him to *drink* the blood . . . like a vampire.

"Jesus Christ."

He held the blood in his hands, the frozen packets representing the end of his old life and the beginning of a strange, unknowable future. Even after everything he had gone through already, the prospect of drinking the blood struck him as some sort of monumental turning point. After this, there could be no denying what he had become.

"And what if I don't?" he asked her. "What if I can't?"

Selene offered him no way out. "Normal food would be lethal. If you don't anticipate your cravings, you will attack humans." Her voice acquired a melancholy tone. "Believe me, you don't want that on your conscience."

Michael had to wonder if Selene was speaking from personal experience. According to her, modern vampires were forbidden from preying on innocent humans. Synthetic blood had been used as a substitute, until replaced by the cloned variety. Still, wasn't it possible that, sometime over the centuries, Selene might have been forced to sample the real thing?

He didn't have the nerve to ask her.

"There really is no going back, Michael. I'm sorry."

He could tell that she meant it. Did she ever regret becoming a vampire herself, especially now that she knew the truth about her family's death? He recalled that he wasn't the only person whose life had been turned upside down tonight.

"Look, I understand what you did, why you bit me back there in the tunnels. I'm grateful. You saved my life." He gave her a wan smile. "I wasn't ready to die."

She nodded. Although her expression remained guarded, he somehow sensed that she was relieved by his reaction. *Heck*, he thought, *I was already a werewolf by then. What was one more bite between friends?*

"I don't know . . . everything's changed." He took a deep breath. "I probably just need a minute to make it fit in my head, you know? It's a lot to process all at once."

"If it's any help," she said quietly, "everything's changed for me, too."

"I know. . . ."

Naked emotion hung in the air between them. Michael stared into her bottomless brown eyes, uncertain what to do next. He had been drawn to her since the first moment their eyes had met down in the Ferenciek Square subway station, before all this craziness had begun. Did she feel the same way about him? They had been so busy fighting to stay alive

71

that they had barely had a chance to get to know each other more intimately. True, she had kissed him once, but only to distract him long enough to handcuff him to that chair. Or had that been her only motive? His lips still remembered the cool softness of her mouth. His neck tingled where her fangs had pierced his skin. His blood now flowed in her veins.

"Look, go," he told her. "I'll be here. You just make sure you come back."

She walked past him without a word, the tail of her long black coat flapping behind her. Michael stood by silently as she left the safe house without a single backward glance.

Same old story, he thought wryly. *Here I am, left holding the blood.*

Chapter Seven

$\mathcal{A}$ heavy fog hovered over the cold, oily waters of the Black Sea. A bell tolled hauntingly in the distance. Salt water scented the frigid night air. The prow of an imposing ship sliced through the mist, cruising toward the coast of Romania.

The *Sancta Helena* was a refitted naval frigate, registered under the Hungarian flag. Over three hundred feet long, from bow to stern, it plowed through the choppy waves without hesitation, despite the limited visibility. Radar and sonar equipment helped the ship navigate through the fog. A powerful diesel engine provided plenty of horsepower. A helipad occupied the aft section of the ship, behind the rear control room, funnel, and upper decks. A radar tower rose like an old-fashioned mainmast behind the elevated bridge. Gun turrets were no longer visible upon the converted frigate, but that didn't mean the *Sancta Helena* was unarmed.

Samuel looked down on the ship as his helicopter approached the vessel. "Easy does it," he instructed the pilot. Strong winds buffeted the sleek Lynx military copter, making for a bumpy ride. A trim-looking Caucasian with close-cropped blond hair, Samuel rode shotgun beside the pilot. The rest of his Cleaner crew were strapped into the seats behind him. Like their leader, they wore unmarked black commando uniforms and fixed, unsmiling expressions. No badges or other insignia betrayed their identity. If the turbulent ride had any of them worried, the soldiers' neutral faces gave no sign of it. Samuel was proud of their professionalism.

The chopper touched down on the ship's landing deck. The Cleaners didn't wait for the Lynx's rotors to stop spinning before piling out of the copter smoothly and efficiently. The deck listed restlessly beneath them, but every member of the team had long ago earned his or her sea legs. Samuel watched silently as the Cleaners began to unload the copter. Crates of specialized equipment and confiscated evidence were stacked neatly on the deck, before being transported into the ship's waiting storage areas. The team moved like a well-oiled machine, as well they might. This was hardly the first time they had pulled off an operation of this nature. Samuel's eyes narrowed as three sealed body bags were removed from the chopper's cargo bay.

Macaro will want to inspect those carcasses personally, he guessed. *No doubt he is impatient to hear my report.*

Samuel decided not to keep his commander waiting. Confident that the team could finish unpacking on their own, he turned and marched across the flight deck toward the forward control center. A reinforced steel door kept the clammy mist outside. Samuel barely noticed the change in the temperature as he entered the enclosed upper deck. He had more important matters on his mind.

A short hike through the ship's corridors brought him to the *Sancta Helena*'s primary operations center. The chamber was a high-tech mecca, equipped with a battery of state-of-the-art computer stations, screens, and speakers. A dedicated team of researchers and technicians manned the surveillance stations. Macaro had recruited them from most of the world's major intelligence services, including the CIA, MI6, and the Mossad. Casting a wide net, he had also cherry-picked the worlds of organized crime and the international computer-hacker community for the best talent available. This usually involved faking the deaths of new recruits; to work for Macaro meant becoming a virtual nonperson as far the rest of the world was concerned. The Cleaners operated in near-total anonymity. Not only did they officially not exist, they had not even become the stuff of myth or urban legends. *The vampires and the lycans get more press than we do,* Samuel reflected, *despite our best efforts to cover their tracks.*

Curious eyes looked up to note his arrival, before turning back to the keyboards and monitors in front of them. As Samuel strode through the busy ops center, he overheard snatches of various news reports and police communications. The latest skirmish in the war had been unusually messy. The control room was abuzz with captured chatter:

". . . no new leads in the case of the brutal subway shootout in downtown Budapest. Police suspect gang activity . . ."

". . . search for bodies continues after private train is found deserted . . ."

". . . gunfire heard in tunnels beneath Metro station . . ."

". . . large quantities of blood found inside the train . . ."

". . . secure crime scene immediately! Repeat, secure crime scene . . ."

". . . heavy snowfall interferes with investigation . . ."

". . . American doctor wanted for questioning . . ."

". . . evidence of a struggle at Corvin's apartment . . ."

". . . interview all known associates and coworkers . . ."

". . . watch all airports and train stations . . ."

". . . contact U.S. embassy for more information . . ."

". . . no eyewitnesses can be found . . ."

And they won't be, Samuel thought. He and his team had seen to that. *Now if we can just lay our hands on this Michael Corvin.* The missing American seemed to be at the center of the current crisis. Listening to the reports, Samuel found himself disturbed by the way the twilight war between the vampires and the lycans had escalated over the last few nights. Bloody shoot-outs in public? A massacre at a train station? The warring immortals were usually more circumspect than this. *I don't like the sound of this.*

The walls of the ops center were plastered with digital photos and video captures of the latest casualties in the ancient blood feud. A dismembered vampire lay in pieces upon the tracks behind a stalled subway train, evidently torn to shreds by an enemy werewolf; one of Macaro's crack researchers had already identified the mangled remains as belonging to a Death Dealer named Nathaniel. Another dead vampire had been found on the subway platform nearby. His body had been thoroughly carbonized, as though exposed to a lethal amount of sunlight. Samuel suspected that the charred corpse was going to be all but impossible to identify conclusively.

The subway battle had occurred three nights ago. His gaze shifted to photos from a more recent bloodbath, one that had taken place earlier tonight. The gruesome shots depicted the plush interior of a private passenger train. Dried blood was splattered all over the red paneled walls and polished gold fittings. Bullet holes perforated the windows and crimson leather shades. A silver candelabra rested on the deep red carpet, next to an overturned divan with crimson upholstery. The bodies of over a dozen butchered vampires were strewn about the luxurious dining car. High-ranking members of the New World Coven and Vampire Council had been torn apart and disemboweled, their mutilated remains joining those of Death Dealers assigned to protect them. Judging from the shocked expressions on their lifeless faces, the undead delegation had been caught completely off-guard by the werewolves' sneak attack.

Sloppy, Samuel thought. The dead bodyguards should have been prepared for anything. He wasn't too surprised, though. The vampires had grown overconfident since hunting the lycans to the brink of extinction over the last few centuries. *They weren't expecting anything like this.*

Frankly, neither were we.

His eyes were drawn to a close-up of a strikingly beautiful vampire woman. Even contorted in fear, her glassy green eyes wide with horror, her face would have been the envy of any aspiring supermodel. A priceless jeweled pendant dangled from her throat. Raven-black hair lay in disarray about her shockingly pale head and shoulders. Her pallid complexion suggested what an on-site examination had already confirmed: every last drop of blood had been drained from the Elder's body.

Even though there could be no mistaking her identity, Samuel still found it hard to wrap his head around the idea that the legendary Lady Amelia was no more.

And Viktor as well. Two Elders dead in a single night!

But the werewolves had taken some serious losses, too. The bodies of several known lycans had been recovered from a known vampire safe house in Pest, their cooling bodies riddled with silver bullets. And more bodies, both lycan and vampire, had been extracted from the underground tunnels and bunkers—including what appeared to be the body of Lucian himself— where an apparently major battle had been fought.

Overnight, it seemed, the leadership of both the vampires and the lycans had been completely uprooted. All the more reason to report to Macaro at once. Samuel could only hope that his leader could make some sense of these troubling new developments.

If he can't, who can?

A staircase at the far end of the ops center led to Macaro's private suite, overlooking the bustling activity below. In contrast to the futuristic ambience of the control room, the palatial suite reeked of Old World opulence. Antique furniture and genuine Persian carpets decorated the office. A nineteenth-century ebony armoire, of Hungarian secession style, held Macaro's personal collection of historic weapons. A crystal chandelier hung from the ceiling, surrounded by swaths of billowing fabric. A life-size wooden carving of a Grecian Muse dominated the back of the suite, ascending from the hardwood floor to the ceiling like Aphrodite rising from the foam. Only the stainless-steel shutters over the windows, and the sturdy metal bulkheads composing the walls, reminded Samuel that he was still aboard a ship and not entering the drawing room of some stately old mansion. It was like stepping from Launch Control at Cape Canaveral into a Merchant-Ivory movie.

The man who called himself Lorenz Macaro sat behind a large mahogany desk, facing the stairs. The carved figurehead loomed behind him like a guardian angel. Despite the ongoing crisis, the man's desktop was clean and meticulously organized. An antique hourglass rested next to an empty in-box. Fountain pens, stationery, and a leather-bound journal were meticulously arrayed atop the imposing desk. A skylight in the ceiling allowed the moonlight to fall across the deck. A Tiffany lamp added a touch of extra illumination.

Macaro looked up from his journal as Samuel approached. The master of the *Sancta Helena* was an elderly man who appeared to be in his late sixties. A neatly trimmed white beard matched his snowy hair and bangs. A maroon coat, which had the look of something that might have been worn by the naval commander of a bygone era, graced his dignified frame. An engraved signet ring glittered upon his right hand.

Despite his apparent age, no trace of infirmity could be seen in Macaro's mien or manner. His cool gray eyes were fully alert. A quiet authority radiated from his presence, along with a certain weary melancholy.

He raised his hand to signal an aide standing near the top of the staircase. Within moments, the hubbub from the ops center grew softer as the investigators below muted all the communications being monitored. Headsets were fastened over the ears of the researchers, so that they could continue their work in relative silence. The glow of the video screens flickered over the ceiling above the control room.

The Old Man did not waste time with pleasantries. "The innocent who witnessed?" he asked Samuel. His voice was strong and clear, undiminished by age. Samuel heard the concern in his tone. "They've been silenced?"

"But otherwise unharmed," Samuel assured Macaro. "As you ordered."

A judicious combination of bribes, threats, and blackmail had been enough to ensure that any eyewitnesses to the immortals' latest escapades would not go running to the press or the authorities. It helped, of course, that most of the witnesses could barely believe their own eyes or lacked any true understanding of what they had beheld. And who would believe them anyway, aside from the most credulous and disreputable tabloids?

Macaro nodded, obviously pleased that no additional mortals had been harmed. He rose from his seat and stepped out from behind his desk. "Come," he instructed Samuel, heading for the stairs. "Show me what you have."

Samuel followed his leader down the steps into the control room. Commandeering an empty workstation, Samuel slid a memory stick into the appropriate slot on the attached computer. The large plasma screen mounted above the computer came to life, displaying raw video footage of his team's recent missions. Miniature cameras embedded in the Cleaners' helmets had recorded the images as the team swiftly went about their work, eliminating any telltale evidence the vampires and lycans might have left behind . . . just as Samuel and his predecessors had done for countless generations.

They're not making it very easy for us this time.

The first batch of footage came from the cleanup operation at the Ferenciek Square Metro station, where a trio of Death Dealers had engaged in an all-out firefight with at least two lycan foot soldiers. Operating a remote, Samuel clicked from one Cleaner's point of view to another's. Jerky, erratic images depicted army boots splashing through greasy puddles below the subway platform, gloved hands snatching up bodies (and body parts) and stuffing them into bags, chisels digging squashed silver bullets out of the tiled walls of the station, flashlights combing the subway tracks for tufts of dark wolfen fur, or anything else that might give away the inhuman nature of the combatants. Samuel recalled that no lycan corpses had been found at the site, although they had discovered traces of lycan blood deeper in the tunnels surrounding the station. Had both lycans survived the shoot-out, or had one of them carried the other's dead body away?

We may never know, he thought.

Macaro surveyed the footage from the Metro station without comment. "Amelia," he said after a moment or two.

"Yes, sir." Samuel used the remote to fast-forward through the images until he reached the footage taken at the blood-spattered dining car. According to their intel, Amelia and her entourage had been en route to Ordoghaz when they were ambushed by what had to have been a sizable pack of werewolves. Video from the helmet cams showed Samuel and the other Cleaners tidying up after the massacre, just as they had at the subway terminal. This time there had been many more vampire bodies to confiscate. Macaro watched as Amelia's bloodless corpse was bundled into a body bag.

Samuel knew what the Old Man wanted to see next and advanced the footage accordingly. The scene on the plasma screen shifted from the luxurious train interior to a murky subterranean bunker beneath downtown Budapest. Rubble and bullet-riddled wreckage hinted at the ferocious battle that had taken place in the underworld earlier tonight. The upper half of a severed head was matched to the remainder of a dead vampire's body. When the two pieces of the head were held together, there was no mistaking the imperious features of Viktor himself. A conscientious Cleaner made sure that both segments of the Elder's remains made it into the same body bag.

"Viktor," Macaro said.

Viktor had clearly not been killed by a werewolf. The fatal cut was too clean, almost surgical in its precision. Under interrogation, a surviving lycan claimed to have seen a female Death Dealer slay the Elder. This jibed with earlier reports linking Selene to Michael Corvin. Samuel was well acquainted with the female vampire's lethal reputation.

How could she have turned against Viktor so quickly? he wondered. *According to our files, she was utterly loyal to the coven and the Elders.*

Macaro had seen enough of Viktor's disposal. He gestured again, and Samuel fast-forwarded to the most recent footage, taken only a few hours ago, shortly after Kraven had been spotted returning to the vampires' mansion. The plasma screen lit up with scenes of Ordoghaz in flames. Yellow and orange flames leaped toward the winter sky as Viktor's historic mansion, the coven's home for nearly a thousand years, was consumed in a blazing inferno. Samuel kept the remote set on fast-forward so that the manor's destruction seemed to take place at an accelerated rate. The time-lapsed images sped by until the mansion had completely burned to the ground. In the end, all that remained of Ordoghaz was a heap of red-hot embers piled atop the hidden crypt.

Samuel felt a twinge of regret. All that history . . . lost forever. He wondered how many vampires had perished in the conflagration. Few immortals could withstand being burned alive. He slowed the footage down to the standard speed, allowing the smoking ruins to smolder in real time. Had any of the mansion's inhabitants managed to escape the blaze?

"And no trace of Marcus among the ashes?" Macaro asked.

Samuel shook his head. Their preliminary investigation had found no body in the Elder's tomb, where their intel had last placed him. It would be days before the site could be excavated in its entirety, but Samuel felt in his gut that Marcus had not been among those killed in the fire. Indeed, some evidence suggested that many of the mansion's residents had been torn apart before Ordoghaz had caught fire. "It seems he destroyed his own coven."

"It was never his coven," Macaro replied.

The morgue was located on one of the ship's lower decks. As opposed to the palatial decor of Macaro's office, the atmosphere within the morgue was cold, stark, and antiseptic. Heavy steel bulkheads insulated the chamber from the rest of the ship, not to mention the restless sea outside. Fluorescent lights mounted in the ceiling cast a harsh white light on the stainless-steel slabs, sinks, and gurneys below. Razor-sharp surgical implements rested atop metal trays. Freshly developed X-rays were displayed upon illuminated viewboxes. By design, the temperature was kept suitably refrigerated.

Macaro could practically smell the embalming fluid. "Give me a moment," he instructed Samuel.

The loyal soldier stepped outside and closed the door behind him, leaving Macaro alone in the morgue. The older man knew he could count on Samuel to see that he was not disturbed while he did . . . what had to be done.

Amelia's body was already laid out on a slab, awaiting a full autopsy. Macaro suspected the procedure would tell them nothing they didn't already know: the exquisite Elder had been bled to death by the same lycans who had butchered her retinue. *An ugly death,* he thought, *especially for one so beautiful.*

A pair of sealed body bags occupied slabs of their own. Macaro took a deep breath, then unzipped the nearer of the two bags. Lucian's lifeless face stared up at him. The blackened veins crisscrossing the lycan leader's gray countenance testified eloquently to the cause of death: acute silver poisoning. Macaro guessed that Lucian had suffered horribly before he died. Had the rebel commander been united with his beloved Sonja at last? Macaro hoped as much.

Perhaps someday I will see my own lost wife again. . . .

Unzipping the body bag farther, he opened Lucian's scuffed brown jacket. A puzzled expression came over the old man's face as he looked in vain for what he had expected to find. He groped beneath the jacket, but came up empty-handed. *Where the devil is that pendant?* he thought in surprise. *Lucian was never without it, not once in six hundred years.*

Baffled by the mystery, he turned his attention to the final body bag. Inside he found the remains of Viktor, along with the severed half of the warlord's skull. The gruesome sight did not repel Macaro; he had seen too much of life—and death—to be taken aback by such things. In his time, he had looked on far greater horrors and expected to do so again.

Such was his curse.

Still, the realization that both Viktor and Lucian now rested in this morgue was enough to give him pause. *This is a historic night,* he realized, *for those few of us who know the truth.* In many ways, Lucian and Viktor had been the architects and prime movers of the immortal war that had raged in the shadows of human history for the better part of a millennium. *Does this mean that the war is finally over?* Macaro would have liked to believe so, but the carnage at the vampires' mansion belied that comforting supposition. *I fear that this is merely the beginning of a new chapter in the endless conflict, God help us all.*

In the meantime, there were serious matters to be dealt with. He glanced at one of the X-rays mounted upon the wall. The glowing film clearly revealed a small, round object attached to one of Viktor's ribs. *Interesting*, Macaro mused. He opened Viktor's embossed leather tunic, exposing the Elder's bare chest, and dragged his fingertips across the cold, stiff flesh. *Aha*, he thought as his fingers detected a peculiar lump just below Viktor's rib cage. Macaro nodded in satisfaction. This time he had found what he was looking for.

Donning a pair of latex gloves, he plucked a scalpel from a nearby tray and rested the tip of the blade against the dead Elder's chest. Macaro's eyes narrowed in concentration as he sliced open the vampire's flesh, creating an incision large enough for him to thrust his fingers inside the unprotesting body. His fingers closed around a small, solid object that seemed to have been deliberately attached to the Elder's ribs.

There you are, Macaro thought. *Viktor hid you well, but not well enough.*

It took a bit of effort to disengage the object from the vampire's ribs, but the Old Man soon succeeded in dragging his prize out into the harsh glow of the fluorescent lights. He held the object up for his inspection.

The lights exposed an ornate, circular bronze device. Intricate runes were inscribed upon the metal ring, whose complexity was matched only by its unsettling beauty. Macaro wiped the device off with a silk handkerchief, then safely tucked it away in his clothes.

A cryptic smile lifted the corners of his lips.

Chapter Eight

*T*he abandoned mine felt much more desolate now that Selene was gone.

Michael stared at the blood-filled packet in his hand. The warmth of his body was already causing the frozen blood to thaw. Reddish purple fluid sloshed inside the sealed plastic bag. Did Selene expect him to drink it cold, or should he zap it in a microwave first? Either way, the very thought of consuming the blood turned his stomach.

Can I actually do this? he thought dubiously. As a doctor, and a surgeon, he had performed numerous blood transfusions, but he had never asked a patient to swallow the blood whole. For a moment, he considered setting up an IV and transfusing the blood into his own veins; at least that didn't seem as gross and unnatural as pouring the stuff down his throat. But would that satisfy the growing ache in his stomach? Michael tried to remember the last time he had eaten anything. It had to have been a day or so. One way or another, he had been on the run ever since Lucian had bitten him three nights ago.

No wonder I'm starving.

He contemplated the blood some more. Technically, it

was only cloned blood, but it looked real enough to him. All he needed to do, according to Selene, was rip open the packet and gulp the blood down. He had to assume she knew what she was talking about. For all he knew, she drank this stuff every day.

He gagged at the thought.

"Forget it!" he blurted. There was no way he could go through with it. Besides, maybe Selene was wrong. She said herself that he was unique, that nobody really understood how this whole hybrid business was supposed to work. Maybe he didn't need blood after all.

He tossed the bag away in disgust. It plopped onto a nearby counter.

That's better, he thought. He definitely felt weak, though, and light-headed. *I need food. Real food.*

On impulse, he threw his leather jacket back on. Selene would not be back until nightfall, if she returned at all. He had plenty of time to go find something to eat and still get back to the bunker before she came looking for him. Besides, he'd go stir-crazy if he had to stay cooped up here all day, alone with his thoughts.

Time for a breakfast run.

He passed a weapons rack on his way to the door. Should he grab a gun or two? The idea made him uncomfortable. He had gone his whole life without packing heat, and he resisted the idea that he had to go armed from now on. *The sun will be coming up in an hour or so,* he rationalized, *so I'm not likely to run into any insomniac vampires or werewolves.* Plus, he could always change into his hybrid form if he had to. He hadn't needed any firepower to defend himself against Viktor before. . . .

Leaving the weapons behind, he exited the safe house. It was still dark outside, and the snow was falling nonstop. A bumpy mountain road, all but buried beneath the frozen precipitation, led away from the deserted mine. Michael figured the road had to connect with civilization at some point. He trudged down the road, feeling the cold night wind blowing against his face. He thrust his hands into his coat pockets in a futile attempt to keep warm.

It was a miserable night for a hike. The arctic wind nipped at his exposed face. The chill seeped into his bones. His jacket lacked a hood, so the snow fell directly onto his head and shoulders. Melting snowflakes slipped beneath his collar, causing ice water to trickle down his spine. He kept his eyes peeled for headlights, hoping that maybe he could hitch a ride to the nearest bar or diner, but apparently nobody was stupid enough to try driving through the blizzard. The only bright side to the storm was that there didn't seem to be any hostile monsters out prowling around either. The only thing taking a bite out of him was the cold.

Was Selene enduring an equally uncomfortable trek? He wondered if she had made it back to the vampires' mansion yet, and, if so, what sort of reception she had run into. *Dammit,* he thought, *I should have gone with her.* He hated the idea of her facing this other Elder, Marcus, alone. She had sliced Viktor's head in two. Did she really think the other vampires were going to forgive that? *What if I never see her again?*

No, he couldn't allow himself to think like that. Selene *had* to come back, and not just because she was his only guide to this strange, secret world of hers. Michael was surprised by the intensity of his feelings. He had known Selene for less than a week, yet already he couldn't imagine going on without her. Selene was nothing like Samantha, the fiancée he had lost so many years ago. Yet somehow he felt closer to her than he had to any woman since Sam's death.

Guess that's what happens when you go through hell together.

By the time he spied the lights up ahead, he felt as if he had been slogging through the snow for ages, even though it had only been about fifteen minutes, tops. His face burned from the cold, and he had lost all feeling in his fingers and toes. Hunger still gnawed at his stomach, but the need for warmth was rapidly overtaking his appetite as a priority. Hopefully, the lights meant that he could take care of both needs simultaneously.

Picking up the pace, he staggered out of the forest. He found himself on the outskirts of a small mountain town consisting of a meager collection of run-down, weather-beaten buildings running along a single main street; you could probably drive from one end of the town to the other in less than two minutes. Michael spotted a service station, some darkened storefronts, and—thank God!—a tavern. Most of the town looked as if it hadn't woken up yet, but Michael was relieved to see lights burning inside the tavern. He mentally thanked the bar's customers for staying up into the wee hours of the morning.

Cars and pickup trucks were parked outside the tavern. Michael dragged himself across the snow-covered parking lot. A neon sign informed him in Hungarian that the place was open all night, which was the best news he had heard all week. He yanked open the front door and was greeted by a rush of hot air. *All right,* he thought, basking in the sudden warmth. *Just what the doctor ordered.*

The interior of the tavern was rustic in the extreme. The patrons sat on wooden benches in front of crude log tables. Kerosene lanterns glowed atop the tables, while a single lamp hung from one of the thick oak beams supporting the ceiling. Sawdust covered the floor. Old-fashioned cracker barrels were stacked in the corners. A horizontal mirror, mounted behind the rough-hewn bar, reflected Michael's bedraggled features. He brushed his hair back in an attempt to look a little less pathetic. A neon sign advertised Kobanyai brand beer. A silent jukebox occupied the back wall, next to a flashing pinball machine. A TV set, propped up in one corner, was tuned to a local news station. A Hungarian weatherman predicted snow.

No shit, Michael thought.

His entrance attracted a few curious stares. Michael guessed they didn't get a lot of strangers in these parts, especially at this godforsaken hour. His heart stopped momentarily as he spotted a pair of uniformed policemen sitting at one of the tables. *Just my luck,* he thought bitterly. Were the police still looking for him concerning that shoot-out in the Metro station? The last two police officers who had picked Michael up for questioning had turned out to be a couple of lycans in disguise, but that didn't mean that he wasn't still in hot water with the authorities. Hell, he had practically attacked one of his fellow residents back at the hospital, while raving incoherently about bite marks and hallucinations. How could the police *not* be after him? He swallowed hard and tried not to look too guilty.

Damn, he thought. *I should have checked out the parking lot more carefully.*

Selene would never have made a mistake like this.

As always, Marcus was amazed at how much the world had changed in two hundred years. When last he had gone into the earth, at the dawn of the nineteenth century, Buda and Pest had been two separate cities, divided by the winding waters of the mighty Danube. Now a unified capital, linked by many imposing bridges, lay beneath him as he soared through the frigid night sky. The modern miracle of "electricity" lit up the sprawling metropolis, so that the city glittered like a crystal chandelier, outshining the full moon above. Even though Kraven's stolen memories had prepared him for the sight, the revived Elder gaped in wonder nonetheless.

Truly, this brave new millennium had wrought many changes, not the least of which was his own unexpected metamorphosis. Leathery wings carried his wizened form above the transformed city. Although his mummified appearance testified to the fact that he had not yet fully recovered from his long repose, despite the blood of Kraven and his decadent underlings, Marcus had wasted no time embarking on this vital quest. With Viktor dead at last, the time had finally come to fulfill an ancient vow, solemnly sworn upon a bygone night of blood and fire. For over eight hundred years he had bided his time, but now the long wait was over.

But first I must find this errant kinsman of mine.

"Michael Corvin."

Following Kraven's blood memories, he swooped down from the sky toward an unprepossessing neighborhood in central Pest. Night's umbrageous cloak, and the swirling snow, concealed his descent from whatever mortals might be awake at this ungodly hour. His eyes fell upon his destination: a broken-down, old brownstone on a dimly lit block in a bad part of town. The lonely streets looked devoid of life.

In contrast to the city's starry appearance from on high, this region of Pest had declined dramatically since Marcus had last walked these streets. Little remained of the gorgeous baroque architecture erected by the Hapsburgs after over a century of Turkish occupation. The dilapidated brownstone was an ugly pile of bricks, blackened by decades of smog and soot. Steel-shuttered windows and garish graffiti suggested that the homely edifice had been abandoned for some time.

Which was not exactly the case.

Marcus touched down upon the snow-covered roof of the building. According to Kraven, this site was often used by the Death Dealers as a "safe house." A locked door barred entrance to the brownstone, but the Elder easily ripped the door from its hinges. He tucked his wings against his shoulder blades as he passed through the narrow portal.

The smell of rotting corpses and foul lycan blood struck him the minute he entered the building. Descending a flight of stairs, he found a scene of utter carnage. Lycan bodies littered the floor, surrounded by pools of clotting blood. Broken glass, chipped plaster, and bullet shells added to the clutter. Many of the lycan soldiers still clutched their formidable-looking modern muskets in their lifeless hands. Marcus was saddened, but not surprised, to see with his own eyes that William's subhuman spawn still infected the earth. Over the centuries, they had proven damnably hard to exterminate, especially after the coven's ill-advised attempt to domesticate them back in the Dark Ages. Lucian had taught them the folly of that enterprise.

Perhaps it is just as well, he mused. *Destiny surely has its own plan for William and his breed.*

Turning his thoughts away from the past, Marcus contemplated the bloody detritus before him. Obviously, a battle had been fought here, mere hours ago. He searched the faces of the dead lycans but was disappointed to discover that Michael Corvin was not among them. *That would have been too easy, I suppose.*

Broken glass crunched beneath the leathery soles of his taloned feet as he strode through the gory debris. Crates and cardboard boxes cluttered the suite. An interrogation chamber boasted chains, shackles, and a heavy steel chair. Snow blew in through a shattered window. Bloody torture implements rested upon trays and counters. A weapons locker contained an arsenal of modern firearms. Fluorescent lights glowed overhead.

He scanned the aftermath of the battle, looking for . . . *ah, yes!* Black eyes widened at the sight of illuminated screens, consoles, and keyboards. Glowing images shifted upon the screen, as if by sorcery. Marcus quickened his pace as he approached the futuristic communications station. His sharpened nails tapped experimentally at the keyboard.

Now came the difficult part. "Computers" and "linked networks" were two hundred years after his time. Ideally, Amelia would have transferred her own blood memories to him upon his Awakening, ensuring a smooth transition into the present, but Amelia was dead, a victim of Kraven's treachery. He would have to rely on the turncoat's own memories instead.

Closing his eyes, he rifled through Kraven's memories at lightning speed. Repetitive images of ceaseless blood orgies and self-important posturing made him despair for the sorry state of the coven under Kraven's regency. Clandestine meetings with Lucian emphasized once again the full extent of Kraven's perfidy. In retrospect, Marcus found it hard to believe that he and the other Elders had ever taken Kraven's lies about killing Lucian at face value. *What fools we were to trust him!* He experienced Kraven's unrequited lust for Selene and recalled that the female Death Dealer, Viktor's beloved protégée, was still on the loose, most likely in the company of Michael Corvin. He owed Selene a debt for slaying Viktor, but that would not spare her if she dared to come between him and his prize. He had already killed an entire coven tonight. The death of one more vampire meant nothing to him.

Only the quest mattered.

It took Marcus only seconds to settle on the memory he required. In his mind's eye, he saw Kraven seated before a similar station. Gold rings, studded with precious gems, glittered upon the regent's fingers as he tapped upon a keyboard. Marcus perused the thoughts that had passed through Kraven's brain at that moment, extracting from them the knowledge he now required. He was gratified to discover that the network had been designed to be "user-friendly."

How very convenient.

Hesitantly at first, but with increasing confidence, Marcus worked the keyboard. A series of graphic interfaces flashed across the monitor in front of him. Pleased by the speed of this ingenious new technology, he quickly located what he was looking for: a digital map displaying the location of various other safe houses employed by the coven. A flashing red icon indicated that one such sanctuary was currently in use.

Withered lips turned upward in a smile. The site in question was not far from here.

No, not far at all.

"There you are," he pronounced.

Chapter Nine

Selene marched through the snowy forest at a brisk pace. She was cold and exhausted from the night's trials, but she could not afford to rest, not even for a second. She had to reach Ordoghaz by dawn or risk being caught out in the open when the sun rose. The daylight would kill her just as readily as any voracious werewolf or vindictive Elder. She glanced up through the canopy of tree branches overhead. From what she could see of it, the sky did not appear to be lightening yet. She still had time to get to the mansion.

I hope.

Granted, she wasn't entirely sure why she was trying so hard to survive, given that her entire reason for being had gone up in flames over the past seventy-two hours, like a vampire in the sun. Her family's deaths had finally been avenged, but at the cost of learning that her entire immortal life had been a lie. So why bother to go on living?

Habit, I suppose.

And Michael.

A frown crossed her face at the thought of the young American doctor. She knew she should be focused on her upcoming encounter with Marcus, but her thoughts kept gravitating back to the flustered young man she had left behind in the bunker. Would he muster the courage to drink the cloned blood as she had instructed? She could tell that he was still struggling to come to terms with his new condition.

Not that she could blame him. What Michael had gone through over the last three nights would be enough to traumatize any mortal. She was impressed that he was coping as well as he was.

He might not be a warrior, she thought, *but he's not without courage.*

Unlike, say, Kraven.

She pushed herself to walk faster, determined to reach Ordoghaz before the treacherous regent. She couldn't allow Kraven to destroy Marcus and take control of the coven. Then she and Michael would truly be fugitives for all eternity.

I almost hope Kraven and I arrive at the mansion at the same time, she thought, *just so I can have the pleasure of personally blowing his head off.* Her cold blood seethed at the memory of Kraven shooting Michael in the chest with the silver-nitrate gun. Kraven would pay for that unprovoked assault, as well as for his copious other crimes. *I'll see to that myself.*

She smiled at the thought, more comfortable hating Kraven than dealing with her confusing feelings regarding Michael. She tried again to push the American from her thoughts. He was attractive, yes, and compassionate, but she was a soldier on a mission, not a lovesick damsel from one of the romantic ballads she'd heard as a child. Besides, he was at least six hundred years too young for her.

So why couldn't she forget the warmth of his blood within her mouth, the taste of his skin beneath her lips? She remembered the thrill she had felt as her fangs had slid gently into his tender flesh. . . .

A flapping sound intruded upon her sensual reverie. Looking up through the snow-laden branches, she was astounded to see a winged figure, like some terrible dark angel, soaring over the treetops. Her jaw dropped and her brown eyes opened wide.

What in the Elders' name . . . ?

Centuries of prowling the shadows had not prepared Selene for the sight of the airborne apparition above her. She had never seen anything like this creature, in either the mortal or immortal spheres. Scalloped bat-wings swiftly carried the figure out of view as it flew south, back the way she had come.

Selene froze in her tracks as a terrifying thought awoke inside her. Could that have been . . . Marcus? She had only glimpsed the winged creature for a few seconds, but something about it set off alarm bells at the back of her mind. The Elders did not possess wings, at least not before tonight, but many things had changed over the last several hours. A sudden chill ran down her spine as she remembered Singe's blood spreading across the floor of the Elders' crypt, beneath which Marcus hung in repose. What had Viktor said again, shortly before he'd crushed the lycan scientist's skull?

"An heir to Corvinus lies there, not three feet from you."

He had been referring to Marcus himself. Was it possible that the lone Elder indeed possessed the same genetic quirk as Michael? Had Marcus also become a hybrid?

The very idea filled her with dread, especially when she recalled that the winged entity had been flying southwest.

Toward Michael.

Possessed of a sudden fearful premonition, she spun

around and started racing back the way she had come. Her boots trampled over the deep tracks she had previously left in the snow, as she sprinted through the forest as fast as her athletic legs could carry her. All thought of reaching Ordoghaz was forgotten. Over the centuries, Selene had learned to trust her instincts, and right now those instincts told her that Michael was in deadly danger. Kraven and the mansion would have to wait.

I'm coming, Michael! she thought fiercely. The winged apparition had a head start on her, but Selene kept on running regardless. She wasn't going to surrender Michael without a fight, no matter what sort of entity was after him. She prayed that he was still safely locked away in the hidden bunker. *Watch yourself,* she entreated him silently. *Don't take any reckless chances.*

The tail of her black trench coat flapped behind her as she ran.

To Michael's relief, the cops gave him only a cursory glance, before turning back to their meals. They seemed more interested in their breakfasts than in the new arrival. The tavern's other patrons left him alone as well.

Thank heaven for small favors, he thought.

Finding an empty table, he dropped down onto a bench. After his long hike through the snow, it felt good to be out of the cold. A weary-looking barmaid took his order and he waited impatiently for his food. His stomach growled like a hungry werewolf. He licked his lips in anticipation.

God, I feel as if I could eat a horse. He shuddered at the thought of the plasma bag he had left behind at the old mine. He was starving, but he wasn't *that* hungry.

Yet.

The feeling was starting to return to his fingers and toes

by the time the barmaid returned with his order. She slid a large plate of paprikás krumpli in front of him, along with a mug of hot coffee. He couldn't complain about the size of the portions; the diced potatoes and peppery sauce was practically overflowing the plate. The spicy smell of paprika overpowered his nostrils. It was rich, heavy fare, exactly what he was in the mood for.

And yet . . . he hesitated before digging in. Selene's words came back to him: *"Normal food would be lethal."* Did she mean that literally?

Best to take it slow. He speared a chunk of potato with his fork and cautiously took a bite. He chewed the food slowly, ready to spit it out at once if he experienced any adverse effects. Contrary to Selene's warning, however, the savory dish went down fine. Better than fine, in fact; it tasted delicious. Throwing caution to the wind, he start shoveling the food into his mouth, wolfing it down ravenously. He couldn't eat the stuff fast enough. Within moments, he had finished half the plate and was thinking about ordering a second helping.

Keep it coming, he thought.

Then it hit him. A sudden wave of nausea washed over him, causing him to choke and sputter. The hot meal started climbing back up his throat. He gulped the entire mug of coffee to try to wash it back down, but the nausea only got worse. He clenched his jaws to keep from vomiting all over the table.

Oh, shit! he thought. *Selene was right.*

His body was rejecting the food.

The TV news program continued to drone in the background. Michael ignored the broadcast until two English words rang out amidst the Hungarian:

"Michael Corvin."

What the fuck? Despite his churning guts, Michael looked up to see his hospital ID photo plastered all over the TV screen. The anchorwoman said something about "wanted for questioning" and "possibly dangerous."

I'm screwed.

Sure enough, the two cops had not missed the news bulletin. Looking away from the TV, Michael saw that the policemen were already out of their seats and headed toward him, guns drawn. "Don't move!" the lead cop yelled at him in Hungarian. He was a stocky-looking Slav wearing a blue winter jacket and a black fur cap. His partner was slimmer and younger. "Hands over your head!"

A spasm twisted Michael's guts. He clutched his stomach, his face contorted in agony. Another seizure rocked his body. A cold sweat broke out over his body. He felt hot . . . feverish. It was kind of like the ordeal he had gone through when he'd first started to change into a werewolf, back in that squad car in Budapest, but different, too. He clutched the side of the table until his knuckles turned white. The veins on his neck stood out like cables. His legs vibrated restlessly beneath the table. His teeth tugged at his gums. He slumped forward, resting his head against the coarse wooden tabletop. More of Selene's warning flashed through his brain:

"If you don't anticipate your cravings, you will attack humans."

"Please," he begged the cops. "Get away."

This was clearly more than the two men had bargained for tonight. "What's the matter?" the younger cop asked, a note of panic in his voice. His gun hand trembled alarmingly. "Is he on drugs?"

"Or just crazy," the older cop said. His aim was steadier. "Go call for backup."

The young cop didn't need to be asked twice. He scrambled toward the front door, leaving his senior partner to deal with the distraught American. "I said, put up your hands!" the older cop repeated. He stepped closer to the table. Michael's head began to pound as the cop approached. It felt as if someone were beating on a war drum inside his skull. His temples throbbed to the same relentless drumbeat.

"What's the matter? Are you deaf?" the cop snarled, waving his gun in Michael's face. "Don't give me any trouble!"

Michael was too sick to obey the policeman's orders. All he could hear was the thunderous pounding in his head, which seemed to grow exponentially louder with every step the cop took toward him, until it sounded like tidal waves crashing against a rocky shore over and over. It was the moon that controlled the tides, he recalled, and there was a full moon out tonight. . . .

His febrile gaze was irresistibly drawn to the bull-like neck of the older cop—and the jugular pulsing beneath the skin. The tempting artery throbbed in perfect unison with the excruciating pounding in Michael's skull. He visualized the hot blood coursing through the other man's jugular and realized with horror that he had been listening to the cop's heartbeat this entire time!

Oh my God, he thought. *What's happening to me?*

Lorenz Macaro stood at the top of the stairs overlooking the ops center. The artifact he had extracted from Viktor's corpse rested securely within one of the inner pockets of his coat. Samuel maintained his post at the foot of the stairs, awaiting further orders. Macaro suspected that he would be dispatching the Cleaners again before long.

The *Sancta Helena* had left the Black Sea and was now cruising up the Danube toward Budapest. The Hungarian capital appeared to be the nexus of the current crisis, so

Macaro had thought it wise to bring his floating headquarters closer to the front lines. Running at top speed, the ship was expected to dock at Budapest by nightfall.

God grant that we are not too late, he thought. A familiar melancholy hung over his soul, leavened only by a growing conviction that matters were rapidly coming to a head. *Can it be that we have come to the final chapter at last?*

Below him, the ops center was still in full crisis mode. Investigators manned every station, monitoring the media and police chatter. The fire at Ordoghaz continued to generate ample news coverage, but Macaro anticipated that there was little more to be learned there. Marcus had burned all his bridges behind him. Macaro could only guess at the Elder's present activities, but he had no doubt as to Marcus's ultimate objective.

He has to be stopped, Macaro knew. *At all costs.*

While each investigator dutifully monitored his or her own assigned frequency, tuning out any and all distractions, their commander strove to listen to every broadcast at once. To anyone else, the babble of competing voices would have been an incomprehensible wall of sound, but Macaro could differentiate each one. His brow knitted in concentration as he mentally sorted through the various reports and snatches of police chatter. That some of the conversations were in Russian, German, and English posed little difficulty for him.

An excited voice, shouting in Hungarian, caught his attention.

". . . Corvin, the American fugitive . . . he's here!"

Macaro's hand shot up. He pointed decisively at one of the receivers below.

"There!" he said tersely.

His people responded with laudable speed. Instantly, all the other transmissions were silenced. Only the voice emanating from the indicated receiver could be heard throughout the ops room. The entire team listened intently.

". . . requesting immediate backup. Repeat, requesting backup . . ."

That's it, Macaro thought. A rush of excitement shot through his veins. He snapped his fingers and shot an urgent look at Samuel.

"Get the men up there now!"

Chapter Ten

Michael gripped the edge of the table. The policeman's heartbeat pounded inside his skull. He tried to look away from the cop's throbbing jugular.

"Please . . . just get away." Desperation tinged his voice. It was an effort just to speak. "You've got to get away."

His eyes remained locked upon the cop's throat. The stupid policeman had no idea of the danger he was in! Brandishing his service revolver, he advanced on Michael until he was only a few inches away from the other side of the table. "Surrender peacefully and you won't get hurt," he promised. "Don't make me use this gun."

Michael clamped his eyes shut. He tried to think of baseball scores, the periodic table, Beatles lyrics . . . anything to fend off his uncontrollable urge to feed. But it was no use. He could still hear the cop's pulse echoing inside his head, drowning out the pathetic squeaking of his conscience. His mouth watered involuntarily. Sharpened incisors slid from his gums. Taloned nails dug deep scratches into the wooden surface of the table. He couldn't hold on any longer.

"Get the fuck away from me!"

The cop stepped up to the table, a belligerent expression on his beefy face. "That's enough!" he grunted. Besides the gun, he had a clear weight advantage over Michael. A pair of handcuffs dangled from his belt. "You're coming with me!"

Michael's eyes snapped open. Jet-black orbs glared balefully. He growled back at the startled policeman, exposing a mouthful of jagged fangs.

"Holy Mother—!" the cop gasped. Too late, he staggered backward, away from the table.

Michael's sanity took a time-out. Driven by an overwhelming physical compulsion, he pounced across the table at the other man, knocking him to the floor. The cop only managed to fire off one shot before his gun went flying from his fingers. The shot went wild, nailing the ceiling instead of Michael. Splinters rained down onto the floor, mixing with the sawdust. The sharp report of the shot echoed against the sturdy timber walls.

Having cleared the table in a single leap, Michael was right on top of his prey. Razor-sharp talons dug into the cop's arms as Michael pinned them to the floor. The policeman's thick fingers groped uselessly for his lost pistol. Michael threw back his head, ready to sink his fangs into the other man's throat. Saliva dripped down his chin. He could already taste the cop's hot blood. He couldn't understand why he had waited so long. . . .

Pandemonium erupted inside the tavern. The other customers shrieked and shouted as they jumped up from their seats, knocking over tables and chairs. They pushed and clawed at one another in their desperate attempts to flee the tavern. Plates and cups crashed onto the floor. Behind the long wooden bar, the bartender dived for the floor. Flailing bodies crammed the front door, blocking each other. A trucker swore loudly in Hungarian. The barmaid let out a hysterical scream as a serving tray slipped from her fingers. Glass steins shattered loudly. Beer spilled over the sawdust.

The commotion momentarily distracted Michael. His fangs still poised over the policeman's jugular, he glanced up at the panicked crowd. Their terrified faces hit him like a sledgehammer. They looked scared to death.

Of me?

The thought was like a splash of cold water, restoring his sanity. He turned to look at himself in the mirror above the bar. He hadn't morphed all the way into his hybrid form, but the reflection he saw was repugnant enough. A blood-crazed beast, with ebony eyes and bestial fangs, stared back at him.

"Oh my God . . ." His own voice sounded alien to him, deeper and more guttural. He looked down at the cop beneath him. The man's face was white with fear. Frantic prayers tumbled from his lips. Michael realized that he had been only seconds away from ripping out the man's throat.

"You don't want that on your conscience," Selene had warned him.

He had come so close!

Sickened with himself, he let go of the cop's arms and clambered away from the man. His mind recoiled from what he had almost done; it was as if he were trapped inside his worst nightmare. He was supposed to be a doctor . . . a healer. Not a cannibal!

His eyes searched the faces of the fleeing patrons, seeking forgiveness and understanding, but all he saw were the panic-stricken eyes of innocent men and women afraid for their lives. They glanced fearfully back over their shoulders as they ran screaming into the parking lot outside. He had become these people's nightmare as well.

It was all too much for him. The room began to spin

around him, and he grabbed on to a tabletop for support. The pounding in his head multiplied and divided; he realized he was hearing the heartbeats of over a half dozen prospective victims, all mixed together in an unbearable cacophony. The smell of their alcohol-laced blood and sweat mixed with the oppressive odor of spilled beer and paprika. His stomach rebelled at the stench. Alternating waves of hot and cold washed over his body as the most violent spasm yet wrenched his insides. He dropped onto his hands and knees, gray-faced and shaking. He vomited explosively. Undigested potato sprayed from his mouth. He gnashed his fangs in agony.

Is this it? he wondered. *Am I dying?*

He half-hoped he was, but no such luck. Once his stomach was empty, he found the strength to lift his gaze from the floor. A lighted sign reading KIJARAT caught his eye. *Exit,* his brain translated, as he scrambled to his feet and ran for the tavern's back door. *I have to get out of here before I hurt someone for good.* That frozen blood back at the bunker was starting to sound like his last hope for salvation.

I should have listened to Selene!

The rear door was locked, no doubt in violation of the local fire codes, but Michael slammed into it with superhuman strength. The door crashed to the ground and Michael found himself lying face-first in a dark alley behind the tavern. Icicles dangled like spikes from the overhanging roof of the building. Frozen puddles filled the potholes in the pavement. Snow continued to blanket the ground. The sun had not yet risen.

Michael was starting to think this night was *never* going to end.

Attracted by the noise, the second cop came running around the corner. His flashlight lit up the alley. Michael's black eyes blinked against the glare. He rose quickly to his feet.

"*Stop!*" the young cop yelled. He drew his gun. "*I'm warning you!*"

No! Michael thought. He couldn't trust himself around anyone right now. He was sane again, but for how much longer? *For God's sake, just leave me alone!*

Turning his back on the cop, he raced toward the other end of the alley. Gunshots rang out behind him and he felt the bullets tear into his back. Blood exploded from his chest as the bullets passed through him. Pain flared along his nerve endings. The multiple impacts staggered him, throwing his stride out of whack, but he kept on running. Apparently the local constabulary did not employ silver bullets.

He winced at the searing pain. How many times had he been shot? He had lost count after the first few impacts. It came as a start to realize that this was the *second* time someone had shot him tonight, Kraven being the first. Selene's blood had healed him the first time around, but this time he was on his own. Ignoring the gaping exit wounds, he dashed out of the alley.

The cop's pounding footsteps chased after him.

Selene was dismayed to find the front entrance to the mine open when she arrived back at the safe house. Had the winged creature been here already? Half-buried boot prints, sunk deep into the snow, led away from the mine. Fresher tracks, made more recently, bore the unmistakable imprint of taloned paws. No werewolf had made those tracks; Selene knew wolfen spoor when she saw it, and these were something different. Hybrid tracks?

"Michael!" She raced into the bunker, afraid that she was already too late. Twin Berettas rested in her hands. Her fingers hovered on the triggers. She called out his name, but no one answered. A quick search confirmed that the bunker was empty. Her heart sank further as she spotted the untouched bags of cloned blood resting atop a counter. Her mouth watered at the sight, but there was no time to satisfy her own thirst. For all she knew, Michael was under attack at this very minute.

Could he defend himself against another hybrid? Selene didn't want to find out.

A series of loud reports echoed in the distance. *Gunshots,* she realized instantly. *Coming from somewhere outside.*

"Shit."

She dashed back out into the snow. The sound of the shots was coming from the east. The boot prints, which she assumed belonged to Michael, seemed to be heading in the same direction. *Toward town,* she guessed. Selene didn't know whether to be relieved or angry that Michael hadn't stayed put in the bunker. Everything depended on who found him first, her or . . . that thing in the sky.

I don't care if he is Marcus. He's not taking Michael away from me.

She glanced to the east, where a faint pink haze was beginning to form on the horizon. The sun would be up soon. If she was smart, she would take cover in the bunker until nightfall. There was no point in getting herself incinerated for a man she barely knew.

Fuck it.

She raced down the mountain road as if her immortal life depended on it.

More shots blared in the night.

The older cop, recovered from his close brush with death, came rushing out into the alley, joining his partner in pur-

109

suit of the fugitive. Michael heard both sets of footsteps pounding on the pavement behind him. Blood streamed from the bullet holes in his perforated black shirt. His chest and back felt as if they had been stabbed over and over with a red-hot poker. If he had still been human, he would almost certainly be DOA by now. Instead he managed to keep on running, despite having been shot repeatedly in the back. The bullet wounds throbbed with every step.

"Halt!" a cop yelled at him. "Stop right there!"

No way, Michael thought. He was less afraid of being captured by the police than of losing control again and possibly ripping both officers to shreds. Even now he could feel the hunger—and the madness—growing inside him once more. His black eyes gleamed in the night. He clenched his fangs together, fighting back the urge to turn around and savage the clueless humans with his bare hands and teeth. His mouth watered at the thought of their blood pouring down his throat. . . .

No! he thought. *That's not who I am!*

The forest beyond the alley beckoned to him. He glimpsed skeletal oak and beech trees through the open end of the alley. If he could just make it to the woods, he might be able lose his pursuers in the dense wilderness. He scooted out of the alley onto a one-lane street leading out of town. The woods were only a few yards away now, on the other side of the road. He was almost there. . . .

A wailing siren and flashing blue light caught Michael by surprise as a black-and-white squad car came squealing around the corner, blocking his path. It screeched to a halt directly in front of him. The glaring blue light hurt his eyes.

Michael didn't even slow down. Using the hood of the car as a springboard, he leaped over the vehicle into the forest. Behind the windshield, the backup cops gaped in amazement. A startled curse was drowned out by the screaming siren.

The two new cops piled out of the car. Toting rifles, they joined the original pair of officers in chasing after Michael. *Great,* he thought. *Now I've got* four *cops on my tail.*

A steep hill tested his dwindling endurance. He limped up the wooded slope, occasionally grabbing on to icy tree trunks for support. Flashlight beams raked the hill behind him as the cops followed him into the forest. He heard them shouting back and forth to each other. They sounded mad, anxious . . . and completely bewildered. Michael couldn't blame them for being confused. They probably weren't used to fugitives who kept running even after they were shot. Despite his injuries, he was still outpacing them.

But for how much longer? He could feel his strength ebbing. Halfway up the hill, he dropped to his knees, exhausted. Every muscle in his body ached. His legs felt like overcooked spaghetti. Glancing back over his shoulder, he saw that the cops were gaining ground, no more than thirty yards behind him. Their flushed, angry faces promised little mercy at their hands. Michael felt like an old-time movie monster being chased by a mob of torch-wielding villagers.

Have to keep going, he realized. Lurching to his feet, he stumbled up the hill. He gasped for breath, the frigid air searing his lungs. Each new step was an unbearable ordeal. Sweat soaked through his bloodstained shirt. Perspiration dripped from his face. Lactic acid built up painfully in his muscles. Michael knew he was nearing his limit. *I'm hitting the wall.*

"Halt! Stop where you are!" The policemen hurled threats and orders at him. He heard them panting in exertion as they clambered up the slope after him. "Stop or we'll shoot!"

Michael wasn't even listening to them anymore. Reaching the crest of the hill at last, he spotted a dilapidated structure a few yards ahead. A rusted tin roof topped a crude stone building missing entire chunks of bricks and mortar. *An old mining shed,* he guessed. He staggered toward it, desperate for any kind of shelter. He tottered upon unsteady legs. The ground seemed to tilt vertiginously beneath his feet. He took a few more steps, then toppled forward onto the ground. Six inches of snow cushioned his fall. The frosty powder chilled his face, so cold it burned. Chest heaving, he lay prone upon the snow, unable to move another inch. He could barely lift his face out of the snow.

Guess I should have chugged that cloned blood when I had the chance. He felt thoroughly drained, as if he had just run a marathon wearing iron boots. Darkness encroached on the periphery of his vision.

He wondered if he would ever see Selene again.

"Get him!" a furious cop yelled in Hungarian. Flashlight beams converged on Michael's fallen form. "Careful! He's a real lunatic!"

The cop's threatening tone sent one last jolt of adrenaline through Michael's system. He started crawling toward the ruined shed, dragging himself through the snow like a wounded animal. Fear drove him onward, but it was no use. His hybrid strength had completely evaporated.

Instinct took over. Looking back over his shoulder, he glared at his pursuers with jet-black eyes. Their flashlight beams all but blinded him as he bared his fangs and roared furiously in defiance.

"Holy shit!" the youngest officer exclaimed. He opened fire and the other policemen joined in. A hail of bullets slammed into Michael's body, which thrashed wildly be-

112

neath the lethal barrage. All four cops kept on firing as they advanced cautiously toward their writhing target.

Then . . .

Thwack! Selene took out the first cop with a ridge-handed blow to the neck. The mortal dropped like a sack of potatoes onto the snow. He wouldn't be getting up again anytime soon.

One down, three to go, she thought. Her Berettas remained holstered to her thighs. Despite their attack on Michael, she wasn't about to employ lethal force against human police officers.

She didn't need to.

Fifty feet away, the second cop heard his partner hit the ground. "Sandor?" Puzzled, he turned his flashlight toward the sound. The bright white beam fell upon the limp body of the other cop, sprawled facedown in the snow. The look on the other cop's face was almost comical in its stunned bewilderment.

"The fuck?"

Selene touched down right in the flashlight's beam, a vision of black leather and pale white skin. Landing only inches away from the startled policeman, she dealt with him up close and personal, inflicting a punishing combination of jabs before spinning him to the ground with a noisy crunch. He was out cold before his head even hit the snow.

Two down.

By now, the remaining cops were aware that something was amiss, but Selene barely gave the men a second to react before attacking them as well. She moved with preternatural speed and efficiency, striking in the night like the veteran Death Dealer she was. The odds against her were not even cause for concern. Selene had been fighting for her life against werewolves since before these mortals' great-great-grandparents had been conceived.

The cops didn't stand a chance.

A third officer took aim with his rifle, yet Selene passed before his sights like a blur. Three deafening blasts from the gun shredded the bark of an innocent chestnut tree, but that was it. He swung the muzzle of the gun around, trying to get another shot at the woman taking him and the other cops apart. "Who—?"

Suddenly, Selene was right beside him. She punched him so hard that his feet left the ground and he went hurtling into the trunk of a massive oak. His unconscious body slid down the side of the tree onto the snowy forest floor, then toppled over onto its side. It was lights out for him, too.

Three down, one to go.

The fourth and final cop spun around with his shotgun, but Selene was no longer where she had been standing only seconds before. In a heartbeat, she was closer than he expected, less than a foot away from him. She grabbed on to the barrel of the gun with surprising strength, and the cop squeezed the trigger in a panic. The shotgun went off, blasting Selene in the ribs.

Damn! she thought, wincing at the sudden explosion of pain in her midsection. The bullets hurt like hell, just as they always did. She closed her eyes and let the pain pass through her. The heated gun barrel burned her palm, but she didn't let go of the rifle. *Stupid!* she thought angrily, castigating herself for her carelessness. *I was overconfident . . . sloppy.*

The policeman stood frozen at the other end of the rifle, paralyzed perhaps by the enormity of what he thought he had done. He gasped as Selene's eyes snapped open. No longer chestnut brown, they now burned with an eerie blue fire. Ivory fangs gleamed between her lips.

114

Next time, try ultraviolet rounds, the pissed-off vampire thought. She was through messing around. With her right fist still wrapped around the barrel of the gun, she hammered the cop with a vicious left hook that damn near took his head off. He collapsed onto the snow, joining his fellow officers in unconsciousness. Selene didn't waste a second feeling sorry for him. *You're just lucky that I don't kill humans.*

An agonized groan from Michael reminded her of what was truly at stake. Hurling the rifle into the snow, she launched herself into the air, before landing as gently as a snowflake next to the injured young American. Packed snow crunched beneath her as she dropped down onto her knees beside him. "I'm here, Michael."

She saw at once that he was in a bad way. He had rolled onto his back and the front of his shirt had been reduced to tatters, exposing a bullet-ridden torso. Blood was smeared over everything, but she counted at least ten bullet wounds, maybe more. Sonja's pendant dangled from a chain around his neck, the crest-shaped emblem symbolizing untold centuries of heartbreak and sacrifice. Michael's eyes were glazed and unfocused. She couldn't even tell for sure that he knew she was there. His breathing came in ragged gasps. Placing a hand against his throat, she could barely feel his pulse. His eyelids drooped alarmingly. Blood trickled from the corner of his mouth, evidence of internal bleeding.

He's dying, she realized. For a second, she flashed back to that stormy night six hundred years ago, when she had knelt in the wet straw beside her father's body. She had been helpless then to preserve the lives of those she cared about. Now she felt as if she were reliving that nightmare all over again.

Except . . . she was no longer the trembling, defenseless maiden she had been back then. She was a very different Selene now, with options her younger self could never have dreamed of. *I'm no doctor,* she thought with grim determination, *but I know what Michael needs.* The last time he had been at death's door, after Kraven had shot him full of silver nitrate, Selene's bite had been enough to save him. *This time the reverse is required.*

Raising her arm to her mouth, she bit her wrist. Blood flowed from the severed veins and she thrust the wound against Michael's lips. At the barest taste of her blood, his eyes opened, growing clear and more focused than before. But as awareness dawned of what he was doing, he turned his face away, denying the salvation she was offering. Selene felt a curious pang of rejection. Was he repelled by her blood, or just unwilling to take of her own strength? Crimson droplets fell upon his cheek, but he twisted his head to keep them away from his mouth.

She urged him to accept her sacrifice.

"Michael, take it."

"No . . ." he insisted, turning his head to the side.

Chapter Eleven

"Michael, you'll die."

He heard her voice as from a great distance. *Selene?* As usual, there was no trace of emotion in her voice, but somehow he sensed just how much this meant to her. She had returned for him, hadn't she? That was the important thing. She wouldn't be offering him her blood if she didn't want to. . . .

I can't let her down.

His mouth found her wrist again and he began to drink. Her blood was as cool as a mountain stream and just as invigorating. He lapped gently at the wound at first, but an all-consuming thirst swiftly overpowered him. He sucked furiously, gulping down her precious blood as quickly as he could swallow it. For the first time in hours, he felt the gnawing emptiness inside him abate. *This* was what he had been craving all this time, even if he hadn't realized it. His tongue probed hungrily at the open wound. He couldn't get enough of her.

She flinched against his draw and let out a tiny gasp of pain. The bleeding clearly stung, but she did not pull back her arm. She cradled his head against her lap as the blood flowed between them. He felt her heartbeat pulse within his head, but unlike the pounding he had experienced before, this rhythmic drumming was oddly soothing, especially as their separate heartbeats began to converge. The more blood he took in, the more synchronized the disparate pulses became . . until at last they merged in a perfect union.

A feeling of ineffable peace washed over him, carrying away all his pains, fears, and doubts. He stared upward at her beautiful face, drinking in every lovely plane and angle of her alabaster features. Slowly, almost imperceptibly, her unearthly azure eyes took on their customary brown tint. White teeth bit down gently on her lower lip, perhaps to keep her from gasping out loud again.

Selene.

He realized that he needed to control his thirst, before he took too much from her. Allowing himself just one last sip, he released her wrist and let his head sag back against her lap. A contented sigh escaped his lips, and for the first time he wondered why exactly she had returned, and how she had happened to arrive in time to rescue him. *What does it matter?* he thought. *She came back . . . for me.*

He smiled woozily up at her, the taste of her still upon his lips.

"I didn't feel like watching you die today," she said coolly, as though what had just transpired between them was no big deal.

Yeah, right, Michael thought. He wasn't fooled by her hard-boiled soldier routine, but he let it slide. If that was how she wanted to play it, he was okay with it for now. *Let her have her shell. I've heard her heartbeat. I know how much she cares.*

She helped him up into a sitting position. He glanced

down at his tattered shirt and was shocked by the sight of nearly a dozen bullet wounds in his flesh. He tentatively fingered the scars. Not even the best emergency room in the world could have saved him the way Selene had. By all rights, he should have been dead.

"Shit."

If he needed any more proof that he was no longer remotely human, this cinched it. Still, maybe there were compensations.

He licked the last few drops of blood from his lips.

Michael's adoring gaze made Selene uncomfortable. Nothing in her experience had prepared her for a moment like this. She had no idea how to respond.

He's alive, she reminded herself. *That's what matters.* Her detached expression failed to convey the overwhelming relief she experienced deep inside. For a few moments there, as Michael was slipping away from her, she had felt utterly bereft and alone. *Just like when I found my father's corpse.*

Away from the natural anticoagulant in Michael's saliva, her sliced wrist was already starting to heal. She glanced up at the lightening sky; the rosy glow to the east was creeping steadily higher. Was Michael strong enough to travel? They had to get a move on. She didn't relish the idea of spending the entire day trapped inside that ramshackle shed up ahead, not with the dazed policemen due to wake up at some point. She could just imagine the irate officers dragging her out into the sunlight—with fatal results.

A distant rustle, like the flapping of enormous wings, drove that scenario out of her mind. Her muscles tensed in anticipation of danger. In her desperate effort to save

Michael from the policemen's bullets, she had almost forgotten the mysterious apparition she had sighted before.

Until now.

Her eyes searched the sky as a score of frightened crows suddenly took wing, erupting out of the trees in a flurry of agitated black feathers. The birds fled the scene en masse.

That can't possibly be a good sign, she thought.

"Can you walk?" she asked Michael. Her eyes continued to search the surrounding treetops. "We need to go."

Before he could answer her, the frantic fluttering of the departing crows was drowned out by a more foreboding rustle. *It's here,* she realized. She reached down and plucked a Beretta from beneath her trench coat. She grabbed on to Michael's wrist and yanked him to his feet. There was no time to be gentle about it. Ready or not, they had to get away from here.

I'll explain later, she thought, *if we get out of this alive.*

Their odds of surviving declined dramatically as a winged demon came swooping out of the night at them. Taloned claws slammed Selene into the wall of the mining shed, knocking the Beretta from her grasp. A single swipe from a colossal pinion sent Michael flying into a nearby snowbank. Her hand, which had been holding tightly to his arm, abruptly found itself empty.

The creature soared over her head, then landed several yards in front of her. It turned around and began advancing toward her, its great wings poised above its mottled shoulders. Despite its incongruous wings and batlike features, Selene recognized the distorted monstrosity stalking toward her. The inhuman visage still bore a warped resemblance to a face well known to her. His intricate golden belt and satin trousers were nearly identical to the garments Viktor had worn when he'd first Awoke.

Marcus?

Once again, an ominous sequence of events emerged from her memory: *Viktor striking Singe dead, the lycan scientist dropping onto the floor of the crypt, his blood flowing across the ancient tiles toward the Elder's tomb. . . .*

"I know what you have done, Selene," Marcus Corvinus declared.

Done? She wasn't sure what Marcus meant. She feared, however, that he already knew what had become of his fellow Elders. Had Kraven placed the blame on her? Out of the corner of her eye, she spotted the Beretta lying on the snow, a good fifteen feet away. Michael also appeared to be down for the count, leaving her to face the transformed Elder alone. *Very well,* she thought. *I shall not apologize for my actions.*

"Viktor deserved his fate." Her chin held high, she looked Marcus squarely in the eye. Her fingers crept quietly toward the other Beretta concealed beneath her coat, just to be on the safe side. "And Kraven was no better."

"Kraven has already reaped the rewards of his own misdeeds." Marcus eyed her thoughtfully, his hideous face inscrutable. He closed his wings, which folded neatly into his back. His voice took on a softer tone. "And, yes, Viktor deserved his fate, many times over. A terrible business, the slaying of your mortal family."

Selene was so stunned by Marcus's reaction that her fingers came away from her gun. Kraven already dead, and Viktor's death dismissed so easily? Hope flared within her heart that the situation might not be nearly so dire as she had supposed. Apparently, the other Elders had been unaware of Viktor's secret propensity for slaughtering humans, and of Kraven's role in covering up such atrocities. Perhaps there was still such a thing as true justice within the vampire community. *I'd like to think so,* she thought, *after defending the coven for six hundred years.*

"Yet so much effort was spent to conceal this matter from me," the Elder observed, taking another step toward her. "What do you suppose Viktor had to hide?" His eyes narrowed suspiciously and a more ominous tone entered his voice. "Or perhaps it is you, Selene, as the last of your wretched family, who has something to hide?"

What? She had no idea what Marcus was referring to.

He gazed down on her like a predator. Thin white lips peeled back to reveal his sharklike teeth. Exploding into motion, he lunged at her with bared fangs. She reached for her pistol, but the Elder was too swift for her. He was upon her in an instant, pinning her to the ground. She struggled to break free, but his powerful limbs held her fast. His head reared back like that of a striking cobra, poised to sink his deadly fangs into her throat.

A burst of automatic gunfire came to her rescue. Marcus roared in pain as a fusillade of 9 mm bullets tore into his face and neck. Dark blood sprayed from his pallid flesh. He turned angrily toward the source of the bullets.

Michael stood several feet away, squeezing the trigger of Selene's Beretta. His eyes were black with hybrid fury, just like Marcus's. Sonja's pendant rested against his chest.

The hail of bullets from the gun blasted Marcus off Selene. He tumbled backward into the snow, and she scrambled back onto her feet. Veering right to avoid being tagged by the Beretta's furious discharge, she raced to join Michael. Together, they watched in horror as Marcus rose from the snow and began stalking toward them, against the scorching gunfire. Blood streamed down his face, but the silver bullets only slowed him down. Michael's jaw dropped in amazement.

He's not just an Elder anymore, she realized. *He's a hybrid Elder.*

"Go!" she shouted.

They turned and rushed through the misty forest. Selene noticed with alarm that the shadows cloaking the woods were rapidly lifting as dawn approached. The ceaseless flapping of mighty wings pursued them as they fled toward nowhere in particular.

Selene wondered what would kill her first, Marcus or the sunlight?

The empty flat-deck truck came barreling down the mountain road. Behind the wheel, Ivan Bogrov yawned and tried to stay awake. He had been driving all night, since dropping off a load of timber at Piliscsaba, and now he just wanted to make it back to Szentendre before his exhausted body completely gave out. The sun would be up soon, and he was sorely in need of a hot shower and several hours of sack time. He scratched at the itchy gray stubble carpeting his jowls; a shave wouldn't hurt either. The snowy road forced to him to drive slower than he would have liked, but at least he had the road to himself.

Or so he thought.

Something dashed in front of his headlights. Ivan slammed on the brakes, and the truck slid to a stop atop the icy road. "What the hell?" he blurted in Russian. He had only glimpsed the figure for a second, but it had looked like a man . . . sort of. There was something *wrong* about it, though. He recalled a fleeting impression of slick, shimmery skin and weird black eyes.

Maybe I've been driving too long without a break.

Ivan peered through the frosty windshield at the road ahead. He was fully awake now, his heart pounding. Had he hit . . . whatever that was? He couldn't see over the hood. *I don't think I hit anything.* He hadn't heard or felt a collision. *Should I get out of the cab and check?*

He found himself reluctant to venture out of the truck, and not because of the cold. What if *it* was still out there? Before he could make up his mind, the driver's-side door was yanked open from the outside. The door clanged loudly against the body of the truck.

Huh? He spun around in his seat.

To his surprise, an incredibly sexy woman stood right outside the cab. Her dark brown hair and glossy black clothes stood in stark contrast to the virgin snow covering the landscape. The tail of her coat flapped in the wind, revealing a svelte figure that appeared to have been poured into skintight black leather. Luscious brown eyes looked him over.

Ivan's jaw dropped. His eyes bulged. "What the fuck?"

Not that he was complaining, of course.

"Mind if I drive?" she answered him in Russian.

The trucker ran his eyes up and down her enticing body. A hot shower and shave were no longer the only things on his mind. *This trip's definitely perking up,* he thought. A smirk showed through his stubble. *What the wife doesn't know can't hurt her. . . .*

"You can sit on my lap and blow the horn," he said with a leer. "How about that?"

Crunch! A body landed heavily upon the hood of the truck, yanking his gaze away from the leather-clad babe at the door. Ivan threw himself backward against his seat as a monstrous figure glared back at him, crouching atop the hood. Black eyes and jagged fangs drove all thought of sex from his brain. Terrified, he looked back at the woman, to confirm that she was seeing the same thing he was.

This can't be happening!

Her glowing blue eyes regarded him with amusement. A sly smile revealed the tips of two sharply pointed canines.

"Maybe next time, sweetheart."

Wampyr! Half-remembered folk tales and horror movies rushed through his mind as he lunged frantically for the passenger-side door. He shoved the door open and literally threw himself out of the cab. His heavyset body slammed into the snowy curb, but he was up and running madly away from the truck before another moment passed. Abandoning his truck, he bolted east toward the rising sun. The daylight called out to him like a life buoy to a drowning man.

Please, God! he prayed. *If you let me get away from these freaks, I swear I'll never fuck another hitchhiker again!*

Crouching in front of the windshield, Michael watched the nameless trucker haul ass into the woods. *Poor guy,* he thought, sympathizing with the panic-stricken driver. *A few nights ago, I would have reacted the exact same way.*

Now he didn't even look like a member of the same species. Acting on instinct, Michael had morphed into his hybrid form during their flight from the winged demon. Beneath his bloodstained shirt and jacket, his chest had expanded, its muscles bulging with superhuman power. His skin had taken on a shimmery, iridescent hue. A mane of wild brown hair framed his bestial features, which were more human than a werewolf's, but still unmistakably feral. Bony claws jutted from his bare hands and feet. The gilded pendant dangled around his neck.

Without giving the trucker another glance, Selene clambered into the driver's seat. "Get in!" she shouted urgently.

Michael started to comply, then something in the sky behind them caught his attention. His black eyes squinted to get a better look. Noticing his reaction, Selene glanced back over her shoulder.

"Oh, shit," he growled.

Marcus came soaring out of the forest. He dived toward them, swooping down over the road like a prehistoric bird of prey.

"Hang on!" Selene yelled. She threw the truck into gear and hit the gas.

The sudden acceleration almost threw Michael off the hood. Instead he scrambled over the roof of the cab and tumbled into the open bed at the rear of the truck. An eight-foot-tall wooden fence ran along both sides of the empty deck.

He rose to his feet and grabbed on to the wall for support . . . just as Marcus slammed into him with bone-jarring force. Michael was thrown backward across the deck, shattering the rear window of the cab right behind Selene's head. The sudden impact left him dazed and seeing stars.

The Elder's wings contracted into his back. His claws dug into Michael's shoulders. He whipped Michael around and hurled him down onto his back. Marcus pounced on his fallen opponent, bearing down on Michael like a ton of steel. Hybrid versus hybrid, they grappled upon the wooden floor of the deck. Marcus's batlike face was only inches away from Michael's slightly more human features. Two pairs of molten black eyes testified to their kinship.

This thing is actually related to me? Michael thought as he fought for his life. He tried to break the Elder's grip, but Marcus was far too strong. The Elder's eyes widened at the sight of Sonja's pendant swinging around Michael's neck. He

126

let out a high-pitched screech of satisfaction as he snatched the pendant, snapping its delicate golden chain with a vicious tug. Then he hit Michael with a backhanded blow that sent the younger hybrid tumbling over the back of the truck.

At the last minute, Michael grabbed on to the floorboards with his claws. He dangled precariously over the edge of the deck, hanging on for dear life. His bare feet hung suspended above the icy pavement behind the truck. Marcus stood astride the deck, watching to see if the other hybrid fell.

Selene! Michael thought desperately. *Help!*

Through the cracked rear window, he saw her looking back over her shoulder. Keeping one hand on the wheel, she raised her Beretta and fired back through the window. Shattered glass exploded outward as she blasted Marcus with round after round of red-hot silver. The Elder wheeled about angrily as the bullets tore through his undead flesh. The pendant slipped from his fingers, the sound of it hitting the wooden floorboards completely lost beneath the noise of the Beretta. The pendant bounced across the empty deck.

Selene didn't let up. The relentless barrage drove Marcus back across the truck's bed and over the edge. His wings snapped open, carrying him up and away from the snow-covered asphalt. He growled furiously as he flapped off into the early-morning murk.

Michael tried to pull himself back up onto the deck.

Is that it? Selene wondered. *Is he gone?*

Glancing in her rearview mirror, she saw Michael hanging off the end of the truck. Should she stop the vehicle and give him a chance to climb back into the empty bed? What

127

if Marcus was still after them? She eased up on the gas, uncertain what to do next. The snowy road stretched before her, leading to God knew where.

She started to brake, only to spy Marcus diving out of the sky once more. He flew alongside the truck, directly to her left, then careened against the driver's side of the cab, using his indestructible body as a battering ram. The five-ton truck rocked to one side as if it had been hit dead-on by a wrecking ball . . . with wings.

"Shit!" Selene cursed. She struggled to maintain control of the truck, the ice-slick pavement not making her task any easier. In the mirror, she glimpsed Michael swinging violently from the end of the truck. Momentum hammered him into the side of the bed. He scrambled to get a better grip on the wooden railing. *Hold on, Michael!* she pleaded with him silently. *Don't let go!*

For a second, she feared that the truck was going to flip over altogether, but, to her vast relief, the vehicle quickly righted itself, planting all four wheels back on the road. Looking ahead, she spotted a tight curve coming fast. She tugged hard on the wheel, barely making the turn in time. Beyond the bend, she saw a high rock wall approaching on the passenger's side of the road. An icy glaze frosted the craggy granite.

It would be nice if I didn't run into that, she thought. She steered with one hand, keeping the other hand locked around the grip of her Beretta. She looked about anxiously for Marcus, having momentarily lost track of the homicidal Elder. *Where the devil did you fly off to?*

A explosion of glass fragments answered her question as a taloned hand smashed through the cab's side window. Powerful fingers closed around her throat, throttling her. Marcus pulled his head and shoulders into the cab.

"Dead or alive," he snarled, "you will give me what I want!"

His jaws opened wide, eager for her flesh and blood. *Not so fast,* she thought, whipping the Beretta around. She opened fire, sending a round right down his throat.

The blast blew him away from the cab and sent him spiraling out of control. Gagging, he coughed up a mass of blood and silver. Selene hoped that would be enough to discourage him permanently, but she underestimated the Elder's persistence. His flight path stabilized and he swooped around the truck to the passenger's side of the cab.

Selene got a bead on him and fired off three shots. Marcus dodged the bullets and she squeezed the trigger again. The gun made a doleful clicking noise. *Dammit!* she thought. *I'm out of ammo!*

A malevolent grin stretched Marcus's monstrous visage as he started to climb into the cab from the passenger's side. Via the mirror, Selene saw that Michael was aware of her danger. Grunting through clenched fangs, he redoubled his efforts to pull himself up into the truck bed so that he could come to her defense.

She knew he wouldn't make it in time.

Marcus's claws reached out for her. . . .

Selene yanked hard on the wheel, swerving to the right. The speeding truck scraped against the solid rock face, smashing Marcus between them. He wailed in agony as his back and wings were crushed against the granite outcropping. Immortal bones snapped like twigs. Selene rode the rocky wall for at least thirty meters, holding hard on to the wheel. Sparks flew where the cab's metal frame scraped against the stone.

Sorry, Michael, she thought. The wild ride threw Michael

against the side panels of the truck, but Marcus had it much worse. Blood gushing from his spinning frame, he torna-doed down the side of the truck and out the back. This time, his battered wings did not spare him a nasty landing. He crashed to earth amidst the snow and gravel, hitting the road headfirst. A cloud of dust and frozen powder billowed up into the truck's taillights as Marcus rolled to a stop in the middle of the road. Watching in her mirror, Selene allowed herself a smile of satisfaction. The mighty Elder looked like roadkill.

But not for long.

As his demonic form receded into the distance, she saw Marcus rise slowly to his feet. The ugly bastard had sur-vived! Grimacing in pain, he tried to close his wings, but the injured pinions refused to tuck back into his shoulders. Scrapes and bruises covered every inch of his unsightly flesh. Blood trickled from multiple wounds. He glared mur-derously at the fleeing truck, but made no move to continue his pursuit . . . for now.

We've hurt him, Selene concluded. *That will have to be enough for now.*

Checking on Michael, she saw that he had finally man-aged to make it back into the truck bed. He watched Mar-cus's dwindling figure warily, before finally accepting that the chase was over for the time being. His hybrid attributes dissolved back into his flesh as he reverted to his human guise. He lifted something from the floor of the bed, then made his way toward the cab.

A weary groan issued from him as he awkwardly climbed through the shattered rear window and dropped into the passenger seat beside her. Cold air invaded the cab through the broken windows. Bullet shells and shattered glass lit-tered the floor and seat cushions.

He was visibly exhausted. Sweat covered his face and chest. He was breathing hard.

She knew just how he felt.

"Are you okay?" he asked.

She massaged her bruised throat, which was still tender where Marcus had throttled her. *That's nothing,* she thought. *I got off easy.*

She gave Michael a reassuring nod.

He stared blankly at the snow-covered road ahead. She could tell he was trying to process what had just happened. "He's a hybrid, isn't he?"

"Yes," she said. There would be time enough later to share her theory as to what might have triggered the Elder's transformation. Her own mind was still reeling at the concept. *Something is seriously wrong here,* she realized, *even more than I had anticipated.* Why had Marcus attacked them, especially if he didn't care about Viktor's death? *What did he think I was hiding?*

She gave Michael a serious look, just to make sure he understood what deep waters they were in. He nodded back at her and held out his palm. She saw that he was holding Sonja's pendant, now splattered with hybrid blood; she realized that was what he had retrieved from the floor of the truck bed.

"He wanted this," Michael said. "Why?"

I have no idea, she thought. He had explained to her the historical significance of the crest-shaped pendant: how it had once belonged to Viktor's daughter, Sonja, before the coven executed her for consorting with a lycan. Lucian had stolen the precious keepsake and treasured it until his death earlier tonight. But what did Marcus want with the pendant?

"I don't know," she admitted.

A brilliant red glow on the horizon, clearly visible in her rearview mirror, reminded her of a much more urgent issue. After creeping up on them for what felt like hours, dawn was finally arriving. Was it just her imagination, or could she already feel the heat upon her skin? Sonja, she recalled, had been destroyed by the sun. . . .

"We have another problem."

Chapter Twelve

*T*he sky above was growing brighter by the second. Selene squinted at the spreading radiance. The daylight obviously hurt her eyes, making it hard for her to see. Michael suddenly wished he was driving instead.

Thankfully, the dawn had no effect on him, perhaps because he started out as a lycan before becoming a hybrid. He leaned forward in his seat, peering through the windshield for some place they could take shelter. At first all he saw was endless trees and snow, then he spotted some sort of structure up ahead, off to the left. "Keep going," he urged Selene. As the truck raced down the road, he got a better look at the building.

An access road led to some sort of huge mining facility, which looked like an enormous brick warehouse built into the side of a mountain. An unmoving ore breaker climbed the slope to one side of the warehouse. Smokestacks rose from the roof of the complex, but Michael didn't see any fumes billowing from them. A sign posted just before the turnoff announced that the mine had been shut down due to environmental concerns, which probably explained the lack of activity. *Perfect*, Michael thought. *If we're lucky, nobody's at home.*

"There!" he said, pointing toward the turnoff.

Just then, the sun peeked over the horizon behind them. Sunlight flashed upon the rearview mirror and the shards of broken glass scattered around the cab. Selene gasped out loud and Michael heard a sound like bacon sizzling in a pan. She yanked her hand away from a stray beam of light. Michael saw that her knuckles were burned bright red. Wisps of smoke rose from the scorched skin. The smell of burning flesh, familiar to Michael from his nights in the ER, filled the cab.

Jesus Christ! He'd known, of course, that sunlight and vampires didn't mix, but he'd never actually witnessed the phenomenon with his own eyes. *That happened so fast!*

Selene ducked her head, trying to keep her face in the shade, but a ray of bright sunlight struck her cheek. Her smooth white skin blistered instantly, and she bit back a scream of pain. She lost control of the wheel and the truck veered alarmingly toward a snow-filled ditch at the side of the road. A wall of oaks and beeches loomed beyond the ditch.

"Get down!" Michael shouted. He grabbed the wheel, experiencing a sudden flashback to the first time he had gotten into a car with Selene. Wounded by Lucian, she had passed out behind the wheel and plunged her Jaguar into the Danube. *No way,* he thought. *Not again!*

Selene crouched down below the dashboard, away from the deadly sunbeams. Michael smelled the smoke rising from her scalded face. The plaintive whimper that escaped her lips offered only the barest hint of the pain she had to be going through. *That's a second-degree burn at least,* he thought. She needed immediate first aid.

The turnoff to the mining complex was right in front of them. Selene floored it as he cranked on the wheel. Acting in tandem, they took the access road leading up to the main building. Michael spotted railroad tracks and empty steel carts lying alongside the road, but didn't see any workers going about their business. He silently blessed whatever environmental agency had shut down the seemingly deserted facility.

Sunlight continued to infiltrate the interior of the cab. Michael knew that the dashboard wasn't going to protect Selene much longer. A wooden garage door blocked their way, but he didn't ask Selene to let up on the gas. "Brace yourself!" he warned her as the five-ton truck crashed through the garage door into the building. "Now . . . hit the brakes!" Their front fender clipped a parked jeep, sending a shudder through the entire cab, before the truck skidded to a halt.

Michael let out the breath he had been holding and let go of the wheel. A quick look around revealed that they were inside the facility's motor pool. Auto lifts, engine stands, lathes, jacks, oil stands, wheel dollies, battery chargers, tire machines, and other equipment were arrayed throughout the cavernous space. Tool racks lined the walls. Dried grease stains marred the concrete floor. A number of freight trucks, in various states of repair, were parked all around them. Their stolen truck fit right in, especially after all the damage they had inflicted on it.

If we get through this, he thought, *we're going to need another car.*

Selene lifted her head, then quickly thought better of it. Deadly shafts of light penetrated the unlit garage through dirty windows and cracks in the brick walls. She curled herself up into a tight little ball upon the floor of the cab. The collar of her trench coat *almost* covered her head.

"Hang on!" Michael told her. He hopped out of the truck

and looked around for something to block the sun. Grabbing a greasy tarp off an abandoned engine stand, he flung it over the truck's windshield. *That should buy us a few more seconds.* He worked frantically to make the vast garage more "vampire-friendly." He punctured some metal cans with a wrench, then splashed black paint all over the windows. Hybrid muscles shoved heavy steel racks and tool cabinets in front of the gaps in the walls. The smashed garage door posed a bigger problem, but the sunlight had not yet made it all the way across the floor of the motor pool. Michael figured he still had time to get Selene to a safer location . . . if they moved quickly.

The garage was noticeably darker by the time he got back to the cab. Tugging open the driver's-side door, he tossed her a gray wool blanket he had found. "Come on!" he said. "Let's get you out of here."

Selene didn't need to be asked twice. He caught a glimpse of her blistered hands and face as she hurriedly wrapped the blanket around her and scrambled out of the cab. Michael hustled her across the garage toward the rear of a semitrailer. A padlock guarded the trailer from intrusion, but he snapped it apart with his bare hands. He rolled up the back door of the semi and helped Selene inside before climbing up into the trailer after her. The metal door clanged loudly as he yanked it back down.

By now he was convinced that the remote mining complex was completely uninhabited. If all this commotion hadn't attracted any agitated guards or employees, then nothing would. *If a truck crashes into a building and nobody hears it,* he thought facetiously, *is there really a crash?*

The back of the truck was loaded with crates of engine parts. It took his eyes a moment to adjust to the dark, while Selene took off the blanket and laid it down on the floor of the semi. He winced at the ugly burns and blisters scarring her face. Years of medical training kicked in, and he bent down to take a better look at the burns. She forced a smile, but he could tell she was still in pain. She tried to turn her seared cheek away from him.

"Hold still," he told her.

"There's really no need," she insisted.

Michael admired her courage, but she didn't need to play the stoic warrior with him, not when there was something he could do to help her. He jumped to his feet and headed for the door. "Be right back," he promised.

There had to be a first-aid kit around here somewhere!

True to his word, he returned within minutes, clutching a bright red first-aid kit. "Found this in a restroom," he explained breathlessly. Selene guessed that he had sprinted all over the building before he'd found the kit.

He dropped to his knees in front of her and popped open the kit. She was struck by his obvious sense of purpose as he rummaged through the kit for what he needed. He really was a born healer, even after everything that had happened to him. She recalled how he had selflessly rescued her from drowning three nights ago and bound her wounds after Lucian had stabbed her with that spring-loaded blade of his. *He didn't even know my name then, but he still risked his life to save me.* He had done the same for that mortal girl who had been caught in the cross fire during the gun battle at the Metro station. Selene remembered Michael dashing across the platform to see to the girl, despite the bullets flying back and forth across the station. She had taken note of his bravery then. She was even more impressed now.

I've never known anyone like him.

He turned toward her, his hands full of clean dressings and antiseptic wipes. His brown eyes radiated care and compassion. She couldn't help being touched, and more, by his anxious concern for her well-being, even though she was not really in need of his ministrations. The vicious burns were already healing; all that remained of the searing pain was a faint stinging sensation. Still, she let him gently lay his hand against her cheek and turn her face toward him, so that he could see for himself that her injuries were all but passed. He gaped in surprise as the last reddened patch of skin grew smooth and white once more. She almost laughed at his dumbfounded expression.

"See." She raised her hands to show him her unblemished knuckles. "No need."

His initial shock gave way to obvious relief. His eyes brightened as he gave her an impish grin. "You don't need much of anything, do you?"

I'm not sure, she thought, suddenly at a loss for words. The moment hung between them, laden with possibility. He put down his first-aid supplies and looked into her eyes. His deep brown orbs seemed to drink her in. Vampires didn't blush, but Selene felt her blood rushing beneath his ardent gaze. She knew how much she meant to him, how much he wanted to take care of her. Not because he was a doctor, but because of the undeniable chemistry between them. For once, it seemed, their enemies were far away. No pressing danger threatened them with immediate extinction. It was just the two of them, alone together.

Selene was no virgin. Over her six hundred years, curiosity—and loneliness—had lured her into the occasional carnal encounter with another vampire; not every immortal was a pig like Kraven, after all. But such liaisons had been infrequent and always without consequence, temporary indulgences quickly put behind her. She had shared her body, but never her heart.

Now, with Michael, she didn't know what she felt. Everything had changed for her, including the ironclad code of conduct by which she had long governed her ageless existence. The prospect was both thrilling and terrifying.

Do I want this?

Taking her silence as consent, Michael leaned forward and kissed her. She responded tentatively for the first few heartbeats, then parted her lips to accept him. His own lips were warmer than any vampire lover's. *Just like his blood.*

He pulled her to him with surprising strength. Her passion rose and she surrendered to the moment. Their mouths still locked in a ravenous kiss, she peeled off his jacket and the tattered remains of his shirt. Her hands explored his naked chest, discovering that his bullet wounds had long since healed. The unmarred flesh was hot and irresistible to her touch.

She shrugged off her voluminous trench coat, which joined the borrowed blanket upon the floor of the trailer. "Help me," she entreated huskily as she tugged on the zippers of her tight black leathers. The tailored bodysuit was like a second skin, but suddenly she couldn't get it off fast enough. Michael's skillful hands came to her assistance, and the leather slid from her body, leaving her exposed and vulnerable before his gaze. His eyes gratefully devoured every inch of her bare white skin. He gazed at her in wonder.

Selene felt a wall crumble inside her, falling away just like her discarded clothes. She fell back against the blanket and scattered pieces of clothing. Her pale arms reached out for him. Michael kicked off his soggy trousers and joined her upon the makeshift bed, resting his weight atop her pliant curves. Their skin brushed together in a tantalizing caress. Her fingers stroked the firm, masculine contours of his back. His hungry mouth found her breast.

There was no biting, no sinking of fangs into tender flesh. Her blood already flowed through his veins, and his through hers. Instead they made love as mortals did, gasping and panting as their intertwined bodies came together again and again. *Yes*, she thought rapturously, as they ascended the heights of passion, *this is how it had to be*. Today she didn't want to be a vampire, a Death Dealer.

Only a woman.

Nestled in the forest, along the side of the road, the mouth of a concrete drainage tunnel protruded from the bottom of a snow-covered ridge. Ice water trickled along the floor of the tunnel, passing through a carpet of dead leaves, silt, and animal droppings. The fetid air within the shaft stank of piss and rot. The dank cement walls were coated with slime and mold. It was a far cry from the luxurious accommodations Marcus was accustomed to.

He dragged himself along the floor of the tunnel, retreating from the dawn. Despite the changes he had undergone of late, he was still enough of a vampire to fear the sun. Vengeance on Selene and her hybrid lover would have to wait until nightfall.

His mutilated wings scraped against the roof of the tunnel. They were already healing, but the sharp pains radiating through his shattered pinions stoked the anger burning within his breast. He cursed himself for letting go of the pendant when Selene had unleashed her gunfire upon him. The prize had been within his grasp, and yet he had let it slip away.

Tonight, he vowed. When the sun went down again, nothing would stop him from reclaiming the pendant—and making Selene and Michael Corvin pay for their defiance. He gnashed his fangs as he inched farther into the dark recesses of the vile tunnel.

Tonight . . .

Chapter Thirteen

Sergeant Sandor Hadik was not in a good mood.

His head hurt from where that dark-haired woman had clobbered him. He was cold and wet from lying unconscious in the snow for at least an hour. A wanted fugitive was missing. And he had no idea what was going on.

How the hell am I going to explain this in my report? he fretted. *Any of it?*

He and his fellow officers searched the woods for Michael Corvin and his female accomplice. Despite the brilliant sunlight filtering down through the tree branches, the morning was still bitterly cold. His breath frosted in front of his lips as he trekked through the snow. Judging from the sullen expressions on the faces of the three other men, they were just as angry and confused as he was. Fresh cuts and bruises made them look as though they had just been beaten up by a large gang of toughs, not a solitary female.

Who was that bitch? And how come Michael Corvin was still alive anyway? The last thing Hadik remembered was he and the other policemen filling the American lunatic full of lead. They must have hit him nearly a dozen times, yet when they had come to, their heads and battered bodies aching, they had found only a puddle of frozen blood where Corvin's body had been. What's more, two sets of tracks had led away from the site.

He tried not to think about the *third* set of tracks they had seen, the ones that looked like the spoor of some ferocious beast, just as he tried not to remember the American's impossible black eyes and fangs. A chill ran down his spine as he remembered the stories his grandmother had told him when he was just a child, about ghosts and vampires and werewolves. *Such things do not exist,* he reminded himself. *I must have been seeing things.*

"Sergeant! Over here!"

The rookie, Olszanski, called excitedly. Hadik and the other men rushed to join him. They emerged from a fringe of trees to find themselves on a narrow road leading up to an old mine shaft at the base of a rocky hill. Hadik vaguely remembered a bauxite-mining operation that had been tapped out and abandoned back when he was a kid. The door to the sealed-off mine was hanging open. Although fresh snow continued to fall from the sky, he could still see the vague imprints of footprints outside the entrance of the mine.

Had Corvin and the woman taken refuge in the old tunnels? It made sense; they could hardly stay outside in this weather forever. Maybe they were in there right now?

"Follow me!" he ordered gruffly. He unclipped a flashlight from his belt and drew his service revolver. Despite his bluff manner, his nerves were on edge as they approached the unlit entrance to the mine. He was in no hurry to face either Corvin or that woman again. Those eerie black eyes and wolflike fangs haunted his memory. He glanced at the bruises on his comrades' faces. The ugly purple marks didn't make him any less spooked.

How had one woman managed to take out four armed cops?

Their flashlights probed the darkened mine. Startled gasps and exclamations burst from the men as the intersecting beams fell upon the face of an enormous wolf. Unblinking cobalt eyes glared at them. Dagger-sized fangs gleamed between the beast's open jaws.

"Holy Mother—!" Hadik almost opened fire on the wolf, before he realized that the animal was neither moving nor making any sort of sound. "Hold your fire!" he called out to the other men. "I think it's dead!"

His heart racing, he swept his flashlight beam over the shaggy monstrosity. To his relief, he saw that the wolf-thing was hanging lifelessly inside some sort of cage. Lowering his gun, he breathed for the first time in several seconds. His shoulders drooped as he gave his heart a few minutes to slow down. *Christ,* he thought, *that thing almost gave me a coronary!*

The other cops lowered their weapons as well. Hadik figured it was a minor miracle that there weren't already bullets ricocheting around the mine. Olszanski stared at the suspended creature with wide, fearful eyes. "Sergeant?" he asked, a quaver in his voice. "What is that thing?"

Hell if I know, Hadik thought. The carcass had the head of a wolf, complete with pointed ears and a protruding muzzle, but its body looked more like a man's, built for walking erect. Fearsome claws dangled at the end of the monster's sinewy limbs. It was at least eight feet tall, larger than any wolf or human he was familiar with. Some sort of ape? No, that wasn't quite right. There was something distinctly *canine* about the beast's head and paws. *It's a werewolf,* his brain shrieked at him, but he couldn't bring himself to say that word aloud. What was that old saying again? *Speak of the wolf and you will see his teeth.*

144

"Maybe it's a fake," Officer Andrassy said. He had a reputation for creative thinking. "A prop for a horror movie?"

"It looks real enough to me," Hadik grunted. He swept his flashlight around the rest of the old mine shaft, which had obviously been refurbished at some point. His jaw dropped at the sight of a computerized communications center, a tray full of bloody surgical implements, and enough guns and ammunition to fight a war. Racks of automatic weapons lined the walls. Packets of whole blood rested on a nearby counter.

Oh my God, he thought. *What the hell have we stumbled into?*

"It's a terrorist base!" Olszanski blurted. "Corvin and the woman . . . they're terrorists!"

"Or CIA," Andrassy added. "He's an American, remember?"

The fourth policeman, Latja, just shook his head in disbelief.

Oddly enough, Hadik found all this talk of spies and terrorists strangely comforting. Terrorism was a fact of life, nothing supernatural about it. Unlike, say, certain mythological creatures . . .

In any event, his course was clear. "We need to call this in," he said decisively. "Back to our cars, on the double!" A thought occurred to him and he turned toward the rookie. "Olszanski, you stay here and watch the exit. Don't let anyone leave or enter until we get back. You got that?"

"But . . ." Before the fresh-faced young cop could object, a sudden wind blew the open door against the wall. The men jumped at the unexpected clang, then looked in bewilderment at the open doorway. Fallen leaves and snow came blowing into the bunker.

The cops rushed out of the mine into the open. Swirling

winds whipped up the cold white powder. A loud whirring sound drew their gaze upward. They gawked in amazement at the sleek black helicopter hovering directly above them.

Andrassy's CIA theory was looking better and better.

The nose of the chopper dipped toward the cops. A burst of automatic gunfire chewed up the snow in front of the men's feet. An amplified voice addressed them from the copter: *"Drop your weapons and stand down. Repeat, drop your weapons."* Another spray of bullets punctuated the command.

The other officers looked to Hadik for guidance. He shrugged his stocky shoulders. *I know when I'm outgunned.* He glumly tossed his pistol onto the snow. His fellow cops followed suit.

"Remain where you are," the anonymous voice instructed, not bothering to identify itself. A half dozen long cables came tumbling out of the chopper, followed by a team of commandos who came sliding down the cables like goddamn ninjas or something. They wore black uniforms with no markings. Balaclavas covered their faces. Automatic rifles were slung over their shoulders.

Who? Hadik wondered impotently. *Allies of the woman in black?*

Boldly striking in broad daylight, the nameless commandos quickly eliminated any threat posed by the four police officers. Within minutes, Hadik found himself lying on his side on the snow, his wrists zip-tied behind his back. He strained to free himself, but the heavy-duty plastic cable ties were too strong to snap apart. He heard Olszanski and the other men grunting and swearing as well. For the second time that morning, the cops were freezing their asses off in the snow.

They were *not* having a good day.

At least we're conscious this time. He watched helplessly as the commandos went about their business, emptying out the converted mine with practiced efficiency. They hauled out the computers, the crates of ammo, the medical supplies, and even an overstuffed body bag that almost surely contained the shaggy carcass of the dead wolf-thing. The potential evidence was quickly loaded into the helicopter, which had touched down on the road in front of the mine entrance. By the time the commandos were done, Hadik guessed, the bunker would be stripped clean of anything remotely incriminating. *I wonder if we'll ever find out what this was all about?*

The armed cleanup crew finished in less than fifteen minutes. The last commando out of the mine reported to the man who seemed to be in charge, a tall, rangy individual with a military bearing. The leader nodded and removed a handful of metal disks from a pouch on his belt. The polished silver disks resembled oversize coins. He hurled them into the bunker.

Hadik heard the disks skitter across the concrete floor of the mine before coming to rest somewhere deep inside the hidden base. A faint hissing noise reached his ears.

A commando unsheathed a knife as he approached the immobilized sergeant. For a second, Hadik thought he was done for, then the masked trooper stepped behind him and neatly sliced through the ties binding the cop's hands together. As the circulation returned to his fingers, Hadik saw that other cops were being freed as well.

"If I were you, I wouldn't stick around," a commando said tersely. He spoke Hungarian without any discernible accent. "And stay away from the mine."

Don't tell me what to do, Hadik thought angrily. He rubbed his chafed wrists as he stumbled to his feet. His bones felt as if they had turned to ice. *I'm getting damn tired of being pushed around by strangers.*

The commandos left as briskly as they had arrived. The helicopter lifted off from the lonely mountain road, stirring up a blinding cloud of fine white powder. Hadik and the other cops watched the chopper vanish into the sky. Like the men, the black aircraft bore no identifying insignia.

"I told you," Andrassy said. "CIA."

Inside the mine, unseen by the four cops, the metal disks sprayed a fine mist from the tiny holes that had opened up along their edges. Gas fumes soon filled the bunker, which had been stripped to its bare walls. A timed mechanism caused one of the disks to split in half. Two shiny contacts were exposed to the volatile atmosphere inside the mine. A crackle of electricity arced between them. . . .

The explosion destroyed what little the anonymous men had left behind. A roiling ball of flame erupted from the mouth of the mine. The accumulated snow and ice was vaporized instantly. A deafening bang rocked the morning.

"Wha—?" Hadik gasped, a second before the shock wave sent all four policemen flying backward into the woods. His head slammed into an unyielding oak and the world went black once more.

It would be hours before any of the cops stirred again.

An engine roared to life, waking Selene from a sound sleep. She sat up with a start and grabbed for her gun, but the weapon was not resting on the table next to her bed the way it usually was. In fact, there didn't seem to be a table.

Or a bed.

It took her a moment to get oriented. *Right.* She was naked in the back of the semitrailer, the gray wool blanket draped over her body. Her gun was with her clothing, scattered about on the floor of the trailer, surrounded by crates of engine parts. Sonja's pendant rested on the floor next to where her head had been.

"Michael?"

He was nowhere in sight, but she thought she heard him stirring outside the trailer. A closed window was built into the wall at her right. Wrapping the blanket around her, she retrieved some fresh ammo from the pockets of her trench coat and reloaded the Berettas. Then she cautiously approached the window. Wary of sunbeams, she stood to one side of the window as she slowly drew open the metal blinds. No lethal shaft of light invaded the trailer, so she took a chance and peered out the window.

Outside the trailer, several meters away, Michael was working on the engine of an old Land Rover. He had the hood up and his hands were busy performing surgery on the vehicle's innards. She wondered if he could get the abandoned Rover up and running by nightfall.

Why not? she thought. *Michael is blessed with many talents. As I learned this morning.*

She watched him silently for a moment, then retreated back into the darker corners of the trailer. Sonja's pendant caught her eye and she sat down to take a better look at it. She smiled at the thought of Michael leaving it for her to find when she woke up. No doubt he had been thinking of Lucian and Sonja, the star-crossed lovers whose forbidden romance had incurred Viktor's terrible wrath, setting off long centuries of internecine warfare. Like Lucian and Sonja, she and Michael came from two different worlds, but had somehow found each other regardless. *I only hope our tale ends somewhat less tragically . . . as unlikely as that seems.*

Her thoughts drifted back to their lovemaking earlier today. Despite her earlier doubts, she felt strangely at peace with what had transpired between them. There was no turning back now. For better or for worse, she had let Michael past the barricades that had long guarded her heart. Her old life was over. All she could do now was fight for their future together. It was the end of an era, and the beginning of a risky new campaign.

Did Sonja feel this way, Selene wondered, *after she slept with Lucian for the first time?* She held up the crest-shaped pendant before her eyes. Dried blood caked its gilded design, marring its beauty. She frowned. Far too much blood had been spilled over this emblem for her liking.

Licking her finger, she started to clear away the clotted gore.

Click. Her fingertip accidentally depressed a concealed latch, triggering some sort of internal mechanism. Selene's eyes widened in wonder as delicate bronze blades came sliding out of the pendant, not unlike the petals of a clockwork flower. Selene was briefly reminded of the silver throwing stars she often used against werewolves, but, no, the blades were not sharp enough to serve as weapons. Rather they resembled the teeth of some sort of complicated gear, as though the opened pendant were merely a component of a larger mechanical puzzle.

But that wasn't the strangest part of her discovery. What was truly unexpected, and disturbing, was the realization that she had seen this apparatus before, a long time ago. . . .

The dungeon was damp and cold. No more than six or seven, little Selene shivered beneath her woolen kirtle. The fair-haired child wandered down the gloomy stone corridor, fascinated by the gilded pendant in her hand. Torches mounted in sconces on the wall provided just enough light for her to admire the intricate runes inscribed on the newly made pendant. The shiny metal blades projecting from the device reflected the flickering glow of the torches. Selene thought she had never seen anything quite so beautiful.

A heavy thud caught the little girl by surprise. She spun around, terrified. . . .

"Selene?"

She snapped back to the present, startled to find Michael sitting across from her. Somehow he had slipped back into the trailer without her even noticing. *He's getting stronger,* she realized; catching a Death Dealer unawares was no small matter. *We still don't know the full extent of his new abilities.*

"Sun's setting," he declared. Selene realized she had slept most of the day away. She knew she should get dressed; they needed to keep moving, if only to stay one step ahead of Marcus. But the forgotten memory, if that was indeed what it was, had left her deeply unsettled. She tugged the blanket tighter around her trembling body. She felt confused, uncertain, quite unlike herself. Her own past had caught her unawares.

Michael noted the difference in her. "What's wrong?" he asked anxiously.

The *Sancta Helena* was docked at the pier in Budapest. Lorenz Macaro heard the Danube lapping against the hull of the ship as he sat behind his mahogany desk in the suite above the ops center. Samuel's voice emerged from the intercom. He spoke loudly, to be heard over the whirring of the helicopter blades in the background.

"Supplies were taken, used weapons were left behind," the Cleaner reported. "The incident at the tavern occurred just before dawn. They couldn't have gotten very far."

Macaro wished he had dispatched a team to the safe house in the mountains earlier. Perhaps they could have apprehended Michael Corvin and Selene before this situation

151

had escalated further. He glanced at an antique clock. Dusk was approaching. Marcus would soon be on the move again, as would Selene and Michael. If Marcus hadn't killed them already.

"Remain airborne for the present," he instructed Samuel. "I'm certain they'll reappear in good time."

"Yes, sir."

Chapter Fourteen

Selene handed the pendant to Michael.

"I've seen this before," she told him, "when I was a child. I held it. When it was open like this."

Michael didn't understand. "How's that possible?" He hadn't seen Selene in any of Lucian's memories of the Dark Ages. Was this before Sonja died, before Lucian had claimed the pendant as his own? *It has to be,* he thought. *That's the only scenario that makes sense.*

"I don't know," she said, obviously troubled. He found it hard to imagine that Selene had ever been a child, even though he knew that she had once been human. Her eyes lit up as an idea popped into her head. "But I know someone that might."

Throwing aside the blanket, she hastily slid back into her leathers and geared up. Unafraid of the cold, she left her torn trench coat behind. Michael got into the passenger seat of the Land Rover, his own bloodstained jacket having seen better days. He was tempted to drive, but she knew where they were going, not him. Selene got behind the wheel and slammed her door shut.

"Andreas Tanis," she explained on the run. "He was the

official historian of the covens, back when there was such a post." She jammed the key into the ignition. Michael felt a surge of satisfaction as the engine fired up; his repair job seemed to have paid off. "But he fell out of favor after documenting what Viktor considered 'malicious lies.' Of course," she added bitterly, "that means he was probably telling the truth."

She threw the Land Rover into reverse and hit the gas. The stolen SUV roared out of the garage in reverse, then expertly spun around on the icy pavement. Michael was thrown back against his seat and thanked God for his seat belt. Not for the first time, he wondered why he kept getting into cars with Selene. The Rover peeled out of the mining complex and took off into the night. Their headlights cut through the wintry darkness. Selene shifted gears and put the pedal to the metal. A sudden burst of acceleration sent them rocketing down the remote mountain road. It was no longer snowing, but there was still plenty of white stuff all around. Michael couldn't see any other vehicles ahead or behind them. They seemed to have the road all to themselves.

"He was exiled over three hundred years ago," she continued, keeping her eye on the road.

"Three hundred years?" Michael still had trouble grasping the huge spans of time in which Selene and the other immortals seemed to operate. "What makes you think we're going to find him now?"

She shot him a look. "I was the one who exiled him."

Deep within the slimy drainage tunnel, Marcus sensed the sun go down. His wings were wrapped around him like those of a sleeping bat. They were strong and flexible once more, restored to health by the day's long slumber. His black eyes opened and he flexed his deadly talons. All the scars and bruises he had received in this morning's clashes were long since healed. He felt stronger and more vigorous than ever.

At last! he thought. His daylong repose in the fetid tunnel had tried his patience, but now he need wait no longer. The golden pendant shone brightly in his memory, sharpening his resolve. Hatred flared within his heart as he recalled how Selene and Michael had dared to come between him and his prize. They would pay with their lives for their impertinence. *Before the sun sets once more,* he vowed, *they will be punished . . . and the key will be mine.*

He had waited eight centuries already. He could not wait another night more.

His wings rustled like dry leaves as he crept toward the mouth of the tunnel. . . .

They headed east, higher into the hills.

The Land Rover thundered through a remote canyon. Towering walls of granite loomed above the road on both sides, all but blocking out the moonlit sky. Michael hadn't seen a service station, telephone pole, or any other sign of human habitation for over an hour. *That's it,* he thought, *we're officially in the middle of nowhere.*

Selene had spoken little during the long drive. Michael could tell she was deeply disturbed by this latest revelation, whatever it might mean. As if her whole life hadn't been turned upside down already! He couldn't begin to guess how her past could possibly be connected to Sonja's pendant. The disgraced princess had died, and Lucian had stolen the pendant, years before Viktor had turned Selene into a vampire. By then, Sonja's very existence had been stricken from the history of the coven, never to be spoken of again. Michael remembered Selene telling him that the Elders had forbidden the other vampires from probing too deeply into the past.

I guess I shouldn't be surprised, he thought, *that a pack of vampires has a whole bunch of skeletons in their closet.*

He looked at Selene with concern. After their intimacy earlier, he had hoped that she would be quicker to open to him when she was going through a rough time. He wanted to be there for her, especially at moments like this. *Give her time,* he told himself. *This is all pretty new for her.*

The Rover came tearing around a bend and into a valley. "Whoa!" Michael said as an impressive stone structure came into view. Shaped like a monumental Celtic cross, with granite crossbeams the size of Neolithic monoliths, the breathtaking edifice had literally been carved into the face of a craggy hill. Cracked stone and faded marble mosaics hinted at centuries of neglect. A primitive wooden gate guarded the barren grounds in front of the giant cross. Michael didn't spot any sort of lights either inside or outside the structure. The only illumination came from the Rover's headlights, and the full moon waxing overhead.

"Looks like a monastery," he guessed.

"It used to be," Selene confirmed. "More like a prison now. Tanis has been hiding here since Viktor's decree. We may be the first people he's seen in centuries."

The blonde was Olga. The brunette was Grushenka.

Or perhaps it was the other way around.

Happily smothered between the two sumptuous female vampires, Andreas Tanis wasn't worried about keeping the women's names straight. He had more important matters to occupy him right now, such as their lush breasts, smooth thighs, and delectable rumps. Enmeshed in a tangle of naked flesh, he barely knew what to grope or suckle first.

Choices, choices . . .

The monastery's capacious wine cellar had been transformed into an opulent love nest. Faded mosaics looked down on a sprawling bed liberally strewn with expensive sheets and cushions. A profusion of candles cast flickering shadows over the threesome cavorting on the bed. Elegant tapestries were draped over the venerable stone walls. Corinthian columns supported the vaulted ceiling. Antique furniture had replaced the absent wine racks. Bookshelves sagged beneath the weight of numerous dusty tomes. Bartók's String Quartet No. 1 played softly over a concealed sound system. Discarded clothing littered the floor. Life-size marble statues of departed saints occupied recessed nooks in the far corners of the cellar. Their sculpted eyes gazed voyeuristically at the orgy taking place only a few yards away.

Kneeling upon the bed, Tanis was sandwiched between his avid lovers. The brunette (Grushenka?) pressed her bare breasts against his back, her moist lips cool against his throat, while he embraced the blonde in front of him. He fondled the blonde's succulent ass with both hands, even as the brunette reached around him to toy with the other woman's left breast. Busy fingers teased the straining nipple. The blonde arched her back in delight.

Blood flowed between them in a continuous three-way circuit. The brunette drank from Tanis's neck, while he lapped at the pulsing throat of the blonde, who fed in turn from the brunette's left wrist. Ecstatic groans and whimpers mixed with wet, sucking noises. Tanis gulped down the blonde's cold blood with abandon, relishing the salty taste of the delicious nectar. His tongue swirled the plasma around the inside of his mouth. For all he knew, it might very well be his own blood, returning to him via the throbbing veins of the two vampire women. His eyes eagerly devoured the sight of the blond beauty lustily sucking on the brunette's arm. Her wanton desire inflamed his own.

Drink your fill! he silently urged her. *There's enough for all!*

Gasping in pleasure, Tanis withdrew his fangs from the blonde's neck. He savored the sensation of the brunette nuzzling his neck, her insistent tongue digging into the open bite, even as the blonde's clever hands slowly stroked his engorged cock. His face was flushed with borrowed blood. His luminous blue eyes were dreamy and unfocused, like a drug addict's. He took a deep breath, inhaling the pungent aroma of blood and sex. His senses were awash in sybaritic excess. Nothing existed anymore except the banquet of nubile flesh enveloping him on all sides. His entire world had been distilled down into the naked limbs wrapped around him and the hungry mouths swallowing him whole.

He licked his lips, then dived back down for more, this time sinking his teeth into the blonde's upturned breast.

Selene drove the Land Rover up to the locked wooden gate. Aside from the snow, the former monastery looked much as she remembered. "Take the wheel," she instructed Michael as she handed him one of her Berettas. She kept the other pistol for herself as she hopped out of the SUV. Multiple rounds of silver ammunition had done little to deter Marcus before, but she still felt better with a gun in her hand.

Besides, it was always possible that Tanis bore a grudge.

A rusty padlock sealed the gate. Selene crushed the lock in her fist, then pushed the massive oak doors open. Her lithe figure was silhouetted by the Rover's headlights as she marched through the gate, carrying the gun.

Michael slowly followed her in the SUV, its wheels rolling over the bumpy terrain. The Rover's high beams lit the way before her.

The monastery grounds were a frozen wasteland. Brown weeds and granite outcroppings sprouted from the rocky soil. A fresh layer of snow blanketed the ground and boulders. No footprints had soiled the pristine whiteness. In theory, no one besides Tanis had walked these grounds for generations. Selene imagined he would be greatly surprised to receive visitors after all these years. *I wonder, what's he been doing to pass the time?*

She listened carefully for the telltale rustle of Marcus's wings, but detected no trace of the mutated Elder's presence. BEWARE OF DOGS read a faded metal sign in Russian posted to one of the gateposts, yet no indignant barks or growls greeted her arrival. All she heard was the wind whistling through the dying weeds. The desolate courtyard was as quiet as a graveyard

Stepping toward the monastery itself, she failed to notice the electric eye beam in her path.

Beep!

The strident alarm jolted Tanis from his delirious rapture beneath Olga and Grushenka. A supple breast slipped from his mouth as he lifted his head in alarm. The mood abruptly broken, he shoved his lovers aside. The blonde yelped as she tumbled off the bed onto the cold stone floor. "Wait!" the brunette protested. Fresh blood was smeared all over her pouty lips. "Come back!"

He ignored his lovers' cries. Fear instantly snuffed out his ardor. *Who is it?* he fretted anxiously. *Has the coven learned of my recent illicit activities?* He shuddered at the thought. *Or have the damn lycans betrayed me after all?*

Snatching up a brocaded silk dressing gown from the floor, he hurried over to the security monitor on the southern wall. The mounted video screen clashed sharply with the cellar's antique furnishings. He silenced the alarm with the push of a button, then stared at the monitor. His eyes widened as, to his dismay, he immediately recognized the silhouetted figure walking ahead of a slow-moving vehicle.

"Shit!"

She faced the mammoth stone cross, which loomed impressively before her. Thankfully, the idea that vampires were repelled by crosses was nothing but a foolish mortal myth, as was the notion that they required an invitation to enter another's domicile. *What nonsense,* she thought as she approached a heavy wooden door built into the base of the cross. She didn't intend to ask for Tanis's permission.

Another padlock guarded the door. She reached for the lock, only to be interrupted by a faint metallic rumbling whose origin she could not immediately place. Her muscles tensed beneath the skintight leather and she raised the Beretta. Senses on edge, she turned around to look behind her . . . as a trapdoor suddenly opened beneath her feet.

Gravity seized her and she plummeted at least sixty feet onto a hard stone floor. A mortal would have broken a limb or two, but Selene managed to land more or less nimbly, ending up in a squatting position upon the floor. The trapdoor snapped shut above her, stranding her in some sort of subterranean catacomb beneath the monastery. Flickers of candlelight permeated the tunnel from deeper within the underground chambers.

Tricky, she thought with grudging admiration. Tanis had clearly not been idle during his long confinement. Picking herself up, she looked around. The trapdoor was a long, steep climb above her; she could barely see the top of the shaft. A dead end was at her back. The best way out seemed to be straight ahead.

An ominous growl sent her adrenaline racing. She knew a werewolf when she heard one. The growling grew louder as it hurried toward her. She reached for her gun, but . . .

"Selene!"

Michael couldn't believe his eyes. One second she was standing in the glow of his headlights, the next she dropped completely out of sight. *Shit!*

He slammed on the brakes and threw the car into park. To his dismay, the Rover's high beams showed him Selene's pistol lying on the ground, only inches from where she had been standing only heartbeats before. *It must have missed falling through the trapdoor,* he realized. Not only was Selene missing, she was unarmed.

I have to find her! Michael thought. He gripped his own pistol and turned toward the door . . . just as an enormous gray werewolf came lunging from a secret passage beneath a nearby boulder. A forged metal harness partially concealed the monster's bestial face, but there was no mistaking its bloodthirsty intentions. The beast slammed into the car with so much force that it smashed in the driver's door and caused the entire SUV to bounce up off its wheels. The seismic impact sent Michael flying across the front seats and crashing headfirst out the passenger's-side window. Safety glass shattered against his skull, and the pistol slipped from his fingers, as he was catapulted out of the car and down a rocky slope.

He tumbled out of control.

Damn! Selene thought as she realized the Beretta was missing.

Pounding footsteps filled the death trap as a massive werewolf charged at her from around a bend in the tunnel. The creature came at her so fast that she had no time to defend herself before the werewolf rammed her into the damp limestone wall behind her. Historic masonry cracked from the force of the collision. The beast's hot breath blasted her face, and its bloodthirsty roar thundered in her ears, as it bared its fangs and opened its jaws wide. Foam dripped from its rubbery black lips in anticipation of the vampire's raw flesh.

Selene didn't give it a chance. In one fluid motion, she drew a silver-bladed hunting knife from her ankle sheath. Aiming for a gap in the werewolf's steel harness, she drove the blade into its skull all the way up to its hilt. Bright arterial blood sprayed the crumbling wall behind her.

That's better, she thought coolly. The werewolf collapsed into a lifeless heap at her feet. In death, the beast reverted to its human form. She regarded the carcass with satisfaction. Much may have changed in her life over the last few nights, but if there was one thing she still knew for certain, it was how to kill lycans. *Nice to know I haven't lost my touch.*

Looking more closely, she saw that the lycan's metal harness and collar were attached to an unbreakable titanium chain leading deeper into the catacombs. *A werewolf chained up like a guard dog?* Selene recalled the BEWARE OF DOGS sign she had glimpsed up above, but was unamused by Tanis's apparent sense of humor. Then she realized the sign had referred to *dogs.*

Plural.

Another roar echoed through the tunnels.

Tumbling pell-mell down the slope, Michael started transforming before he even reached the bottom of the incline.

Rocks and branches assaulted his skin as it took on an iridescent sheen. His eyes turned jet-black. His toes and fingers turned into claws.

It was as an inhuman hybrid that he jumped to his feet once he finally rolled to a stop. He cast aside his constricting winter jacket and leaped back up the slope. The hood of the Land Rover crumpled beneath his weight as he bounded over the SUV and into the werewolf on the other side of the car. The other monster yelped in surprise as he slammed the creature down onto the frosty ground. Michael barely recognized the feral rage fueling his attack. Instinct took over as he surrendered to a primal compulsion to rend and kill. He growled like an animal.

But the werewolf fought back with lightning reflexes. A savage claw smacked into Michael's side, throwing him off his foe. He crashed against the side of the Land Rover, denting the car's back panel, before hitting the ground hard. Pain exploded inside his skull, causing spots to appear before his eyes. His whole head was ringing.

He shook off the blow. A clattering noise attracted his notice, and he saw that a steel chain connected the werewolf's harness to the secret exit from which the monster had emerged. The heavy links rattled along the ground beside him.

Seizing the opportunity, Michael grabbed the chain with both hands. He pulled it taut, yanking the werewolf by the neck. It growled angrily and snapped at the chain, but its fangs didn't even scratch the titanium links. *Hold on, Fido!* Michael thought. *You're going for a ride!* Calling upon his hybrid strength, he braced himself against the ground and swung the howling werewolf around by the chain like a giant hammer throw. The beast's paws left the earth as it was flung into the Land Rover's back driver's-side window. The glass imploded with a tremendous crash. The stunned were-wolf dropped to the ground. A pitiful whine emerged from its muzzle.

Michael allowed the monster no time to recover. He dropped the chain and pounced on the fallen beast. The werewolf squealed in pain as Michael took hold of the creature's jaws and forcefully wrenched them apart. Meat and gristle tore loudly as, tugging with all his strength, Michael ripped the werewolf's jaw off. Blood gushed from the monster's mutilated face, pooling atop the frozen ground. Violent convulsions rocked the beast's shaggy body as its limbs slashed wildly at the side of the SUV. Then, with a final spasm, it stopped moving. Bristling black fur retracted into naked human skin as the werewolf transformed into a dead human body.

About time, Michael thought. He stared at the lycan corpse in disbelief. Despite his transformation, part of him still couldn't believe that he had killed a full-grown werewolf with his bare hands. He glanced down at the unattached jaw in his grip. The lycan's tongue was still twitching. A gory froth spilled onto the snow.

He hurled the jaw away in disgust, then checked out the hidden passageway by the boulder. *I still need to find Selene,* he reminded himself. Remaining in hybrid form, he saw that the dead lycan's chain stretched from a second trapdoor leading below the grounds of the monastery. He rushed toward the unlit shaft without hesitation.

Hang on, Selene! I'm coming!

The second roar offered Selene only an instant's warning before another chained werewolf came springing at her. It ran toward her on all fours, closing in fast. Its musky odor filled the narrow catacomb.

Fortunately, an instant's warning was all she needed. With the grace of an acrobat, she leaned back and plucked her hunting knife from the dead lycan's skull. Its brains leaked out onto the floor stones as she spun around and expertly twirled the blade in her hand before launching it at the charging werewolf with perfect aim. The knife sliced through the air, missing the beast's steel harness and penetrating deep into a moonstruck cobalt eye.

The beast was dead before it even knew it had been hit. Momentum alone carried the lunging carcass down the tunnel before it slid to a stop only inches short of Selene's boots. The dead animal morphed into a human corpse. She knelt down and quickly retrieved her blade.

How many of these "watchdogs" does Tanis have? she wondered. *And what's happening with Michael?* She hoped that he was still safely aboveground, but suspected that he was already searching for her. *He's not very good at staying put.*

Knife in hand, she advanced cautiously down the tunnel, heading for the flickering lights up ahead. Her patience with Tanis's snares had long since evaporated.

I wouldn't want to be him when I catch up with him.

Michael dropped through the trapdoor into the tunnel below. He found himself in a murky catacomb, lit only by the moonlight coming through the open trap. The werewolf's chain stretched away into the darkness, leading to some hidden lair deep beneath the monastery.

What the fuck? he thought. There was much he still didn't know about the secret world of the immortals, but he knew that a chained werewolf guarding an exiled vampire was not exactly kosher. What was that lycan doing here anyway? Selene hadn't said anything about werewolves. *Then again, she probably wasn't expecting that trapdoor either.*

His hybrid eyes quickly adjusted to the dim lighting. Nails scraped against the floor up ahead and he sensed something coming toward him from around a bend in the tunnel.

"Selene?"

A shadow appeared on the wall ahead, just beyond the bend. The shadow of a werewolf.

Oh, hell, Michael thought. He dropped into a defensive stance, raising his claws before him. His lips peeled back from his fangs.

A bestial hiss disturbed the silence.

It took Michael a second to realize that the hiss was coming from him.

Chapter Fifteen

Michael?

Selene thought she heard his voice coming from one of the adjacent tunnels. She rushed forward . . . just as the tunnel tilted sharply downward. Taken by surprise, she slid feetfirst down the steep incline. Musty air, rank with the scent of lycan shit and piss, blew against her face as she sped down the slide on her back, finally landing on her feet in a cavern far below the monastery. Straw crackled beneath the soles of her boots.

Where was she now? Looking around, she saw that the slide had deposited her in a circular chamber with several sloping entrances like the one she had just stumbled onto. Titanium chains, radiating from a central anchor, led up various of the tunnels. Selene counted four chains, which left at least two chained werewolves unaccounted for. She kept her silver blade ready.

This must be the lycans' lair, she realized. The fetid stench of the beasts was even stronger here than in the tunnels. Torches mounted in the walls allowed her to see more than she would have liked of the lycan's squalid den. Piles of bones, many of them recognizably human, were scattered around the lair. Yellowed femurs, humeri, and tibiae had been cracked open, the better to extract the tasty marrow inside. Gobbets of raw meat still clung to a fractured skull and rib cage, implying that the victims had been consumed fairly recently. All the bones bore evidence of having been thoroughly gnawed. Selene could only hope that the unfortunate humans had not been eaten alive. *What the devil have you been up to, Tanis?*

A mournful howl echoed down one of the slanted tunnels, reaching a poignant note before trailing off into silence. Something, she knew, had just died painfully. A steel chain extended up the passageway in question. Selene was reluctant to follow the chain, for fear of running into yet another hungry werewolf.

No point pushing my luck, she thought. One way or another, the battle at the other end of the chain was over. *I just have to hope that Michael was the victor.*

The sputtering glow of the torches revealed an actual staircase, leading up to the ground floor of the monastery. Selene thought she glimpsed more light at the top of the stairs. With luck, she would find Tanis above, and not more of his ravenous guard dogs.

After all of this, he'd better have some answers for me.

Holding her knife before her, she climbed the stairs. Every sense was at a heightened state, alert to the slightest hint of an ambush. Emerging from the stairwell, she found herself in a vaulted corridor heavy with the weight of ages. Time and decay had taken their toll on this part of the monastery. The plaster walls were cracked and crumbling. Wooden crosses and other holy relics, resting in niches along the walls, were covered by many decades' worth of dust. Cobwebs cloaked the hanging tapestries. The paving stones were broken and uneven, forcing Selene to tread carefully. Melted snow dripped from the ceiling, forming puddles upon the floor. Rats scurried away at her approach. Moonlight shone through broken stained-glass windows, casting a spectrum of eerie colors upon the ancient stones.

As Selene entered a particularly murky intersection, she heard muffled breathing to both sides of her. *Not werewolves*, she realized instantly. After centuries as a Death Dealer, she knew a lycan when she heard one; this was something different. She remained on guard regardless. Werewolves were not her only enemies these days. She also had to watch out for her own kind.

Two pairs of bare feet crept toward her. Then, like hissing alley cats, a pair of female vampires exploded from the shadows. Their blue eyes glowed in the darkness as they bared their fangs and came at her with both knives and claws. Bizarrely, they wore only a few pieces of skimpy lingerie.

Despite their frivolous attire, Selene did not underestimate her foes. She herself was living proof of just how deadly a female vampire could be. She took out the blonde with an elbow jab to the gut, then delivered a sideways kick to the brunette that sent the dark-haired vampiress tumbling backward. The blonde doubled over, vomiting blood onto the paving stones. Selene jabbed the point of her own blade into the back of the blonde's head and the woman dropped lifelessly onto the floor. The brunette made the mistake of trying to get up again, still clutching a silver dagger in her hand, but a roundhouse kick snapped her neck in half and she joined her companion in death. Selene retrieved her blade from the blonde's skull. Cold blood stained its length.

Who? Selene glanced quickly at the women's faces. She didn't recognize them from the coven. *Tanis must have turned them himself,* she guessed. Most mortals died immediately from the bite of an immortal, but a small percentage of victims became immortal themselves. *How many human girls did he have to bite to provide himself with these pretty playthings? How many mortal girls had to die?*

Selene felt a pang of regret. Before tonight, she had never killed another vampire. Now she was becoming an old hand at it.

A bullet slammed into the wall behind her, missing her face by inches. Pulverized stone and plaster pelted her cheek. An intense beam of light blinded her. Throwing up a hand to shield her eyes, she squinted past the harsh white light.

Andreas Tanis stood a few yards away, gripping an AK-47 assault rifle. A powerful searchlight was mounted beneath the barrel of the gun. "I knew it was you, Selene," he said venomously. "The stench of Viktor's blood still lingers in your veins."

The exiled historian had changed little in appearance. He was a slight man, with mousy brown hair, who looked to be in his midthirties. A brocade dressing gown with a thick fur collar was draped over his shoulders. A pair of velvet slippers protruded from beneath the hem of the gown. He had a depleted, dissipated look, as though he had spent rather too much of his immortality indulging in hedonistic pursuits. And, judging from the baleful look in his bloodshot brown eyes, he had neither forgotten nor forgiven Selene's role in his banishment.

"Tanis," she greeted him. Her face and voice held a warning. "I see your aim hasn't improved."

He smirked at her from behind his gun. "You haven't changed. You don't scare me, Selene."

"Well, we're going to have to work on that."

Without warning, Michael dropped from the ceiling, landing right behind Tanis. The historian spun around and gaped in shock at the hybrid. Michael's singular black eyes dilated in the light. "What—?"

With but a swipe of his arm, Michael knocked Tanis into the wall, shattering a centuries-old mosaic. He grabbed the struggling vampire's throat and pressed him against the wall. Tanis was as strong as any ordinary vampire, but he was helpless in the hybrid's grasp. The Kalashnikov clattered onto the floor as Tanis released the weapon.

Selene calmly took possession of the rifle. Beneath her icy exterior, she was thrilled to see Michael alive and well, but that wasn't an emotion she wished to share with their new prisoner. Better that he remember the old Selene, who cared for nothing but vengeance.

"We need to talk," she said.

The converted wine cellar was as good a place as any to interrogate Tanis. At their mercy, the disarmed historian sat himself down on an antique wooden chair. His attempt to present a nonchalant attitude was belied by the trickle of sweat running down his temple. He fidgeted restlessly in the chair, obviously more apprehensive than he let on.

Good, Selene thought. *He ought to be scared.*

She glanced around at the lavishly appointed cellar. Tanis had obviously made himself quite at home over the years. Her frosty gaze fell upon the discarded female clothing lying on and about the decadently oversize bed. Disordered cushions and covers hinted at a recent bout of vigorous activity. Incriminating drops of fresh vampire blood stained the rumpled sheets.

"Your exile seems a bit more comfortable than I remember," she remarked drily. The bodies of his undead paramours rested in the corridors outside, leaving Tanis to face the music alone.

He looked nervously at Michael. Although Michael had resumed his human form, now that Tanis was no longer a threat, the memory of the hybrid's fearful appearance was apparently not far from the historian's thoughts. He watched nervously as Michael sorted through a rack of stylish designer jackets, looking for something to wear. At the moment, Michael's entire wardrobe consisted of a single pair of bloodstained trousers.

"How does a vampire have lycan bodyguards?" Michael asked.

Good question, Selene thought. She'd been wondering that, too, although she had her suspicions. Her eyes narrowed as she spotted an unusual glow coming from behind one of the elaborate tapestries adorning the walls.

"A gift," Tanis volunteered. "From a most persuasive client."

As were the mortal girls you turned into your undead concubines, Selene suspected. Her boots carried her across the cellar toward the faint blue glow. She had a pretty good idea who Tanis's mysterious benefactor was.

"Lucian," she guessed.

Michael reacted in surprise to the name. He looked at Tanis in confusion. "Why would Lucian want to protect you?"

Why indeed? Selene thought. She ripped the tapestry from the wall to reveal a huge weapons rack lined with a wide variety of guns, blades, and crossbows. Vials of luminous blue fluid emitted a solar radiance that hurt her eyes. The same fluid filled multiple rounds of ammunition clips. Selene recognized the lethal ultraviolet ammo that Lucian's lycan soldiers had recently added to their arsenal. One of her fellow Death Dealers, a longtime comrade named Rigel, had been killed by the UV rounds only three nights ago. Selene had watched in horror as Rigel had literally been burned alive from the inside out, until only his carbonized corpse remained. The UV ammo was nothing less than weaponized sunlight.

"Because he's been trading with him," she said angrily. She swiped up one of glowing clips. Even through its insulated casing, the glow from the irradiated fluid stung her fingers. "UV rounds." She had previously suspected a mortal arms dealer, Leonid Florescu, of supplying Lucian with the experimental tracer rounds, but now it appeared that Florescu had only been a middleman at best. She glared at Tanis. "How long have you been in the business of killing your own kind?"

He shrugged. "I've done what was necessary to survive," he said without apology. "But my decision was made easier the day your precious Viktor betrayed me."

Michael pulled a dark wool jacket over his bare torso. Tanis moved to object, then thought better of it. Apparently he valued his life over his wardrobe.

"Betrayal was something he did well," Selene said bitterly. She took down a silver-plated throwing star from the weapons rack and examined it with an expert eye. The make was unfamiliar to her.

Tanis looked at Selene in surprise. "Did?"

"Viktor's dead," she informed him. "I killed him."

He chuckled, as though this was the most ridiculous thing he had ever heard. "You? Killed Viktor? No, I think not. Unless . . ." Understanding dawned in his eyes. "You learned the truth." A grin stretched across his face. He was enjoying this now. "So your eyes are finally open. Isn't it interesting how truth is even harder to absorb than light?"

Selene scowled at the historian's mockery. The worst part was knowing that he was perfectly entitled to his scorn. *I was blind for so long.*

His voice took on a wheedling tone as he craftily tried to turn Selene's shattered illusions to his advantage. "You know, I tried to stop him, of course." He feigned a shudder of repulsion. "An unspeakable travesty, committing such a horrible crime. And then turning you . . . that was just too much to take. My protests are why he put me here."

Right, Selene thought. She didn't believe a word of it.

He gestured at the throwing star in her hand. "Careful with that, dear. It makes a terrible bang. Open the blades and they're active."

"Good to know." Selene pocketed a few of the explosive *shuriken,* then selected a gleaming steel crossbow from the armory. She loaded a silver-tipped bolt into the crossbow and peered down the length of the stock. *Time to get down to business,* she decided. "Viktor put you here for a reason, but I doubt it was because you had moral qualms." She swung the crossbow in his direction. "What do you know?"

Tanis chose to ignore the implied threat. Getting up from his chair, he strolled over to a rough-hewn wooden table where he began to pour himself a glass of bloodred wine. "Very little about anything, I'm afraid."

Not the response I wanted, Selene thought. Taking aim, she squeezed the trigger. The silver bolt took flight, whizzing over the historian's shoulder and into the wineglass in his hand. Tinted glass exploded and wine splashed over the walls. Tanis jumped backward, a shocked expression on his face. His blasé pose shattered just as readily as the wineglass. "Son of a bitch!"

Joining her by the weapons rack, Michael smirked at Selene's inimitable people skills. She was glad that he was starting to understand how her world worked. *Just so long as he never expects me to play the good cop.*

"He wanted this," Michael said, drawing Sonja's pendant from his pocket. He tossed the pendant at Tanis, who caught it in one hand. "Why?"

The historian's face paled.

Chapter Sixteen

$\mathcal{T}$he stable was dark and quiet. Having been put away for the night, the weary workhorses dozed in their stalls . . . until a noise upon the roof roused the horses from their equine dreams. They whinnied in alarm and circled frantically inside their stalls. They reared up in fright and kicked at the gates with their hooves. Their eyes rolled wildly as they worked themselves into a lather.

Noisy claws tore apart the timbers overhead, allowing the cold night air into the barn. Then a fearsome winged figured crashed through the roof before alighting on the hay-covered dirt floor below. The hybrid's abrupt entrance made the trapped horses even more panicky. They hurled themselves against the walls of the stable in their crazed attempts to get away from the invader.

Marcus listened to the horses' racing hearts. He licked his fangs.

Tanis was ready to talk.

A smart decision, Selene thought. She leaned against a tile wall, feeling infinitely more at ease now that she had thoroughly rearmed herself from the historian's weapons rack.

New automatic pistols, Walther P99s, replaced her Berettas and now rested against her hips.

Michael stood in the shadows nearby. Fully dressed once more, he kept a close eye on Tanis, who was seated at a long wooden table. Leather-bound tomes, obviously many centuries old, were stacked atop the table, with more books crowding the shelves behind him. The historian eyed his captors nervously, no longer trying to hide his fear behind a sardonic manner.

"Some history is based on truth," he said. "Other on deception. Viktor was not the first of our kind as you were led to believe. He was once human, and the ruler of these lands."

Tanis flipped through yellowed parchment pages as he spoke. A beaded crystal lamp provided him with enough light to read by.

"Marcus. He is the one. The source." Tanis looked up from the pages. "The first true vampire."

Attracted by the panicky cries of the horses, the farmer came running into the stable. Clutching a shotgun, he flicked on the barn's interior lights. A gasp tore itself from his lungs as he got his first look at the slaughterhouse his stable had become.

Dead horses lay in heaps upon the ground, their throats savagely torn out. Excess blood soaked the hay covering the floor. The barn reeked of blood and mutilated horseflesh.

The shocked farmer made an inarticulate, gagging noise. He threw a hand over his mouth to keep from throwing up. The loaded shotgun trembled in his grip.

Marcus emerged from the shadows. No longer a wizened relic, he looked just as he had in his prime. A reddish beard framed his youthful, aristocratic face. His wings were tucked neatly into his back. He casually wiped the blood from his lips with the back of his hand.

This latest feast had done much to restore him.

"Mother of God!" The nameless farmer stared at Marcus in horror. Shaking visibly, he swung his shotgun toward the intruder.

But the Elder's reflexes were infinitely faster. Before the farmer could pull the trigger, Marcus lunged forward and knocked the mortal aside with a vicious slap. The shotgun went off, blasting another hole in the ceiling, as the hapless farmer sailed headfirst into a wall. His neck snapped loudly.

Marcus eyed the corpse with interest. Having glutted himself on the horses' blood, his appetite was sated now, but maybe this unfortunate wretch could still be of use. Marcus glanced down at his silken trousers and gilded belt. The ancient garments did nothing to conceal the wings folded against his back. Moreover, it struck him as rather unseemly to be striding about half-naked. Perhaps a bit more clothing was in order?

Kneeling beside the farmer, he fingered the dead man's weathered overcoat.

Marcus? The first true vampire?

Selene's eyes widened at the revelation. She had always believed Viktor to be the oldest and most powerful of the Elders. Her mind instantly flashed back to the night before, when Viktor had taunted Singe in the crypt below Ordoghaz:

"The three sons of Corvinus," Viktor had mocked the lycan scientist, heaping ridicule on what Selene had believed to be an old wives' tale about the secret origin of the immortals. "One

178

bitten by bat, one by wolf, and one to walk the lonely road of mortality."

"So the legend is true," she declared. Viktor had implied that the story was nothing but a preposterous fairy tale, but Viktor had lied about many things. She searched Tanis's face, but found no hint of deception. Michael listened just as raptly to the historian's words. According to Singe, she recalled, Michael was a direct descendant of the mortal son mentioned in the myth. She regarded him thoughtfully. Although new to their world, Michael was nonetheless a physical link to the very birth of her kind.

Perhaps he was always destined to be part of this?

"Near the end of his ruthless life," Tanis continued, "when his next breath meant more to Viktor than silver or gold, Marcus came with an offer, a reprieve from sickness and death. Immortality."

Selene could readily imagine the scene. In her mind's eye, she saw Viktor, perhaps less than sixty years old, lying upon his deathbed, succumbing to some incurable mortal ailment. Viktor's face would have been drawn and ashen, his life guttering out like the beeswax candles lighting his gloomy bedchamber. Marcus would have been there, looking as young as ever, while he sat beside the dying warlord, whispering promises of eternal life. . . .

All of this centuries before Viktor made me the same promise, she realized, stunned by Tanis's revelations. Up until a few nights ago, she would have regarded such an account as nothing short of heresy. *How can I have spent six hundred years fighting in Viktor's name without ever hearing this story before?*

"In return for immortality for both he and his army," Tanis continued, "Viktor was to use his military might to aid Marcus."

"To do what?" Selene asked.

"To defeat the very first werewolves, a dangerous and highly infectious breed created by Marcus's own flesh and blood. His twin brother, William."

Marcus tugged the brown leather overcoat over his shoulders. With his wings tucked away, it was a decent fit. A gash torn in the back of the coat would allow him to unfurl his wings if need be. He silently thanked the dead farmer at his feet.

He dabbed a stray drop of blood from his beard. This stopover at the stable had been worth the while, but now he had more important matters to attend to.

Soon, William, he promised his cursed brother. *We will be reunited at last.*

Leaving a scene of utter carnage behind him, he strode out into the night.

Tanis wrested another dusty tome from his bookshelves. He slapped it down onto the table in front of Selene and Michael. After blowing a thick layer of dust from the moldering volume, he opened the book to a specific page. A woodcut illustration showed a pack of wolflike creatures running wild through a medieval village. The shaggy monsters looked even less human than any werewolf Selene had ever encountered. *Artistic license?* she wondered.

Apparently not.

"These weren't the lycans we know," Tanis explained. Having been informed of Michael's hybrid nature, he directed his next remarks to the young American. "Disgusting as your contemporary brethren may be, they are at least evolved to a degree. These were raging monsters, never able to take human form again. It is only the later generations that learned to channel their rage enough to mimic humanity at times."

He flipped the pages until he came to another illustration. This one depicted a single werewolf taking on an entire contingent of medieval Death Dealers. The beast looked larger and more powerful than the other early lycans. Judging from the artist's rendering, the lycan's fur was lighter in color as well, perhaps even as white as snow.

An albino werewolf? Selene speculated. She had never heard of such a thing.

"William's appetite for destruction and rampage was insatiable. He had to be stopped, before he infected the entire continent. And so, once Viktor's army was turned, creating legions of vampires under his sole control, he tracked down and destroyed the animals created by William. And, finally, after a long and bloody campaign, captured William himself."

Tanis slammed the book shut. He plucked another tome from the shelves. "Then they locked him away, Viktor's prisoner for all time."

Thus were born the Death Dealers, Selene realized, *and we've been hunting the lycans ever since.* "Why let William live?"

"The same reason Viktor never conspired against Marcus. Fear." Tanis opened the book, scanned a few pages, then snatched up a third volume from the stacks. "He was warned that should Marcus be slain, all those in his bloodline—including Viktor—would follow him to the grave."

Selene thought she understood. "So, in Viktor's mind, William's death could very well mean the end of all lycans . . . his slaves." She wondered why Viktor had continued to keep William alive even after the lycans had risen up in revolt. *Perhaps as a concession to Marcus, to keep peace within the coven?*

"Yes," Tanis stated. "A clever deception, but one Viktor was hardly willing to put to the test. And so Marcus was protected at all costs. By keeping both brothers alive, Viktor ensured—so he believed—the livelihood of the bloodlines. Both species."

Tanis leafed through the book, looking for a relevant passage.

A faded etching caught Selene's attention. She jammed her pistol into the pages like a bookmark, bringing a halt to Tanis's hasty page-turning. He backed off and let her take custody of the hefty tome. She slid the book around so that she and Michael could get a better look at another medieval woodcut.

The black-and-white etching depicted a time of war and plague. Mounted soldiers, clad in the armor of the Middle Ages, rode past a mass grave that held a jumble of lovingly detailed skeletons. Scythe in hand, the Angel of Death hovered over the morbid scene, but Selene was more interested in the unique crest that adorned the shields of the armored soldiers. The crest incorporated an ornate letter *C* that reminded Selene of the stylized letters emblazoned on the Elders' tombs.

C for . . . Corvinus?

Michael saw what she was looking at. "Vampires?"

Tanis shook his head. "Mortals . . . men loyal to Alexander Corvinus."

"Alexander?" Selene recognized the name, of course. According to Singe, Alexander Corvinus had been the original immortal, a fifth-century Hungarian warlord who had somehow survived a devastating plague that had killed

182

everyone else in his domain. In Alexander, the virulent disease had mutated in an unprecedented fashion, granting him eternal life. Years later, so the story went, he had fathered his infamous three sons.

And so our long war began . . .

"Indeed," Tanis confirmed. "The father of us all." He reached for the book. "If I may?"

Selene nodded, and the historian took back the volume. He quickly flipped the pages to another illustration. Unlike the previous woodcuts, this was more of a technical blueprint, like one of Leonardo da Vinci's sketches.

At the center of the diagram was a drawing of Sonja's pendant. Sketched around the pendant was what looked like a locking mechanism embedded within a reinforced stone door. Tanis borrowed the real pendant from Michael, then gently laid it down atop the fragile parchment. He clicked the hidden switch and watched in fascination as the delicate bronze blades slid out into the open once more. "The Lost Pendant," he said in a hushed tone, "still functioning after nearly six centuries."

Selene grew impatient. She had already seen this trick before. What did any of this have to do with her own fragmentary memories? She tapped the sketch of the lock. "What's this?"

"You should know." Tanis gave her a cryptic smile, as though he was enjoying a private joke at her expense. "It's the door to William's prison. The prison your father was commissioned to build."

My father? Unbidden, the buried memories came rushing through her brain:

. . . the dungeon was damp and cold. Along with her sister, little Selene perched atop a stack of wooden crates as she playfully painted a shining sun on the wall of a stone passage-

way. A seashell held their bright yellow paint, which was a mixture of tree sap and ground-up dandelions. Selene used a hog's-hair brush to add the sun's bright rays. Less than a foot away, Cecilia used the red paint, made from powdered madder roots, to add some cheerful flowers to the blank stone wall.

The passage echoed with the sound of picks and hammers pounding away at solid rock. Sweating laborers hauled carts of debris up to the surface. It looked like hard work to Selene, who was glad she didn't have to do it.

Her father strolled by, calling out instructions to the work crew. He paused to smile at the two girls. Twinkling brown eyes inspected their handiwork. "What beautiful paintings," he said warmly. He grinned at them through his bushy brown beard. "How lucky I am to have such talented artists as daughters."

Selene beamed back at her father. She was proud of him. A master mason and smith, he was in charge of constructing these new dungeons beneath the mighty fortress above. He clutched a roll of parchments in one hand. A mason's compass was tucked into his belt. Selene knew that his was an important and demanding job. Not every man would be up to such a task.

Lord Viktor must think very highly of my father, she thought.

. . . many days later, she watched intently as her father inserted the open pendant into a decorative impression on the wall. Stone ground against stone as hidden machinery came to life. Invisible gears engaged behind the wall, and a section of seemingly solid stone split apart, revealing a shadowy alcove leading to a staircase whose upper steps were shrouded in darkness.

Selene shuddered at the thought of where that staircase might lead. Even as a child she knew what a dungeon was, and a hidden dungeon struck her as many times worse. She couldn't imagine who could possibly be so bad as to deserve being locked away and forgotten forever.

. . . the pendant rested in the little girl's hands. The shiny metal blades projecting from the device reflected the flickering candlelight. Selene thought she had never seen anything quite so beautiful.

A heavy thud caught Selene by surprise. She spun around, terrified, only to find her father gazing down at her with an amused smile. She let out a sigh of relief. For a moment, she had been afraid that an ogre or brigand had found her.

Her father bent down so that he could look her in the eye. "Oh, so you've been the one keeping a watch over this for me, have you?" His affectionate chuckle assured her that she was not in trouble for borrowing the pendant. "Much obliged, darling. I've been searching everywhere for this."

He kissed her forehead, then gently took the pendant from her hand. . . .

The memories hit Selene like a wooden stake through her heart. She turned to Michael for comfort, shock and distress written all over her face. The icy mask she had maintained throughout her interrogation of Tanis was melted away by the volatile emotions bubbling up inside her. At the moment, exposing her vulnerability to their prisoner was the least of her concerns.

"What is it?" Michael asked anxiously. He gently took hold of her shoulders. "What's wrong?"

Tanis knew, even if Michael hadn't figured it out yet. "She now understands why her family was killed."

Selene didn't want to believe it. She had thought Viktor had attacked their home at random, merely to indulge an illicit craving for human blood. She had never connected the slaughter with the pretty pendant she had once played with as a child.

"That was many years later," she protested. "I was nearly twenty."

The historian remembered it well. "The winter of Lucian's escape," he observed. "Your father knew too much. Too much for Viktor to risk, especially when Lucian had this." He held up the pendant. "The key to William's cell."

The pieces started to fall into place, creating a hideous picture in Selene's mind. A chill ran down her spine as the full implications sank in.

"And I'm the map."

Tanis smirked, amused by Selene's growing horror. "Yes, the only one still living who has seen its location. Viktor counted on you being too young to remember the site explicitly. But Marcus knows that the memory—and therefore, the exact location—of his brother's prison is hidden away in your blood."

Michael was still a few steps behind. "Why is Marcus looking for him now, after all this time?"

"The great covens are led by those still loyal to Viktor," Tanis said with a touch of impatience, as though Michael should have been well aware of that. He seemed more interested in confronting Selene with the coven's dirty little secrets. "Marcus was never a true equal amongst the Elders. Viktor used his followers to undercut Marcus at every turn, ensuring his own primacy."

All of this came as news to Selene. Unlike Kraven, she had never had any interest in the coven's often byzantine politics. As long as there had been lycans to hunt, she had been content to let the Elders govern the coven, each in their own turn, according to the never-ending cycle of the Chain. That there might actually be serious dissension among the Elders themselves had never even occurred to her. That was what the Chain was for, after all. She wondered briefly what part Amelia had played in this centuries-long power struggle between Marcus and Viktor.

Perhaps I don't want to know.

In any event, Marcus was now the only Elder left. No wonder he felt free to go searching for William after all these centuries. *All he needs is the pendant—and a taste of my blood.*

"Now that Marcus is of . . . mixed nature," Tanis continued, Selene having previously informed him of the Elder's shocking transformation, "well, the coven will certainly never bow down to . . . an abomination." He spit out the last word with disgust, then realized his faux pas. "Present company excluded, of course."

Michael glared at Tanis, who offered a feeble smile in apology. Michael took back the pendant.

"That still doesn't explain why Marcus needs William," Selene pointed out.

Tanis shrugged and threw up his hands. "That I cannot say."

Wrong answer, Selene thought. She clicked off the safety on her new handgun and lifted the weapon into firing position.

Tanis got the message. "But I know who can stop him," he added hastily.

Selene lowered her weapon.

"Perhaps I can arrange a meeting," Tanis volunteered. "In exchange for your discretion."

She gave him a withering look. "Of course." *What a double-dealing snake,* she thought. *He gives vampires a bad name.*

Ten minutes later, they were on the road to Budapest in a

new SUV provided by Tanis. Another of Lucian's gifts to the turncoat vampire, hidden away in a concealed garage beneath the old monastery. Selene assumed that Tanis considered the car a small price to pay in exchange for their leaving him alive.

I wonder which of us got the greater bargain?

Chapter Seventeen

Tanis dropped Grushenka's lifeless body onto the heap of bones in the lycans' lair, where it joined Olga's corpse among the moldering ruins. Selene and that hybrid freak had finally departed, thank the Fates, leaving him to deal with the Death Dealer's unfortunate victims. He wished there was time to give his paramours a more dignified burial, but the monastery was clearly no longer a safe refuge for him. And with Viktor dead at last, he no longer needed to worry about incurring the Elder's wrath by leaving.

The sooner I'm out of here, the better, he resolved. He lingered in the squalid lair, thinking ahead to his departure. Choosing what to take and what to leave behind would be excruciating, especially where his library was concerned, but Tanis knew that he needed to travel light if he wanted to escape the bloody chaos that seemed to have broken out among his fellow immortals. He wondered where he could go to hide from the tumult. China maybe, or Australia? America was no good; Amelia's followers in the New World Coven would be looking for a scapegoat for her death. *I'm not taking the fall for that one. That was Kraven's doing, not mine.*

His mind raced, compiling a list of what to pack. He was going to need weapons, money, and a new identity. Too bad Olga and Grushenka had not survived their encounter with Selene; he was going to miss their company and their bodies, not necessarily in that order. It was a bloody nuisance, too, that Selene had stolen his only vehicle, but if he could just make it over the hills to the nearest mortal town or hamlet, he should be able to buy or steal a new getaway car. Then it was simply a matter of reaching an airport or rail station.

Maps, he thought. *I need maps.* He made a mental note to extract an atlas from his library, even as he winced at the thought of all his precious volumes he would have to leave behind. *Just as well,* he assured himself. *I've spent enough time reading these past centuries.* It was time he rejoined the world.

If he could just get away fast enough.

Crash! The sound of heavy doors flying open echoed from above. Plus, was it just his imagination or did he hear an ominous flapping as well?

Fear seized the historian's heart. Leaving the bodies of his lovers behind, he ran frantically up the steps toward the moonlit corridors of the old monastery. Terror pursued him all the way back to the wine cellar, even as the fearsome flapping grew louder. Tanis knew only too well the source of that dreadful noise.

Marcus!

Tanis dashed across the cellar and slammed shut a pair of heavy oak doors. With no more caged werewolves to guard the monastery, the terrified historian was left to his own devices. He bolted the doors shut and backed away from them fearfully. Sweat dripped from his brow. His mouth went dry with fear. To think that less than an hour ago he had been lolling in bed with two beautiful, naked vampiresses . . . !

Something pounded on the other side of the door. Tanis nearly jumped out of his skin. He glanced at his weapons rack. Was there anything there powerful enough to stop a hybrid Elder? Tanis rather doubted it; according to Selene, Marcus had practically shrugged off the blasts of her pistol. Still, perhaps the UV cartridges might stand a chance?

He took a step toward his armory, but not quickly enough. The heavy doors buckled inward, then exploded off their hinges. They hit the floor with a resounding crash that stirred up a huge cloud of dust. Tanis stared with fear-stricken eyes as Marcus strode through the arched doorway.

The Elder looked just as Tanis remembered, aside from the demonic wings sprouting from his back. Tanis's gaze was riveted by the unnatural wings, which emerged from the back of the battered leather overcoat draped over Marcus's shoulders. Obviously, Selene had not exaggerated the extent of Marcus's transformation, not that Tanis really thought that she had. Killing was Selene's forte, not deceit. In many ways, she was the most honest vampire he knew, and this time was no exception.

Marcus had indeed become an abomination.

The Elder came between Tanis and his armory. Panic overcame the cowardly historian. He scrambled in the opposite direction, into one of the many underground catacombs connected to the cellar. The echo of his own footsteps pursued him as he raced randomly through the tunnels. Hanging cobwebs brushed against him, clinging to his face and hands. Rats scurried away from his slippered feet. He sucked at the musty air, unaccustomed to such exertion. His robe tangled awkwardly around his legs. A stitch in his side felt like a dagger in his flesh.

Tanis wished that he had never heard the word *hybrid*.

He rounded a corner, then another, then another. It was like a maze down here, he reminded himself. Perhaps he could lose Marcus in this murky subterranean labyrinth?

"Hello, Tanis," said the Elder, directly in front of him.

Tanis suddenly found himself face-to-face with Marcus. *How?* Yelping in fright, he spun around and took off back the way he had come. Almost by accident, he stumbled back into the wine cellar. A long wooden table, laid out with copper plates and goblets, gave him something to lean against. Exhausted, he wasted a few precious seconds catching his breath.

"Tanis . . ."

He started, almost losing his balance. He turned around to see Marcus standing at the other end of the table.

"You seem anxious," the Elder said. "Why do you flee from the very sight of me?"

Tanis was too frightened to form a coherent response. He stepped nervously away from the table.

Marcus flashed him a predatory smile. He took a seat and politely motioned for Tanis to do the same. "Please, sit. There's no need for this to be unpleasant. I've always rather enjoyed your company." Tanis hesitated, and glanced toward his recently depleted armory. The Elder's voice took on a more threatening edge. "Now you're being rude."

"Sorry." Tanis sat down at the opposite end of the table, as far from Marcus as possible. This appeared to satisfy the Elder, who nodded approvingly.

"Viktor struck two keys," he stated. "What do you know of them?"

Tanis resisted an urge to glance over at his library, where not long ago he had shown Selene and her cohort the original diagrams of the lock. He tried to remember if that particular volume was still lying open on the other table.

"Keys? I don't know of any keys," he lied.

Marcus cocked his head. An instant later, his wings snapped forward like the jaws of a trap. Razor-sharp talons pierced Tanis's shoulders, slamming him facedown onto the table. Tanis shrieked in shock and agony. Kicking and screaming, he tried to tear himself free from the Elder's vicious pinions, but the talons were inserted too deeply into his flesh. Using his wings, Marcus effortlessly dragged Tanis across the table. Copper plates and cutlery clattered to the floor.

Tanis felt like a fish twisting upon an angler's hook. Lifting his head from the rough wooden tabletop, he came face-to-face with the Elder's saturnine visage. He saw neither patience nor mercy in Marcus's eyes.

"Oh, yes, *those* keys," Tanis stammered. "One was kept in plain sight, draped around his daughter's lovely neck . . . right there for you to see."

Marcus didn't like the implication. He lifted his wings, violently hauling Tanis up closer to his face. "And the other?"

"Kept with Viktor," Tanis said hastily. "At all times."

"Where?"

"Within him . . . beneath the flesh."

Marcus glowered balefully at Tanis, weighing the historian's words. Tanis dared to hope that maybe, just maybe, he might come through this night with his immortality intact. *If I do,* he vowed, *I'm going to bury myself so deep that no vampire, lycan, or hybrid will ever find me again. My books will be my only companions.*

Then Marcus smiled, baring his teeth, and Tanis realized it was already too late. "No, I beg you . . . no!"

Marcus paid no heed to his frantic cries. Still holding on to the impaled historian with his wings, the Elder drove his fangs into Tanis's throat.

                              *   *   *

As the blood poured down his throat, Marcus sifted expertly
through the scribe's memories. As the sole surviving Elder,
he alone now possessed the knowledge and experience required to control the flow of the blood memories, so that
they presented a cohesive narrative rather than a flood of in-
coherent images. As with Kraven before, Marcus readily
found the moments he required:

*"But I know who can stop him," Tanis informed Selene, in a
shameless attempt to curry her favor and preserve his own miserable existence. "Perhaps I can arrange a meeting. . . ."*

Marcus lifted his mouth from Tanis's neck and withdrew
his talons from the historian's shoulders. The vampire's head
slumped lifelessly onto the table. Andreas Tanis would
never again betray the buried secrets of the past. Now he
was nothing more than history himself.

His wings folded around him, Marcus left the cellar without a backward glance. He now knew where to find Selene
and Michael, and in whose company they were likely to be.

Of course, he thought. *I should have anticipated as much.*

Chapter Eighteen

*T*he *Sancta Helena* was docked on the east side of the
Danube, between the Chain and Elizabeth bridges. Piers
and warehouses dominated the sleeping waterfront. Towering steel cranes, abandoned for the night, perched over dilapidated wharves. Rusty freighters, bearing goods from all
over Europe and beyond, were anchored along the shore.
The *Sancta Helena,* sleek and immaculate, looked rather out
of place among the weather-beaten cargo ships berthed
nearby. No doubt Lorenz Macaro had his own reasons for
staying away from the more upscale docks.

Selene and Michael were parked in a narrow alley overlooking the pier. Their view of the stationary vessel offered
few clues regarding what sort of reception they might encounter aboard the ship. "How do we know Tanis isn't setting us up?" Michael asked.

"He's not brave enough to set me up," she replied.
Seated behind the wheel, she questioned whether this was
a good idea. She had heard of these so-called Cleaners before; the Death Dealers had been aware for centuries that a
secret society of mortals was determined, for reasons unknown, to conceal the existence of the immortals from

their fellow humans. The origins and motive of the Cleaners had been the subject of constant rumor and speculation, but the Elders had always discouraged Selene and the other Death Dealers from probing too deeply into the matter. *Why was that?* she wondered. *What were Viktor and the others trying to hide?*

At this point, she didn't trust any of the Elders' edicts anymore.

She considered how best to approach the ship. *Maybe I should do some reconnaissance first?* Michael wouldn't like being left behind again, but she was reluctant to walk into the lions' den without assessing the ship's security first. *If nothing else,* she thought, *we should know where the viable escape routes are.*

Furious barking, coming from right outside the car, startled her. A snarling rottweiler threw itself against the driver's-side window, planting its front paws up against the glass. Selene reached for her guns, but held her fire. The slobbering rottweiler was just a dog, not a werewolf.

With a sharp command, the dog was pulled back away from the window. A flashlight beam searched the interior of the car. Squinting into the glare, Selene saw that the light was attached to an AK-47 assault rifle being held by a looming figure in a black, paramilitary uniform. A second beam entered the car from the opposite direction. Glancing over, she saw another guard and watchdog standing watch outside Michael's door.

So much for casing the ship in advance, she thought. *Looks like we're meeting the Cleaners even sooner than I anticipated.*

The first guard stepped forward and shouted at her through the window. "You're trespassing," he declared in French. "Get out of the car slowly so I can see your hands."

Selene resisted the temptation to draw her own weapons. They were here for information, not a firefight. "We're here to see Lorenz Macaro."

Ignoring her explanation, both guards raised their weapons and took aim at the windows. "I told you to exit the vehicle so I can see your hands."

"You want to see my hands, do you?" She slowly raised her arms, then slammed her open palms against the window.

Sonja's pendant gleamed in the light of the first guard's search-beam.

That did the trick. Within minutes, she and Michael found themselves being escorted through a high-tech operations center aboard the ship. Selene was impressed at the scale and sophistication of the setup. The advanced, state-of-the-art equipment rivaled anything possessed by the coven. She allowed a flicker of hope to enter her heart. Perhaps this Macaro really did have the resources to deal with the threat posed by Marcus.

If he doesn't, she mused, *we're out of options.*

A short flight of stairs brought them to Macaro's private office overlooking the ops center. The elegant furnishings reminded her of the opulent decor back at Ordoghaz. She felt a minor pang at the thought that she might never again set foot in the mansion, her home for so many generations. She was hardly the sentimental sort, and yet . . .

Moonlight filtered through the skylight in the ceiling, adding to the illumination provided by the crystal chandelier and Tiffany lamps. Selene eyed the skylight with a touch of apprehension; Marcus's newfound wings had her on guard against aerial attacks.

Lorenz Macaro greeted them from behind a large mahogany desk, beneath the watchful gaze of a carved wooden goddess. Selene noted the man's dignified bearing and concerned expression. For a human, he conveyed an aura of quiet authority. If he had any misgivings about being in the presence of a vampire and a hybrid, no trace of it showed upon his regal features.

He nodded at the pendant in Selene's hands. "May I?"

Selene handed it over. Lucian's precious keepsake had brought them this far. Maybe the pendant could somehow convince Macaro to help them stop Marcus.

It was a worth a try.

The elderly human contemplated the infamous pendant, running his finger over its intricate detail. Selene noticed his signet ring, although she couldn't quite make out the design upon it. She wondered what was going through the old man's mind. His inscrutable expression defied her attempts to read his reaction to the pendant.

Four armed bodyguards stood by the stairs, watching Selene and Michael warily. Lifting his gaze from the pendant, Macaro motioned for the men to leave. "But, sir," one of them protested, looking with alarm at the Death Dealer and her companion. He was obviously reluctant to leave his employer unguarded.

"You can go," Macaro insisted brusquely. He waited for the men to depart before resuming his inspection of the pendant.

"You're familiar with this then?" Selene asked.

Macaro gave her a cryptic smile, then gently nudged the hidden switch with his fingertip. The concealed blades emerged from the pendant like clockwork. "Intimately."

She and Michael exchanged a startled look. Did everybody know about the pendant's secret workings except them? A thought occurred to her and she took a closer look at Macaro's signet ring, even as she recalled that woodcut illustration of the armored soldiers marching across a plague-

198

ravaged countryside. The stylized *C* upon the ring matched the crest upon the knights' shields.

By the Elders! she thought as the truth struck home. She looked at the aging human with new eyes. Although she tried to maintain her cool, her hushed tone betrayed the awe she felt.

"You're Alexander Corvinus."

The man who called himself Lorenz Macaro blinked in surprise at the name. He glanced at his ring with a rueful sigh. "There was a time that I was known by that name." He rose from his chair and circled around his desk to face Michael. He laid his hands upon the younger man's shoulders. Parental pride showed upon his face. "But by any name, I am still your forefather."

Corvinus, as Selene now thought of him, handed the pendant back to Michael, who refastened the chain around his neck. He gaped at the older man, seeming uncertain how to respond. Selene recalled Michael telling her that his grandparents had immigrated to the United States after the Second World War. Surely, when he had decided to move to Hungary after his fiancée's death, he had never expected to come face-to-face with an ancestor from the fifth century.

"How have you stayed hidden all these years?" Selene asked. Truth be told, she was feeling slightly overwhelmed herself. By her reckoning, the man standing before her was over sixteen hundred years old, an impressive span even for an immortal. The legendary Corvinus was indeed what Tanis had called him.

The father of us all . . .

"For centuries I've stood by and watched the havoc my sons have wrought upon each other . . . and upon humanity." He sighed wearily and turned away from them. "Not the legacy for which I prayed the night I watched them enter the world." He sat back down behind his desk. "And a tiresome duty: keeping the war contained, cleaning up the mess, hiding my family's unfortunate history."

"Couldn't you have stopped them?" Michael asked.

"Yes," Selene insisted.

Corvinus looked sadly at his descendant. "Could you kill your own sons?"

"You know what Marcus will do," Selene said. She leaned across the desk to confront him. "If he finds me, he finds William's prison. You need to help us stop him."

He regarded her skeptically, then laughed harshly. "You are asking me to help you kill my son? You? A Death Dealer?" His face was stern and unforgiving. His cultured voice dripped with scorn. "How many innocents did you kill in the six-century quest to avenge your family? Spare me your self-righteous declarations. You are no different than Marcus, and even less noble than William. At least he cannot control his savagery."

Selene was taken aback by his verbal attack, but only for a moment or two. She wasn't about to be treated with contempt, not even by Alexander Corvinus. "Anything I've done can be laid at your feet. Hundreds of thousands have died because of your inability to accept that your sons are monsters. That they create . . . monsters." She was honest enough to include herself in that category. "You could have stopped all of this."

"Do not come groveling to me," he said, scowling, "simply because you are weaker than your adversary."

Selene refused to be intimidated. She found it ironic that, essentially, she was taking Viktor's side in his long dispute with Marcus. "You know what kind of devastation William caused before he was captured. He can't be set free."

Corvinus had no ready response. He shifted uneasily in

his chair, obviously wrestling with his conscience. *He knows I'm right,* she thought, *no matter how much he hates to admit it.*

"Let me tell you about what your other son has become. . . ."

The sentry paced the deck of the *Sancta Helena,* keeping an eye out for trouble. Colin Langely had served with the Cleaners for nearly three years now, after being recruited from Her Majesty's Secret Service, but tonight he felt unusually on edge. You didn't need to be a top-grade intelligence analyst to know that things were up. Elders assassinated, the vampires' headquarters burned to the ground, now a Death Dealer and a suspected lycan visiting the Old Man in person. All of this was unprecedented in Langely's experience.

Sounds as if this cold war is becoming hot.

Shallow waves lapped against the hull. A full moon cast its reflection on the surface of the Danube. Langely scanned the shoreline with a pair of night-vision binoculars. Beyond the silent docks and warehouses, traffic flowed upon the Belgrade Parkway. In the distance, the lights of central Pest lit up the night. Despite his apprehensions, he spotted nothing amiss.

Without warning, a dark figure dropped into view. Langely caught a glimpse of huge, demonic wings. Clawed feet smacked down upon the deck. A hideous face, with flared ears and a batlike snout, glared at him.

Bloody hell! Langely thought, dropping the binoculars. The grotesque creature before him bore no resemblance to any vamp or lycan he had ever encountered before. He reached for his Uzi, but the winged monster was too fast. His shots went wild as a savage claw ripped off half his face.

The sound of gunfire, coming from topside, electrified Michael and the others. Corvinus leapt to his feet, while Selene drew her new Walthers. They heard anxious gasps and chatter from the ops center below. Michael recognized the sound of automatic weapon's fire, something he had become all too familiar with over the last few nights.

Now what? he worried. *Has Marcus found us already?*

Corvinus opened his mouth to demand a report, but was interrupted by an enormous crash directly overhead. Michael jumped backward as a body, wearing the black uniform of a Cleaner, came smashing through the skylight, landing on top of the desk amidst a shower of splintered glass. Corvinus and Selene also reacted with shock.

Michael saw at once that the guard was dead. His face and chest had been ripped to shreds. An Uzi, strapped to the Cleaner's chest, had obviously done the poor guy no good. Blood dripped off the edge of the desk onto the expensive carpet.

Instinctively, Michael clutched the pendant hanging around his neck. He understood that at all costs they had to stop Marcus from getting his claws on the key. A hybrid Elder was bad enough; they couldn't allow Marcus to free William as well.

He looked to Selene, hoping she would know what to do. But before she could answer, the window behind him exploded inward. Vicious talons tore through steel shutters as if they were tissue paper, then stabbed all the way through Michael's shoulders. He screamed in agony as he was abruptly hoisted off his feet and yanked out of the office through the broken window.

A cold wind rushed against him, but was not frigid

enough to numb the searing pain in his shoulders. Looking down, he saw the *Sancta Helena* shrink away below his dangling feet. Guards upon the ship's deck fired up at them, apparently none too concerned about hitting Michael as well as Marcus. He heard the Elder's powerful wings flapping in his ears.

Michael cried out. High in the air above the dock, he thrashed wildly upon the talons spearing his shoulders. Blood streamed from the wounds, falling hundreds of feet to the pier below. Vertigo threatened as he gazed down at the empty air beneath his feet. How high up was he?

Not that it mattered. A heartbeat later, Marcus hurled Michael at the ground. A scream tore itself from Michael's lungs as he plunged downward at heart-stopping speed. Hitting the run-down wharf, he smashed straight through the rotting timbers into the ice-cold water below. The sudden immersion came as yet one more shock to his system, on top of his crash landing and skewered flesh. The moonlit waters took on a reddish tinge.

Stunned, he sank toward the bottom of the river.

"Michael!"

Selene rushed over to the ruptured window, just in time to see Michael crash through a nearby pier. Splinters flew from fractured wooden beams, followed by a tremendous splash of water erupting from the river below. A second later, a winged figure dived after him.

Was Michael strong enough to survive the fall? Probably, provided he didn't drown before Marcus got to him. But that still left the ruthless Elder to deal with.

Hang on, Michael, she thought desperately. *You don't have to fight him alone.*

Thrusting her handguns back into their holsters, she

swiped the dead guard's Uzi and racked another round into the chamber. Turning away from Corvinus, she headed for the open window. "No, wait," he called after her. "You're no match for him."

She hesitated, but only for a moment. Corvinus was undoubtedly right, yet that wasn't going to stop her from coming to Michael's aid. *Hell,* she thought, *I've already killed one Elder this week. Let's go for another.*

She dived headfirst out the window, then landed like a panther on the dock below. She raced across the wooden planks to the gap Michael's falling body had punched through the floor of the dock. She peered through the hole into the murky shadows beneath the pier. Rusty iron struts supported the crumbling wharf. Excess crates and barrels were stacked on slime-covered wooden planks along the shore. A set of concrete steps led up to the pier. Lengths of thick, knotted rope helped hold the dock's substructure together. Crimson water lapped against the riverbank.

"Michael!"

Oily water sprayed against her face as Marcus burst from the surface of the river, clutching Michael's bleeding body. The Elder, in his monstrous hybrid form, hurled Michael onto a muddy bank beneath the pier. Selene felt a surge of relief as she saw Michael roll to his feet upon the shore. Marcus touched down in front of him. The shattered pier was high enough above their heads to allow the Elder to unfurl his wings to their fullest.

Michael snarled at the other hybrid. His eyes shifted to black.

But Marcus did not give Michael time to complete the transformation. The deadly wings snapped forward, spearing Michael in the chest. Blood sprayed freely as the lethal talons stabbed Michael again and again, like the stingers of an angry scorpion. Michael recoiled from the furious on-slaught. He stumbled clumsily, too overwhelmed to strike back. He swiped impotently at the darting wings, trying and failing to fend them off. His face was contorted in agony. Blood trickled from the corner of his mouth.

No! Selene thought. Michael was being tortured to death before her very eyes. *Leave him alone, damn you!*

She dropped through the hole in the dock, splashing down into the shallow water along the shore. Raising the Uzi, she took aim at Marcus, but . . .

With a wicked growl, Marcus seized hold of Michael and rammed him into one of the rusty iron struts supporting the dock. The metal split in two and Michael's body smashed down on the bottom half of the sundered strut. The force of the collision drove the steel beam up through Michael's chest, impaling him from below. Blood gushed from his open mouth.

Selene froze in horror, transfixed by the awful tableau. She felt as if an iron bar had just been run through her own heart as well. *Please, no,* she thought despairingly. *Not Michael.*

Marcus, on the other hand, was not at all dismayed. He tore open Michael's shirt and wrapped his claws around the blood-spattered pendant. A look of triumph crossed his malevolent face as he claimed the precious ornament once and for all.

The sight of the pendant snapped Selene out of her grief-induced paralysis. Screaming in fury, she emptied the Uzi, peppering Marcus with red-hot silver. The muzzle of the submachine gun flared like the anger erupting inside her. *Die, you ugly bastard!* she thought, wishing she could make the heartless Elder feel just a fraction of the pain she was going through. *Die!*

Marcus hissed loudly, whether from pain or annoyance she couldn't tell. With preternatural speed, he retreated into the shadows, taking the pendant with him.

Shit, she thought.

Aboard the ship, Corvinus strode briskly to the ebony armoire on the starboard side of his office. He opened the cabinet to reveal an impressive collection of antique weapons: broadswords, battle-axes, rapiers, daggers, pikes, maces, scimitars, stilettos, and other mementos of his martial past.

A fitting memorial, he mused, *for one whose legacy has long been written in blood.*

Selecting a seventeenth-century broadsword from the armoire, he withdrew the double-edged weapon and prepared to meet his vampiric son for the first time in centuries. He eyed the sword dubiously. If and when the moment of truth arrived, was he truly willing to take arms against his own flesh and blood? Chances were, he would soon find out.

Not for one moment did he expect Selene to defeat Marcus on her own.

Murder in her eyes, Selene crept along below the dock, searching the shadows for her foe. Part of her wanted to rush to Michael's side, see to his injuries, but she knew she couldn't afford to let her guard down for a moment. Even though Marcus had claimed the first part of the key, he still needed a taste of her blood to discover the location of William's hidden prison.

Come and get it, she thought coldly.

The empty Uzi lay in the mud behind her. She gripped a loaded Walther in her left fist. She regretted that all she had was silver bullets to work with; the experimental UV ammo had not been the right caliber for her new handguns.

Excited voices shouted up above. Racing footsteps pounded across the pier, as though the *Sancta Helena* was being abandoned en masse. Selene did her best to tune the distracting noises out, trying to listen for the flutter of bat-wings instead. All she heard, however, was the sound of the water against the shore . . . and Michael's dying moans.

Dammit, she cursed silently. Where the hell was Marcus?

Suddenly, the misshapen hybrid leapt out at her from behind a large wooden pillar. His wings lashed out at her, but Selene instantly flipped into the air, grabbing on to the underside of the pier with her right hand. The deadly pinions passed beneath her, missing by inches.

Hanging by one hand from the rotted timbers, she fired down at Marcus with her Walther. Nine millimeters of solid silver tore through the Elder's flesh, causing him to grimace in pain. Instead of falling down, however, he flapped off the ground at Selene. Gritting his teeth against the impact of the bullets, he flew toward her like the Angel of Death, while she fired ceaselessly at his misshapen hybrid face.

His wings lashed out, his left nailing her right hand to the wooden crossbeam, while his right wing pierced her hip. Selene bit down on her lip to keep from crying out, while squeezing the trigger of her pistol until it ran dry. Gory bullet wounds marked the hybrid's mottled hide, but Marcus kept on coming. A sadistic grin twisted his lips.

Selene screamed in frustration as her gun clicked uselessly. Marcus drove his taloned wings even deeper in her flesh as he positioned his open jaws beneath her skewered hand. She watched helplessly as her blood streamed down toward the Elder's waiting maw. Her heart pounded against her will, speeding the crimson flow.

This is just what he needs!

The blood splattered across the hybrid's face. Closing his eyes to better savor the moment, he gulped it down eagerly, chasing after stray droplets with his tongue. He sighed in rapture as Selene's memories coursed through his brain:

The dungeon was cold and damp. Selene was tired of playing there. "Come on, Cecilia!" she called to her sister as they ran up the stone passageway toward the sun. Giggling, the girls raced past the straining laborers with their heavy carts. "Last one there is a silly goose!"

"No fair!" Cecilia complained as she dashed after her sister. "You've got a head start!"

Cecilia gave her a good chase, but the outcome was never in doubt. Selene burst out of the gloomy tunnel into the bright afternoon sunshine. "I win!" she shouted to Cecilia, who came rushing out of the dungeon only moments later.

Selene turned around to look back the way she had come. The entrance to the dungeon had been dug into the forbidding face of a craggy mountaintop. A river wound its way through the rocky mountain passes, while high above the raging torrents, Lord Viktor's castle sat atop the very peak of the mountain, its magnificent turrets and battlements reaching toward the sky. The imposing sight of the mighty fortress imprinted itself on the little girl's memory.

Marcus's black eyes snapped open. Selene's blood dripped from his chin as he smiled triumphantly.

Bastard! Selene thought angrily. She felt violated by the Elder's attack. Fury helped her overcome the shock to her system as she reached for her spare handgun and blasted Marcus in the chest. The demonic hybrid shrieked in pain and tumbled back toward the water below.

His talons were yanked from her flesh and she fell like a rock toward the river below. The freezing water jolted her as she splashed into the Danube, sinking below the shallow waves. She kicked madly back up to the surface, and her head burst free of the river. Her eyes searched anxiously for Marcus, but the Elder was nowhere to be seen.

Of course, she thought bitterly. *He got what he came for. The pendant and my blood. Now all he needs is the second half of the key, wherever that is.*

Her gaze fell upon Michael, his unmoving body impaled upon the bloody strut, and every other consideration fled her mind. Heedless of her own injuries, she ran out of the river and over to the shattered strut. Icy water streamed down her soggy leather gear as she splashed through the shallows up to the shore.

Michael!

It was even worse than she remembered. At least a foot of rusty metal jutted from Michael's chest. His body was limp and still, his arms drooping at his sides. His agonized groans had fallen silent. His eyes, reverting to their mortal brown tint, stared blankly at the pier above them.

"Michael . . ." She gently lifted him off the impaling iron beam and laid him down on the wooden planks along the shore. Bending over him, she laid her hand against his cheek, hoping to get a response. Her fingers searched for a pulse. "Michael!"

It was no use. His chest had been torn to shreds, with a gaping hole where his heart should have been. Not even an Elder could survive such a wound.

Michael was dead.

"No!" Anger, an emotion she knew far better than grief, rushed over her. "Damn you!" She fell to her knees beside the body. Her clenched fists pounded upon his ravaged chest, coming away stained with his blood. Tears gushed from her eyes, mixing with the cold water dripping from her hair. Six hundred years of loss and heartbreak surged up inside her, spilling over the dams she had erected around her heart. Violent sobs racked her body.

"Fuck!"

Chapter Nineteen

"*H*ello, Father."

Alexander Corvinus recognized his son's voice, even after centuries. The voice approached him from behind, Marcus having dropped through the shattered skylight into the office. Broken glass crunched beneath the intruder's feet, grinding the brittle fragments into the carpet.

In his hand, Corvinus held the second half of the key, the one he had extracted from Viktor's rib cage. Facing his father's back, Marcus could not see the key. Corvinus prayed he never would.

"You are unwelcome in my presence," Corvinus said sternly.

He turned to face his son, but the vital key was no longer in evidence. To his slight surprise, he saw that Marcus looked like the son he remembered, not the hybrid abomination described by Selene. His beard and hair were the same reddish tint they had always been. A leather overcoat was draped over his bare shoulders, concealing his wings. Corvinus recognized his son's cruel, sardonic smile. He wasn't sure whether to be relieved or dismayed by Marcus's deceptively human appearance.

"Ah, the predictable heart that never thaws," his son said mockingly. He placed his hand atop his chest, as though wounded to the core. "Pity it beats within such a fool. The eldest of the immortals, yet you've made no attempt to seize your destiny."

The ancient broadsword rested on the desk between them. The carved goddess upon the wall was the sole witness to their reunion. In hopes of sparing their lives, Corvinus had ordered the ship's staff and guards to evacuate the vessel. What transpired now was between him and Marcus alone.

As it was always meant to be.

"We are oddities of nature, you and I. Nothing more." He leveled a disapproving gaze upon his son. "This is a world for humanity."

Marcus sneered at him. "And that petty sentiment explains why you rejected your sons? Why you stood by for over half a millennium as William suffered alone in darkness?" Contempt registered in his voice. "No Father. I have no respect for your pitiful excuse." He stepped forward ominously, circling around the desk. "Viktor's key. Where is it?"

"Whatever plan you have for William is futile." Corvinus did not quail in the face of his son's advance. "You cannot control your brother."

Lord knows I tried, he thought sadly, *before William's bloodlust grew beyond all control.*

"I am stronger now," Marcus replied, "and our bond is greater than you have ever wanted to acknowledge."

The same old delusion, Corvinus mused. Marcus had never been able to recognize the truth about his beloved twin. "You're wrong. Soon you will be drowning in lycans . . . just like before."

Marcus shook his head. "Not lycans, Father, or vampires.

A new race, created in the image of their maker . . . their new god. Me."

Fervor burned in his eyes, and Corvinus realized that his son had truly gone mad.

"And a true god . . . has no father."

Corvinus reached for his sword, but he had waited too long . . . perhaps intentionally. Marcus's wings unfurled, the unnatural sight causing Corvinus's eyes to widen in amazement. A demonic pinion snapped outward, knocking the older man against the starboard wall. A spear-tipped talon pierced his shoulder, pinning him to the solid steel bulkhead.

Immortal blood flowed from his injured shoulder, but Corvinus had survived worse in his time. He grunted in pain, but refused to beg for his life, not even when he saw Marcus lift the heavy broadsword with one hand. He was still Alexander Corvinus, and he would not give Marcus the satisfaction of seeing his father tremble in fear.

My death is long overdue, he thought. *Let me face it with dignity.*

There was nothing dignified about the hate-filled expression on Marcus's face as he slowly drove the point of the sword through his father's chest. Despite his resolve, Corvinus could not help gasping out loud as the double-edged blade sliced through his body inch by excruciating inch. The sword cut through bone and tissue alike.

Was I truly too slow to defend myself, Corvinus wondered, *or was it that I simply could not bring myself to slay my son— not even to save my own life?*

He suspected the latter.

Marcus thrust the entire length of the blade into his father, all the way up to the hilt. Only then did he withdraw his left wing from his victim's shoulder. Coughing up blood,

213

Corvinus slumped against the steel bulkhead, held up by the broadsword alone. As he writhed upon the blade, his son reached into his wool coat and began searching Corvinus's pockets.

Forgive me, Viktor, Corvinus thought in despair. The deceased Elder had been a liar and a hypocrite, but at least he had understood the importance of keeping William locked away from the world. *You hid it better than I.*

Marcus's eyes lit up with malevolent glee. Grinning evilly at his father, he plucked the key from an inside pocket. Corvinus's dying heart sank at the sight; he had no doubt that, despite Selene's best efforts, Marcus had already obtained the pendant and the location of William's hidden prison. Now his insane son had it all . . . and all of humanity was in danger.

"You will fail," Corvinus said, looking into his son's eyes.

But Marcus wasn't quite done with him yet. Tucking the key into the pocket of his overcoat, he turned to face his father once more. It was time to deliver the coup de grâce.

The talons of both wings sprang forward, converging on the old man's heart.

Whirring blades sliced through the air as the helicopter touched down on the ship's landing pad. Peering from the cockpit, Samuel could have told at once that they had a situation on their hands, even if they hadn't already received an emergency distress signal from the *Sancta Helena.* Dead guards littered the deck, along with blood and empty shells. A gaping hole had been torn in the dock alongside the ship, while the broken skylight testified that even the sanctity of Macaro's private office had been violated.

The *Sancta Helena* had obviously come under attack.

Samuel feared that he and his men had arrived too late. Was the Old Man still alive?

Rifles and machine guns ready, the Cleaners piled out of the copter and raced toward the ops center. They found the corridors of the ship strangely deserted, which suggested that most of the crew and staff had managed to escape the assault. Samuel dared to hope that Macaro might be among the survivors, but in his heart he knew otherwise. Their commander was definitely one who would want to go down with his ship.

Leading the way, Samuel rushed through the abandoned ops center and up the stairs to the palatial suite. A quick glance confirmed the worst: Macaro sat slumped against one wall, barely breathing. A bright red streak upon the steel bulkhead testified to how the Old Man had slid onto the floor. A bloodstained broadsword rested on the polished wooden planks a few feet away, its grisly work accomplished. Scanning the office, Samuel spotted the inert body of another Cleaner sprawled atop the mahogany desk. Colin Langely, he believed, although the corpse's mutilated face threw some doubt on the matter.

"Look sharp!" he ordered his team. Searching the office, they quickly determined that the enemy was no longer present. Then, and only then, did Samuel hurry to see to Macaro. A look of horror transformed the soldier's usually impassive features as he registered the full extent of his commander's injuries. Gaping wounds perforated Macaro's chest, many of them passing all the way through the man's body. A crimson froth bubbled up from his punctured lungs. Blood pooled beneath him, seeping through the cracks in the hardwood floor. His face was drawn and pale. Pain showed in his ageless gray eyes.

Samuel was one of the few operatives Macaro had trusted

with the secret of his true identity. The Cleaner realized that any other man would already be dead by now; only Macaro's immortal nature had kept him alive so far.

But for how much longer?

Samuel found it hard to believe that even Alexander Corvinus could survive such grievous wounds. Urgently, he called for a first-aid kit and started applying pressure to the worst of the sucking chest wounds. If he could just stop the bleeding, maybe there was still a chance to save him!

Macaro waved him away. "No," he insisted. "The time has come, my friend." Gasping for breath, he hurriedly explained the nature of the threat posed by Marcus. "Find the girl." He coughed up blood. "Bring her to me."

Beneath the pier, Selene tried hopelessly to revive Michael. Her blood had saved him once before; perhaps it could do so again? She squeezed her hand, forcing the blood to stream from her wounded palm onto the gaping wounds in Michael's chest, which nevertheless stubbornly refused to heal. In desperation, she pressed her bleeding palm to his lips. *Drink,* she pleaded with him silently. *Drink, please.*

His lips were cold to her touch. His mouth did not welcome the blood.

It was no use. Michael was past saving.

Hunched over his body, she cradled his head with one arm. Only days ago, she recalled, Michael had tended her own wounds beneath a similar pier, after he'd rescued her from a sinking car. Perhaps he would have been better off letting her die; in the end, she had brought him nothing but a violent death.

Fresh tears streaked her face as she wept openly. It was all too much. She had lost everything, including any last

216

hope for happiness. She felt as though her own future had died with Michael.

Caught up in her grief, she didn't even hear the Cleaners coming down the steps until their flashlight beams cut through the darkness below the dock. A hand landed on her shoulder and she spun around violently, knocking the hand away. She sprang to her feet and raised her gun.

The leader of the Cleaners stepped back and raised his hands to signal that he didn't want a fight. "No, wait." Behind him, his men lowered their weapons. Selene held her fire, but kept her gun ready. As far as she knew, Corvinus's soldiers were not her enemy, but she wasn't about to take any chances.

"Well?" she demanded hoarsely. Her throat ached from sobbing.

"My name is Samuel," the lead Cleaner identified himself. "If you want Marcus, you'll need Alexander's help."

Marcus! The Elder's name inspired a burst of volcanic rage. Selene realized that she still had one thing left to live for: stopping Marcus and avenging Michael's death. But to destroy the hybrid Elder she would need all the assistance she could get.

She nodded, then glanced down at Michael.

"We're not leaving him here."

The opulent suite had changed little since Selene had last seen it, aside from the bloodstains on the wall and the gore-covered sword lying upon the floor. She found Corvinus propped up against one wall, surrounded by his own immortal blood. A museum-quality medieval dagger rested upon his lap.

She could tell at glance that he was at death's door. His face had taken on a grayish cast and he was breathing with great difficulty. Her mind reeled at the very idea of the near-mythical Alexander Corvinus succumbing to death at last, but now was not the time to dwell on the historic significance of the moment. According to Samuel, the ancient warlord had only a short time left to live. They had to make it count.

"Did he get the pendant?" he gasped.

Selene remembered Marcus wrenching his prize away from Michael. "Yes."

"He is too powerful for you alone," Corvinus said, unsurprised by her admission.

It took her a moment to realize what he had in mind. Her gaze darted at the waiting dagger.

"You're the only one older than he is," she protested, "the only one stronger. You could have killed him yourself."

Corvinus shook his head. "No matter what he has become . . . he is my son."

"Well, he's not mine."

He nodded grimly. "You are the last hope left," he told her. Selene wondered if he had even tried to defend himself. "There is only one way to defeat him." Picking up the dagger, he drew the tip of the blade across his wrist. A crimson line seeped up from beneath his skin. "Quickly now, before there is no more legacy left in my veins."

Selene recalled offering her own wrist to Michael only one night ago. Her heart ached at the realization that her sacrifice had only kept her lover alive for another twenty-four hours or so. She hoped that Corvinus's blood would not be similarly wasted.

She knelt beside the dying immortal and lifted his wrist to her lips. His blood touched her tongue and an unexpected shock rushed through her body. Her brown eyes instantly flashed to a luminous blue. Corvinus's blood, the font from which both the lycan and vampire races had been born, possessed a dynamic energy like nothing she had ever tasted before. Already she felt its powers coursing through her veins.

Startled, and more than a little frightened, she drew back her lips. Her eyes stared anxiously into his. She spoke in a whisper:

"What will I become?"

Corvinus lifted his wrist toward her mouth. His voice, when he answered her, was suffused with a near-religious fervor.

"The Future."

What does he mean? She contemplated his bleeding wrist, uneasy about the momentous step she was about to take. Even without knowing the full consequences of the act, she knew that she faced a crucial turning point that would change her immortal existence forever. After this, nothing would ever be the same. She hesitated briefly, then realized she had no choice. Marcus had to be stopped, and this was the only way she could become strong enough to oppose him. Also, if she was completely honest with herself, the lure of Corvinus's potent blood was just too intoxicating to resist.

Opening her mouth wide, she sank her fangs deeply into the immortal's wrist. An electric thrill raced through her quivering flesh as she hungrily gulped down the potent elixir flowing through the old man's veins. Her body convulsed in sync with Corvinus's fading pulse. Her own heart pounded like the hooves of medieval warhorses. Blue fire blazed in her eyes as the blood of the First merged with her own. For the first time since Michael's death, she felt alive once more.

Is this what Michael felt, when my bite made him a hybrid?

Finally, she could drink no more. She tore her mouth away from the old man's wrist. To her surprise, she saw contentment on his face, even though his end was near. He gazed up at her with an enigmatic smile upon his lips, as though he knew something both sublime and wonderful:

What she would become. What worlds she would bridge.

"Go now," he told her.

The console lit up as the helicopter pilot flipped the switches. The aircraft's powerful turboshaft engine whined to life. The rotary blades spun into motion.

Selene settled into her seat aboard the chopper. Her lips still tingled from coming into contact with Corvinus's blood, but now she thirsted only for vengeance. Her face was a mask of icy determination. Her eyes glittered coldly.

I'm coming for you, Marcus, she thought. Before this night was over, either she or the murderous Elder would be dead. And, if fortune was kind, William would still be locked away for all eternity. *I have to end this madness, once and for all.*

The alternative was unimaginable.

The Lynx's pilot calmly went through his takeoff procedure. Selene was impressed by the smooth professionalism of the Cleaners, who reminded her favorably of the Death Dealers. Besides Samuel, who was riding shotgun beside the pilot, their strike team consisted of the pilot, a gunner, and four additional commandos. The armed soldiers sat beside her in stony silence, seemingly committed to carrying out Corvinus's final orders. She was struck by the loyalty the ancient warlord commanded even as he lay dying.

Michael's corpse, sealed up in a body bag, rested beside her. Selene could not bring herself to leave his body behind and fully intended to give him a decent burial, provided she survived her final confrontation with Marcus. It was the least she could do for him, after all he had meant to her. She unzipped the bag, and her throat tightened at the sight of his lifeless body, with its cold, clammy skin and gaping wounds. Dried blood was crusted over his punctured chest. Tears welled up in her eyes.

Had it really been less than a day since they had made love?

She choked back a sob. The time for weeping was over.

She had a mission to fulfill.

Nearby, the gunner swung his fifty-caliber machine gun into position. He unlatched the safety and racked the slide back. Selene was glad to see that the copter was ready for an aerial attack. She wondered if even Marcus would willingly take on an armed helicopter.

Welcome to the twenty-first century, she thought.

The rotors engaged fully and the chopper lifted off from the deck. It banked sharply, leaving the *Sancta Helena* behind.

Selene didn't look back.

Alexander Corvinus sat behind his desk in the blood-spattered office. Samuel and his men had carted the body of the unfortunate guard away, but broken glass was still scattered all over the desktop. The cold of winter invaded the suite through the splintered skylight. Through the open ceiling, he watched the helicopter carry Selene and his men away.

Godspeed, he thought. *The future depends on you now.*

He was alone now. Samuel had assured him that no other living soul remained aboard the *Sancta Helena.* This was as it should be; it was almost time to perform one final cleanup operation. He reached into the pocket of his coat and extracted one of the explosive disks he had removed from the weapons cabinet earlier. Ultimately, he had lacked the will to use the destructive device against Marcus, but it could still serve a useful purpose.

A coughing fit racked his body and he hacked up a gobbet of clotted blood. He was almost surprised there was any blood left in him after satisfying Selene's thirst. He felt like a hollowed-out shell, dried-up and ready to blow away in the wind. He wheezed painfully, every breath an ordeal. A numbing chill swept over his body. Darkness encroached on his vision.

So this is dying, he thought. It was a peculiar sensation, after sixteen centuries of immortality. "We owe God a death," the Bard had written centuries ago. *If so,* Corvinus thought, *my payment is long past due.* He turned to look at the elegant face of the massive carving behind him. The Muse's divine countenance was modeled on that of Helena, his long-dead wife and the mother of his children. He was grateful that she did not live to see the monsters their sons had become. *At long last, Helena, we shall be reunited once more.*

He depressed the disk, activating it. The miniature holes opened in its side, releasing the concentrated gas fumes into the air. The acrid smell of the accelerant offended his nostrils. He tossed the disk into an open crate filled with over twenty identical devices. Understanding his purpose, Samuel had been good enough to fetch the crate before departing with Selene.

That should do quite nicely, he thought.

The original disk automatically split in half, exposing the contacts inside.

Corvinus closed his eyes for the last time.

A spark of blue electricity arced between the contacts. . . .

A gigantic fireball tore the *Sancta Helena* apart. The devastating explosion shook the waterfront. Jagged shards of flaming shrapnel spiraled into the night. Churning black smoke billowed up from the sinking wreckage.

Selene heard the blast even over the noise of the chopper. The shock wave sent a shudder through the Lynx, but the helicopter kept on flying. A muscle twitched beneath Samuel's face, but that was the only sign of emotion displayed by the stoic Cleaner. "Oh, man," one of the younger soldiers whispered, before a glare from his leader shut him up.

So much for Alexander Corvinus, she realized. Sixteen hundred years of life had come to an end, perhaps many centuries too late. *Better he should have died of the plague in the first place.* Selene didn't know how to react to the first immortal's death. Too many cataclysmic events in too short a time had left her numb.

Alexander. Viktor. Amelia. Lucian. All the giants of the past lived no more. Now only Marcus and William remained.

But not for much longer, she vowed.

Chapter Twenty

Over time, waters had infiltrated the underground passageway. Marcus waded through waist-deep water as he trekked through the ancient tunnel he had seen in Selene's memories. The dark, silty water was bitterly cold, but Marcus barely noticed. This close to the end of his sacred quest, he was not about to let a little freezing water slow him down.

Soon, William. Your long captivity is almost over.

His right hand held aloft a blazing torch. In human guise, he navigated the subterranean labyrinth. His eyes searched the shadowy nooks and crannies. The passage of time had taken its toll on the flooded tunnel. The granite walls were crumbling and coated with fungus. The air within the corridor was dank and smelled of mildew. Water dripped from the arched ceiling.

A dash of faded color caught his eye. Above the waterline, vestiges of red and yellow paint still clung to the moldering stonework. His finger traced the lingering smears of paint and he chuckled in amusement. Although the design was barely discernible now, he recognized the sun and flowers that little Selene and her sister had scrawled upon the walls some six hundred years ago. He felt destiny's multifarious strands coming together at last.

Almost there, he thought.

The primitive drawings were the final proof that he had come to the right place. Indeed, he felt as though he could almost sense his twin's presence nearby. Their shared blood called out to him, urging him onward. He quickened his pace through the turbid waters.

At long last, I will fulfill my vow—and the sons of Corvinus will be united once more.

Just beyond the childish paintings, he came to a wall of blackened stone. The barrier appeared solid enough, yet an ornate design had been cut into the heavy granite blocks. In the center of the pattern was a depression in the shape of the open pendant.

Marcus smiled.

Traveling at over 250 kilometers per hour, the Lynx headed southeast, crossing the border into Romania. Soon the jagged peaks of the Carpathian Mountains loomed before them. At six thousand feet in altitude, dense forests of firs and pines gave way to desolate outcroppings of barren rock, now surmounted by tons of accumulated snow and ice. Selene felt a pang of nostalgia at the sight of the mountains, familiar to her from her long-vanished childhood, but swiftly thrust the feeling aside. This was no time for bittersweet reminiscences. She had an Elder to kill.

She sat beside Michael's body in the cockpit. The top of the body bag was still unzipped, so that she could gaze upon his lifeless features. Even in death, his face retained its rugged good looks. She found it hard to accept that his eyes would never look upon her again. The gross injustice of it all stabbed at her heart. After six centuries of solitude she

225

had finally found the love of her life, only to lose him in a matter of days.

Her face hardened as she took her grief and converted it into anger. A hunger for revenge came easily to her, and she let her all-consuming need for vengeance fuel her determination to end Marcus's obscene existence. Forget the threat posed by William and his highly infectious brand of lycanthropy; Marcus would pay for taking Michael from her. She would see to that . . . or die trying.

Marcus stood where Selene's father had once stood, six centuries before. He ran his fingers over the intricate design etched into the wall, then inserted Sonja's pendant into the matching depression. He flicked the switch upon the pendant's side and its bronze blades emerged from hiding. The blades fit perfectly into the slots intended for them, locking the key into place. Marcus reached out and gave the key a decisive turn.

Click. Concealed machinery came to life after centuries of slumber. Reanimated gears creaked loudly, before being drowned out by the grinding of stone against stone. A sizable portion of the wall began to lift from the floor, receding into the ceiling. The newly exposed doorway opened onto a hidden corridor, just as Selene's childhood memories had promised. Through a shimmering curtain of dripping water, Marcus glimpsed the flooded alcove beyond. For a moment, he feared that the frigid waters might have filled the dungeon entirely, drowning William in his forgotten cell, but then, to his relief, he saw a dusty stone staircase rising up from the water on the other side of the alcove. The polished stone steps, which looked as though they had been untrodden ever since the dungeon had first been sealed off centuries ago, led off into the darkness.

Marcus's eyes gleamed in anticipation. He smirked at the thought that, somewhere beyond the grave, Viktor's restless spirit was crying out in dismay.

You hid my brother well, he thought vindictively, *but not well enough.*

He removed the pendant from the lock, then stepped forward through the falling water.

The chopper soared above the frothing waters of a rushing river. This high in the mountains, the rocky passes churned the river into turbulent rapids. White water tumbled down a winding path toward the dense pine forests below. The tumultuous course of the river matched the turmoil in Selene's soul, although she did her best to hide her heartache behind the cool, emotionless mask of a warrior. She needed to be a Death Dealer now, more than ever before.

"We're getting close," Samuel announced.

Good, she thought. Reluctantly looking away from Michael, she focused on the mission before her. The Lynx banked sharply, roaring around a bend in the river, and the ruins of a medieval castle came into view.

Viktor's once-mighty fortress had been destroyed by centuries of warfare and neglect. Selene recalled it rising proudly from the craggy slopes of the mountain. Now, however, nothing more than a skeletal remnant of its former glory remained. Its formidable walls had collapsed altogether in places. Fallen stones dotted the snowy landscape. The wooden roofs had rotted away, exposing the castle's gutted interior to the elements. The drawbridge leading up to the gatehouse was long gone, discouraging visitors, although that was hardly likely to keep out the winged Elder. Frost-covered spires and parapets jutted upward from the packed snow and ice like the stumps of amputated limbs.

Thick black clouds obscured the moon, adding to the impenetrable shadows veiling the lower levels of the abandoned citadel. Selene tried not to remember playing with her sister on the sunlit slopes below the castle.

The last time she'd seen Cecilia, many years later, her throat had been ripped open by Viktor's fangs. . . .

Samuel leaned forward in his seat, peering out over the nose of the chopper. "I don't see a way inside."

"Head back around," she instructed the pilot. "Toward the river."

The pilot glanced at Samuel, who nodded his consent. The Lynx swooped down toward the water, then leveled out several meters above the choppy surface of the river. Selene looked at Samuel and motioned toward a rocky riverbed up ahead. The raging waters crashed along the side of the steep granite slope.

Samuel peered through the windshield. "I don't see a way inside."

"There used to be a river entrance just there," she explained. "It must be submerged now, but it should lead straight into the catacombs beneath the dungeon."

Samuel did not question her assertion. He turned toward his men.

"Looks like we're getting wet."

The strike team immediately went into action. Locker doors were slammed open to reveal multiple wet suits and other pieces of diving gear. Selene was impressed; apparently Corvinus's men were prepared for anything.

As the Cleaners suited up, Selene glanced at Michael's body one last time. It was possible, she knew, that she would never leave the ruined castle alive. She wanted to think that they might have beaten Marcus to the site, but she knew that was highly unlikely. Chances were, the hy-

228

brid Elder was waiting for them below. They could only hope that he had not yet liberated his equally fearsome brother.

Marcus is bad enough, she thought. *Heaven help us if we have to take on William, too.* She recalled the fearsome albino beast depicted in the ancient woodcut. Viktor and Amelia had needed an army of Death Dealers to capture William the first time. *What hope do we have, especially now that he's allied with Marcus?*

A fatalistic mood descended upon her. She would do her best; what other choice was there? Perhaps Corvinus's blood would give her the edge she needed. Perhaps not.

Bending down over Michael, she lightly kissed his forehead. The inert flesh felt cold against her lips. She rose and turned away from the body, her eyes shimmering like ice crystals. She wiped away the incriminating moisture, then strode over to the chopper's side door. Unfastening the latch, she yanked the door open in midflight, allowing a gust of freezing air to buffet the interior of the Lynx. Her fingers wrapped around the edge of the doorframe as she checked their position.

"Closer," she shouted to the pilot.

The Lynx descended into a low hover above the river. The wash from the copter's blades stirred up the already foamy water, sending concentric waves crashing against the rocky shore. Selene felt the cold spray against her face.

By now, Samuel and the other Cleaners had geared up for the dive. He tossed Selene a transparent face mask. She glanced at it briefly, then tossed it back to him. She didn't bother with a wet suit either; her slick black leathers were still damp from fighting Marcus beneath the pier. Staying warm and dry were the least of her concerns.

Instead she reached out and claimed a Remington 870

combat shotgun from the weapons rack. She deftly slung the weapon's strap over her shoulder.

"Ladies first," Samuel said.

Selene wouldn't have it any other way. Shooting him a look, she leapt from the chopper without hesitation.

Gravity grabbed her and didn't let go. She plummeted, falling fifteen feet toward the river below. Her boots broke the surface of the water with a tremendous splash as she sank beneath the waves. Five more splashes confirmed that Samuel and his men had hit the water as well.

The icy water was even colder here in the mountains than it had been in the city. The freezing cold came as a shock, but Selene's undead nature protected her from hypothermia. Moonlight filtered through the murky water above her. She surfaced long enough to conduct a quick head count, then dived beneath the waves once more. Waterproof flashlights lit up the way before them as she swam toward the mouth of a submerged tunnel. The Cleaners followed closely behind her.

Darkness swallowed them as they left the moonlight behind.

The French had a word, *oubliette,* which referred to a hidden dungeon in which an unfortunate prisoner could be forgotten forever. It was a fitting term for the granite tomb in which Viktor had confined William. Immortality only added to the diabolical cruelty of the concept.

Marcus stood before another stretch of seemingly impervious wall. A second ornate design, twice as large as the one before, was carved into the solid rock. Lodging his torch in an empty sconce, he extracted both parts of the key from the pockets of his overcoat. He carefully inserted the pendant, its inner blades once more withdrawn, into the larger component he had captured from his father. Making sure the pieces fit together securely, he again activated the hidden hinges inside the pendant. The bronze blades blossomed outward, engaging with the larger key. A new set of intricate blades opened along the outer edge of the joined keys.

What exquisite workmanship, Marcus thought. He spared a moment to admire the ingenuity and skill of Selene's late, unlamented father. The long-dead metalsmith had been quite talented for a mortal. *A pity his craft cost him his life.*

Delaying no longer, he inserted the master key into the depression upon the wall. He held his breath as he turned the key clockwise. His action was rewarded by the sound of clandestine machinery fulfilling its destined function. Harsh grinding noises echoed within the gloomy catacombs as a vertical sheet of rock descended into the floor. Marcus glimpsed a cramped, coffin-shaped alcove almost completely shrouded in darkness. Straining his eyes, he spotted only a few stray glints of metal, reflecting the flickering glow of the torch.

"William?"

He impatiently snatched the torch from its holder and stepped toward the open sarcophagus. The claustrophobic dimensions of the cell both appalled and angered him. Bad enough that Viktor had condemned William to eternal imprisonment, but in so small a space as well? There was barely enough room to move, let alone rest in comfort!

The sputtering torchlight revealed the enormity of his brother's torment. The snow-white albino werewolf hung limply within the upright sarcophagus. Silver manacles were clamped around his forelimbs, chaining him to the rough brick wall at the rear of the cell. His eyes were closed in uneasy slumber. His muzzle twitched restlessly. Deep

grooves had been scratched into the granite floor of the oubliette, where the beast's paws had clawed uselessly for at
least six hundred years. His fur was matted painfully. So had
his brother hung all these centuries, Marcus realized, de-
prived of food, water, and even light for countless generations, all thanks to Viktor's perfidy!

How has he endured it? he wondered. *I would have gone mad.*

He could not bear to see his brother suffer so a moment
longer. He rushed forward, intending to liberate William
from his sadistic bonds.

The werewolf's eyes snapped open. Bloodred orbs stared
at the world with feral rage. Taken aback, Marcus stumbled
backward as his brother lunged at him from the cramped con-
fines of the sarcophagus. A ferocious roar reverberated against
the damp stone walls.

William's chains were longer than Marcus had anticipated. The crazed werewolf drove his startled brother across
the corridor into the wall opposite his tomb. He drew back
his bestial head and opened his jaws wide.

"Be still, Brother," Marcus said in a soothing tone. Re-
gaining his composure, he knew nonetheless that his life
was in deadly jeopardy. The werewolf's bloodlust had often
been beyond his control, even before he had been starved
for centuries. It was possible that he didn't even recognize
Marcus. Still, the Elder stared coolly into his brother's crimson eyes. "I would no sooner hurt you than I would myself."

For a second, he feared that the long centuries of confinement had indeed driven William mad. Then the werewolf's eyes narrowed as he studied Marcus's face.
Recognition dawned upon the beast's inhuman features.
Rubbery black lips lifted in a smile.

That's better, Marcus thought. Even after all this time,
their bond remained strong. Marcus regretted that he had

ever conspired with Viktor to capture his brother, no matter how urgent that necessity had appeared at the time. *This is how it should have always been. The two of us united against the world.*

An unexpected sound intruded upon their reunion. Marcus cocked his head to listen. William looked distinctly puzzled by the unfamiliar noise, but Marcus recognized the muffled *whump-whump* of an approaching helicopter.

It seemed they had company.

Chapter Twenty-one

Selene was almost out of breath by the time they reached the end of the flooded tunnel. She kicked her way to the surface and gratefully inhaled the dank air within the castle. Samuel and his Cleaners followed her lead. She heard the men suck in the air as they splashed to the surface all around her.

Their flashlight beams darted around the ruins, checking out their surroundings. They appeared to be in one of the lower levels of the castle's sprawling dungeons, at a junction between two shadowy passageways. A damp stone floor beckoned to them, and they waded out of the sunken pool onto slightly drier terrain. The Cleaners stripped off their diving gear, while Selene slipped the shotgun off her shoulder and hefted it in her arms. A searchlight was mounted beneath the barrel of the pump-action rifle. Ice-cold water dripped from her hair.

She scanned the waiting junction. Intersecting tunnels led off in separate directions. Both paths were riddled with treacherous puddles and sinkholes. Cobwebs hung from the ceiling, further obscuring her view. Mold glistened upon the stone walls, whose ancient mortar had practically turned to dust. A lizard slithered into a crack in the wall.

"Which way?" Samuel asked.

Selene closed her eyes, calling up long-forgotten memories:

Giggling, she and Cecilia raced along the murky passageway, dodging the straining laborers with heavy carts. "Last one there is a silly goose!"

Without a word, she turned and headed off down the tunnel on the left. She didn't trust herself to speak, not when her voice might betray the powerful emotions the fleeting memory had stirred up inside her. She was quite literally treading the ruins of her own lost childhood. The past seemed to lie in ambush for her around every corner.

Never mind that, she scolded herself harshly. She had to keep her mind on the mission. *The past is the past. Stopping Marcus is all that matters now.*

Samuel motioned for his men to follow her. Weapons ready, they stalked warily through the blighted dungeons. Empty prison cells and abandoned instruments of torture made it clear that these subterranean chambers had borne witness to unspeakable pain and suffering. A human skeleton hung in shackles upon a crumbing wall, its fractured bones hinting at the abuse the poor prisoner must have received before he died. Faint brown bloodstains could still be glimpsed upon the uneven paving stones. An iron maiden rested against one wall, its lid hanging open to reveal a battery of rusty metal spikes. Metal pokers and branding irons lay on the floor beside a toppled iron brazier that had once been used to heat the vicious implements until they had glowed as red as molten lava. A wooden rack had all but rotted away, the tortured screams of its victims now lost to history.

Selene found it disturbing, yet strangely appropriate, that this hellish place had once been her childhood playground.

Had her father realized the dreadful purpose to which these catacombs would be put when he'd accepted Viktor's commission to oversee their construction? She wanted to consign such barbarism to the Dark Ages, where it belonged, yet were the interrogation rooms in which she and her fellow Death Dealers had extracted vital intel from captured lycans all that different from this medieval torture chamber? Selene had lost track of how many lycans she had killed and interrogated over the centuries, in the mistaken belief that their kind had been responsible for her family's death. All she knew for certain was that no lycan had ever survived being captured by her; disposing of them afterward had been one of the perks of the job.

I belong here, she thought ruefully. *This place is a part of me, in more ways than one.*

A rat scurried somewhere above her and she glanced upward. Stone arches curved off into a stygian blackness that was beyond the ability of her eyes to penetrate. Her searchbeam probed the darkness, but with only slightly better results. Large sections of the ceiling had crumbled away, and she could tell that there were definitely more levels above them, but the pervasive gloom made it difficult to make out the details. *Only Viktor would need so many dungeons for his enemies,* she mused. How many innocent lycans had he confined here back in the early days of the war?

They turned a corner, only to discover that the passage ahead was partially flooded. The floor before their feet sloped downward into the stagnant water. A slimy layer of algae coated the surface of the water. One of the Cleaners groaned audibly. No doubt he regretted taking off his wet suit.

"This it?" Samuel asked. Going back for the diving gear was not an option; for all they knew, Marcus was only mo-

236

ments away from liberating William—if he hadn't done so already.

"Yes," Selene confirmed. She kept a close eye on the murky water, half-expecting Marcus to burst from beneath the concealing liquid as he had under the pier. Her shotgun was primed and ready.

Samuel turned toward his men. "Parks, Hapka," he addressed two of the soldiers. "Keep watch and hold this position." The men nodded in assent. "Stay sharp."

He and Selene waded into the waist-deep water, accompanied by the other two Cleaners. Sludge covered the slippery floor stones beneath her feet, forcing her to tread carefully. A lizard swam across her path. Corroded iron chains dangled from the ceiling.

Six-hundred-year-old memories guided her forward, until she reached the point where the secret door should have been. To her dismay, she saw that the concealed entrance was no longer hidden. Only a curtain of falling water guarded the forgotten alcove beyond.

Fuck, she thought. *We're too late.*

She threw up her hand, bringing the procession to a halt. Samuel followed her gaze to the open portal. Selene nodded, confirming his fears.

"He's already here," she whispered.

Which almost surely meant that William was loose as well. She gripped the shotgun securely as she moved cautiously toward the exposed doorway. Then, out of the corner of her eye, she spotted a splotch of color to her left. She froze in her tracks. Her eyes turned involuntarily toward the wall beside her.

There, faded almost to the point of nonexistence, were the sun and flowers she and Cecilia had painted upon the wall six centuries ago. Her throat tightened as the carefree laughter of two happy children echoed at the back of her mind. Cecilia was long dead, as was the innocent girl Selene had once been, yet this chilling memento of their golden childhood had somehow survived all these years, lying in wait to stab Selene in the heart when she least expected it.

"What is it?" Samuel asked, sounding both puzzled and concerned.

"Nothing," she replied tersely. Through sheer force of will, she silenced the heart-tugging laughter in her head. She tamped down any and all distracting emotions, at least as much as she was able. Her voice and face were as cold as the frigid water lapping at her hips. "Let's go."

She turned away from the painted sunburst and stepped through the unlocked doorway. A sheet of falling water drenched her head and shoulders. Ice-cold droplets wormed their way beneath her collar and trickled down the length of her spine. Samuel and his men followed her through the alcove until they reached the low staircase leading up to the crypt beyond. Selene was disturbed, but not surprised, to see the empty sarcophagus open before them. Shattered silver manacles lay on the floor in front of the vacant tomb.

"We're too late," she said.

Her eyes fell upon the key, still lodged into the wall beside the sarcophagus. Marcus must have left it behind, now that he no longer needed it. She tugged it free of the lock and removed the pendant from the other component of the key. The crest-shaped emblem felt heavy in her hand, weighed down by centuries of loss and thwarted romance. Sonja had worn the pendant to her death, as had Lucian hundreds of years later. Selene remembered finding the pendant beside her head after she and Michael had made love, then watching Marcus rip the pendant from

Michael's chest while her newfound lover lay impaled upon the iron strut.

She fought back tears. For Marcus, the pendant had been merely a means to an end, to be discarded after it fulfilled its preordained function, but for Selene, the centuries-old relic represented everything she had lost over the years, from her family's slaughter to Michael's tragic end. All could be traced back to Viktor's machinations—and her father's unwitting part in the ancient conflict between the Elders. For a moment, she wished that Viktor was still alive, just so she could kill him again.

Then her Death Dealer training reasserted itself as she forced herself to concentrate on the matter at hand. Their situation was not good: Marcus, the very first vampire, and William, the first werewolf, were both at large and unaccounted for. Her searchlight scanned the corridor around, but Selene found no sign of either brother. Had they already fled the castle, or were they lurking in the shadows at this very minute, waiting for the right opportunity to fall upon Selene and her mortal companions? Despite the personal danger posed by the latter scenario, it was still better than the alternative. The entire world would suffer if William escaped to spread another epidemic of uncontrollable lycanthropy throughout Europe and beyond.

The mission was now all about containment. Neither William nor Marcus could be allowed to leave these ruins alive.

Works for me, she thought grimly. Her fist tightened around the pendant.

Karl Hapka stood tensely at the entrance to the flooded corridor, just as Samuel had ordered. Part of him was relieved that he hadn't been required to wade through the freezing water again, yet he couldn't help wondering what the rest of the team might have found up ahead. Along with the other guard, Parks, he listened nervously for growls, gunfire, screams . . . or any combination thereof. Bracing himself against a crumbling stone wall, so as not to be attacked from behind, he swept the beam of his searchlight back and forth along the sepulchral tunnel. His finger rested on the trigger of his Uzi.

"Quite a night, eh?" Parks commented from a few feet away. Like Hapka, he was alert and ready for action. His black uniform blended into the heavy shadows infesting the catacombs, making him hard to see even though Hapka was practically beside him. "Crazy stuff."

"Tell me about it," Hapka said gruffly. Although a veteran in the Cleaner corps, with over six years of experience in the field, he found himself unusually on edge. This mission was unlike any other operation he had ever taken part in. He had never expected to see a vampire in charge of a mission, for one thing, let alone a goddamn Death Dealer. Yet here he was, letting this Selene chick lead them into the bowels of some creepy old castle in search of a couple of renegade Elders. It was enough to make any soldier nervous.

"So what happens after this?" Parks asked. He was a rookie, with barely a year of active duty under his belt. Hapka guessed that the chatter was the kid's way of keeping his fears at bay. "I mean, is this it? Are we, well, unemployed now that the Old Man is . . . gone?"

"Just keep your mind on the job," Hapka said, not too harshly. Under the circumstances, he couldn't blame the rookie for being spooked. Hell, he was pretty creeped-out himself. In many ways, waiting like this was more unnerving than actual combat. Hapka almost wanted something to happen soon.

Watch it, he warned himself. *Be careful what you wish for . . .*

A whiff of wet fur was the only warning he got before a shaggy white beast suddenly pounced from the darkness, its savage claws and fangs flying at them like ivory shrapnel. The Cleaners whirled around and fired their rifles and submachine guns, but the snarling werewolf kept on coming. A fierce roar bellowed from the creature's open jaws.

Unemployment was not something either man needed to worry about again.

The sound of gunfire galvanized Selene and the three commandos. She realized instantly that the alarming noise was coming from the soldiers they had left behind. The blaring gunshots quickly gave way to the bloodcurdling screams of men in mortal pain and terror.

Guns in hand, she and Samuel and the other two men charged back the way they had come. The chain attached to Sonja's pendant was wrapped around her hand, while her fingers tightly gripped the Remington. The team splashed noisily through the water as Selene wondered who exactly was tearing the hapless Cleaners apart. Marcus? William? Both? Reaching a bend in the tunnel, she peered around the corner—and laid eyes on William for the first time.

The great white lycanthrope was hunched over the body of the younger Cleaner, looking just as fierce and formidable as that ancient woodcut had suggested. If anything, the nameless illustrator had failed to do the primordial werewolf justice; the beast before her eyes was larger and less human-looking than any other lycan she had ever encountered. His bristling pelt was the color of virgin snow, his kill-crazed eyes were as red as blood. Gore dripped from his mammoth jaws as he ripped out the soldier's intestines with

241

his teeth. Selene spotted the second Cleaner lying nearby, half-submerged beneath the bloody water, his legs and combat boots propped up against a heap of rubble. She couldn't help wondering whether the upper half of the man's body was still attached to his legs.

William sniffed the air, catching her scent. Abandoning his prey, he reared back on his haunches and unleashed a ferocious roar. His hackles rose along his back.

So much for the element of surprise, she thought. Swinging her shotgun around, she opened fire on William, as did the other Cleaners. The werewolf staggered back in surprise; silver bullets were a new experience for him. Flashlight beams converged on his monstrous form, along with four streams of automatic weapons fire. He yelped in pain as the high-powered fusillade knocked him about, the impact of the bullets causing him to gyrate upon his heels. Lycan blood spouted from the bullet holes, staining his snowy pelt. Smoke rose from the silver embedded in his flesh. Hirsute limbs flailed wildly, trying to ward off the barrage, before he turned and retreated into the pitch-black catacombs.

Still waist-deep in the water, Selene watched the werewolf escape. The amount of silver they had pumped into the creature's hide should have been enough to poison any ordinary lycan, but Selene feared that William would not so easily be killed. In essence, he was the lycan equivalent of an Elder . . . hell, he was *the* lycan Elder. *I suppose I should be thankful,* she thought, *that Marcus hasn't tried to turn him into a hybrid yet.*

She started to chase after William, hoping to catch up with the beast before he had a chance to heal. Samuel and the two remaining Cleaners ran past her and she hurried to catch up with them . . . only to hear a cold, sardonic chuckle behind her!

She spun around to find Marcus standing only inches away. The Elder was in human form, his wings tucked away beneath a soaked brown overcoat. She started to raise her shotgun, but Marcus was way ahead of her. Seizing her by her shoulders, he violently slammed her into the wall, the force of the collision knocking the rifle from her hands. The wall's decaying mortar gave way as the two immortals crashed against it. Dislodged chunks of granite splashed down into the water, sending a spray of silt and algae everywhere. Dust and gravel rained down alarmingly from the ceiling.

Empty-handed, except for the pendant, Selene found herself pinned against the crumbling wall. Ironically, she saw that she was merely a hand's breadth away from the remains of her old painting. The golden rays of the crudely drawn sun taunted her. She remembered Marcus stealing her blood back beneath the pier. Would he now claim the rest of it?

Marcus leaned in close to her, so that she could feel his cold breath upon her throat. He licked his lips in anticipation, then hesitated. He drew back his head and inhaled deeply, taking in her scent. Puzzlement was written on his aristocratic face, followed by a look of stunned realization. Selene realized that he could smell his father's blood in her veins. A hushed voice escaped his throat.

"What have you done?"

Whatever I had to, she thought bitterly. A righteous fury rose up inside her like a gathering storm. Her eyes flashed blue. An angry heart pumped the sacred blood of Alexander Corvinus through her body, infusing her with strength worthy of an Elder . . . or a hybrid. With an unexpected burst of power, she broke free of Marcus's grip and drove him backward with a devastating series of kicks and punches. Her knuckles smashed into the Elder's face, drawing blood. She delivered a one-two combination to his chin, followed by a forward kick to his solar plexus. His grunts of pain were like music to her ears.

Marcus reeled backward, astonished by Selene's newfound power. Framed by the doorway to the hidden crypt, he halted his retreat and glared back at her with utter hatred. His eyes shifted to black. His wings began to unfold. Selene realized that he was getting ready to pull out all the stops

So am I, she thought. Retrieving her shotgun, she opened fire. Silver bullets slammed into his bare chest, tearing open his flesh in a way that reminded her of the gaping chest wounds that had killed both Michael and Corvinus. She was all in favor of history repeating itself. *This is for you, Michael.*

The relentless onslaught drove Marcus farther back into the formerly hidden alcove. He hissed angrily, baring his fangs, but Selene did not let up. She kept pumping the shotgun, then reloading with preternatural speed. The nonstop hail of bullets forced Marcus across the flooded chamber and up the stairs on the other side of the water, back toward William's ancient crypt.

The shotgun rounds made a gory mess of his chest, which was now drenched with his blood, but were not enough to kill him. Ugly scabs gleamed wetly over his heart. He slashed at the air between them. Black eyes shot daggers at Selene. Leathery wings flexed ominously.

Not so fast, Selene thought. She still had one more trick up her sleeve. Holding up the gilt pendant, its inner blades fully extended, she stepped toward the depression in the wall. Marcus's eyes widened in alarm as he realized what she was up to. He rushed forward, even in the face of her steady gunfire, but this time Selene had the advantage. She slammed the key into the lock and turned it forcefully. *You shouldn't have left this behind.*

The hidden door slammed down, trapping Marcus inside the crypt. He threw back his head and howled in frustration. Selene could hear his angry wail even through the heavy stone.

That's one brother taken care of, she thought, reclaiming the pendant from the lock. She thrust the relic into her boot for safekeeping. *At least for the present.* She glanced uneasily at the fallen rubble strewn about the corridor. She couldn't rule out the possibility that, beneath the waterline, some of the debris might have landed under the door, keeping it from closing all the way. *What if Marcus manages to pry his way out?*

Gunfire blared farther down the corridor. Selene realized that the Cleaners had caught up with William, or maybe it was the other way around. Tossing the empty shotgun aside, she drew her pistols. She took off toward the gunfire, with only a single backward glance at the prison door.

She would have to worry about that later.

Chapter Twenty-two

*T*he helicopter circled above the castle ruins, awaiting further orders from Samuel. If necessary, the Lynx could maintain its position for over two hours before needing to refuel. Of the original team, only the gunner and the pilot remained aboard.

Not counting the body of Michael Corvin.

The flaps of the open body bag whipped about in the wind. Michael's face looked just as inert as before, but deep inside his chest cavity something miraculous was occurring. Dead cells sparked to life, dividing and multiplying according to their genetic code. Fractured ribs reknit themselves. Punctured organs healed. A new heart blossomed within his body, growing steadily larger. Brain activity resumed inside his skull.

Intent upon their mission, the two Cleaners didn't even notice Michael's eyelids flicker.

Pistols in hand, Selene sprinted out of the flooded passageway, retracing her steps through the confusing catacombs. She reached a junction to two tunnels, not unlike the one they had found earlier. Maybe it was even the same one; at this point, she couldn't be sure.

The gunfire fell silent momentarily, leaving her uncertain which way to go. Then an Uzi blared somewhere above her. Looking up, she saw muzzle flashes on the next level up. *How the hell did they get up there?* she wondered briefly. A barbaric roar greeted the flashing guns. Selene caught a blur of motion just overhead. A body plummeted toward her.

She jumped out of the way as a Cleaner crashed down onto the stone floor. The man's face and chest had been torn to ribbons; she could tell in a glance that the man was already dead. *At least it's not Samuel,* she thought, grateful that the team's leader might still be alive. It troubled her that she couldn't quite remember the Cleaner's name. Levin maybe, or Levant.

Three dead humans already. William was making up for lost time.

Not if I can help it, she vowed. Choosing a tunnel at random, she charged into the shadows.

There had to be a staircase around here somewhere!

Inside the sealed crypt, Marcus completed his transformation. His reddish hair and beard receded into his skull, leaving his head bald and sickly white. His aquiline nose stretched into a batlike snout with large, flaring nostrils. His ears flattened against his skull, while also expanding in size. His skin took on an opalescent sheen. The furious hybrid banged his claws against the stone door. The talons on his wings dug angrily at the solid rock. Black eyes flashed with homicidal rage. He gnashed his fangs and howled like a banshee.

The irony of it all galled his soul. At long last, he had freed his brother, only to end up trapped inside the very crypt that had been William's prison for six centuries. And Selene—that wretched bitch of a Death Dealer—had the key once more!

He cursed himself for letting her live before. *I should have killed her when I had the chance,* he lamented, *instead of merely sampling her blood.* His impatience to confront his father, and free his brother, had been his undoing, causing him to leave Selene alive to interfere with his designs once again.

I shall not make that mistake again, he vowed. He was not chained into a sarcophagus like William. This crypt would not hold him as it had his brother. *I shall find a way out.*

And when he did . . . Viktor's pet would join her creator in oblivion.

Selene charged up a narrow stairwell, trying to reach the upper level as soon as possible. From the sound of it, the besieged Cleaners needed all the help they could get. By her calculations, only two commandos were left: Samuel and another soldier. At this rate, the entire team would be dead before she caught up with them.

An arched doorway appeared at the top of the steps. Despite the urgency of the situation, she did not forget her training. Playing it safe, she inched around the edge of the doorway and cautiously peered past the threshold. Her twin Walther P99s were poised and ready.

The flash of a muzzle gave her barely enough warning. She ducked back behind the stone arch an instant before an eruption of gunfire that would have taken her head off. Bullets smacked into the ancient stones across from the portal, sending pulverized granite and mortar flying.

"Hold it!" she called out. "Fuck!"

The gunfire ceased as quickly as it had begun. "Sorry!" an embarrassed voice shouted back. Moments later, a sheepish-looking Cleaner emerged from the shadows. He was a young black man with a shaved head and clean-cut features. She seemed to recall Samuel calling him Greenway. The look of relief on his face made it clear that he was happy to see her. Not a response she often got from mortals. To be honest, she wasn't quite sure what to make of it.

"Where is he?" she asked tersely, meaning William.

The young Cleaner gestured to the left. "He went through there."

Turning her head, she saw Samuel standing on what appeared to be a primitive bridge composed of thick, fraying ropes and decrepit wooden planks. Selene admired his courage for actually setting foot on the ramshackle structure, even as she questioned his wisdom. Perhaps he figured that, if the bridge could support William's weight, it should be able to hold up a couple of humans and one fairly trim vampire?

Sounds good in theory, she thought. *It's the practical application that gives me pause.*

She stepped warily out onto the bridge. It swayed and creaked beneath her weight, but appeared to hold together, at least for the time being. She remained on guard, however, ready to leap for safety at the first hint of a collapse. Unlike the fragile humans, she actually stood a good chance of surviving should the bridge give out. After all, she had stepped off tall buildings and cliffs before. What was one shaky bridge by comparison?

She and Greenway joined Samuel on the bridge. Looking across the rickety span, she saw that it led to another section of the ruins. Now that she had reached this upper level, she was able to get a better picture of the overall layout of the dungeons. Although much of the underground labyrinth remained shrouded in darkness, there could be no mistaking the vast dimensions of the castle's subterranean vaults. She thought back to all those heavy carts of debris that the workers had dug out from the earth during the original excavations, all those centuries ago.

My father created all this?

She peered over the edge of the bridge. The Cleaners' flashlights picked out details of the level they had left behind, with its flooded crypts and catacombs. If nothing else, this higher floor might be substantially drier. She wondered if Marcus was still locked away in his brother's prison.

"We think William went this way," Samuel confirmed. Together, Selene and the two Cleaners slowly made their way across the uninspiring bridge. Heavy ropes stretched tautly. The sagging wooden planks creaked and moaned beneath their feet. Selene winced inwardly at every sound. William was definitely going to hear them coming.

Selene held her pistols before her, while Samuel and the other man swept the darkness with the searchlights attached to their rifles. The two Cleaners gripped their Uzis. Amidst all the rubble and shadowy recesses, there was no shortage of places for a crafty werewolf to hide. Selene reminded herself not to underestimate William's intelligence. Despite his bestial appearance and appetites, he could not have eluded Viktor's Death Dealers for so long if he had not possessed innate cunning.

More than once, she thought she spotted movement in the tenebrous gloom, but she couldn't be sure. Perhaps she had merely glimpsed a frightened rat or lizard, or maybe it was just a trick of the light? She didn't want to waste her precious ammo on anything less than William himself.

A stretch of worm-eaten wooden planks broke apart beneath Greenway. Watching out for a werewolf instead, the young Cleaner was caught completely by surprise. He started to fall through the gap, but Selene grabbed him and pulled him to safety with superhuman strength. She steadied him as he regained his footing on a more solid portion of the bridge. He gave her a grateful look.

"Thanks!" he exclaimed, wiping his brow with the back of his hand. "That was a close—"

"You all right?" Samuel began.

A tremendous roar cut him off as William charged up behind him, then bounded onto the bridge from a nearby ledge. His slashing claws struck out at them almost before Selene and the others realized what was happening. Muzzle flashes strobed in the darkness as they opened fire at the attacking beast. In the confusion, Selene saw William's jaws take a gory chunk out of Samuel's throat. His gun fired wildly, winging Greenway. Blood spouting from the severed arteries, the leader of the commandos tumbled over the edge of the bridge. Greenway grunted in pain.

No! Selene thought. Everything was happening too quickly!

Greenway was the next to go. He fired wildly at the unstoppable werewolf, but William's bloody claws tore open his throat and chest with a single slash. The wounded Cleaner collapsed onto the creaking wooden planks, his life's blood pouring out of him. His body twitched once, then fell completely still.

In what felt like an instant, the last of the strike team had been wiped out. Selene suddenly found herself alone with William on the bridge. The werewolf lunged at her, swiping with his claws, but Selene dodged the attack by flipping backward through the open gap in the bridge. William's claws missed her back by inches.

She landed like a panther on the floor below. Hastily reloading her guns, she fired up at the creature on the bridge. Silver bullets erupted from the wooden planks beneath William's paws. He recoiled from the stinging silver, retreating into the shadows once more.

Dammit! Selene thought. She would mourn the murdered Cleaners later; right now she took advantage of William's disappearance to make sure her Walthers were fully loaded again. *Too bad Kraven stole the prototype of the silver-nitrate gun,* she thought. *I could definitely use that right now.* She stepped out from beneath the shadow of the bridge and stared up at the level above her, hoping to catch sight of William. Collapsed stonework and empty ledges helped to conceal the bloodthirsty werewolf from sight.

Then she caught a break. A loud crash came from above, sounding like a pile of loose rubble collapsing. Selene zeroed in on the noise instantly. She caught a suspicious blur of movement and let William have it with both guns blazing.

Bullets viciously raked the walls, sending shards of granite flying everywhere. William burst from his hiding place and scrambled for cover, leaping from ledge to ledge as he defied gravity by climbing higher and higher up the craggy walls looming over the bridge. He jumped across the open shaft above Selene's head, trying to keep one pounce ahead of her bullets. His preternatural agility was astounding to behold.

No way! Selene thought. *You're not getting away from me!*

She rushed across the floor of the dungeon, trying to catch William in her line of fire. She did her best to keep the heat on the fleeing werewolf as he scrambled up the wall of the dungeon, frantic to escape the merciless silver. Automatic firearms were definitely coming as a shock to the ancient werewolf; swords and crossbows had been the order of business when last he had faced off against a Death Dealer. Selene was glad to bring him up to speed, one bullet at a time.

Click. Click.

Selene cursed in frustration as her pistols ran dry.

Afraid of losing her quarry, she kept her eyes locked on William. She experienced a sudden rush of anxiety as she saw that William was heading toward the entrance of a dark tunnel tucked away at the far end of a crumbling ledge.

Had the werewolf found a way out of the ruins? All was lost if William escaped the castle to spread his wolfen taint throughout the unsuspecting populace. If Tanis was to be believed, the world would soon be overrun with rampaging lycans even more rabid and uncontrollable than the ones Selene was accustomed to. Human society was not remotely prepared to cope with such an outbreak. Civilization itself might collapse into a new Dark Age.

William paused before the open archway. Chest heaving, he glared balefully down at Selene. Gloating over his imminent escape?

Like hell! Selene thought. Plucking four explosive throwing stars from a pouch upon her hip, she hurled the rigged *shuriken* in rapid succession. The stars whistled through the cavernous dungeon like harbingers of doom.

Upon the ledge, William saw the razor-sharp stars spinning toward him. Selene watched intently, glued to the action, as the agile werewolf jumped to one side, barely avoiding the hungry blades. They whizzed right past and stuck into the eroded archway above the exit.

William growled defiantly at Selene, as if daring her to take another shot. Behind him, unobserved by the distracted werewolf, the embedded stars began to pulse with light. They flashed faster and faster as their explosive charges armed themselves at an accelerated rate. The flashing was intended as warning, alerting the user to get the hell out of there before it was too late.

And then it was. . . .

The stars went off one after another.

Chapter Twenty-three

"Jesus Christ!"

The helicopter pilot reacted in surprise as a series of violent explosions went off inside the ruined fortress. Shock waves rumbled through the ancient edifice, stirring up clouds of snow. Massive sheets of ice cracked open.

An enormous hole opened up right in the middle of the gutted castle, swallowing up tons of snow, ice, and rock. The pilot gulped as he realized that, in theory, Samuel and the rest of the strike team were somewhere below the gigantic avalanche.

The gunner was equally shocked. "What was that?" he blurted.

"Hell if I know," the pilot said. He frantically tried to raise the strike team via their comm links. "Lynx One to Alpha Team, can you read me? Please respond. Repeat, Lynx One to Alpha Team . . ."

No answer came.

The throwing stars were even more destructive than Tanis had boasted. Selene ducked into a narrow passage as an avalanche of snow and ice came crashing down into the dungeon with a thunderous roar. Chunks of masonry as large as boulders slammed into the floor like meteors. She threw a hand up against the wall to steady herself. Tremors shook the floor.

Selene began to fear that she would be buried alive.

Fine, she thought. *Just so long as Marcus and William are, too.*

Her life would be a small price to pay to rid the world of those monsters.

A tremor shook the hidden crypt. Marcus reacted in surprise as a seismic rumbling penetrated the thick stone walls. Dust and gravel rained down from the ceiling.

An earthquake? he wondered, momentarily pausing in his attempts to break free of his prison. No, more like an explosion, taking place somewhere within the forsaken castle. He had no doubt that Selene and her mortal allies were responsible.

The very thought that his father's soldiers now served Selene, just as his father's blood now flowed in her veins, galled him beyond endurance. Had Alexander Corvinus willingly shared his blood with Selene, or had she stolen it from his dying body? Knowing his father, he suspected the former. Were there no ends to which he would not go to thwart his own sons?

He betrayed us with his dying breath.

More rubble fell from the ceiling as the battered structure settled in the wake of the explosion. Had William survived the attack? Marcus was tormented by his inability to take part in the battle raging outside the crypt. *I have to escape this accursed rathole, join with my brother against our enemies!*

His black eyes tracked the falling debris. Bits of gravel splashed into the water in front of the partially submerged door. A thought occurred to him as he recalled the great chunks of granite that had been sent flying when he had slammed Selene into the wall outside the alcove. Was it possible that some of that debris might have fallen across the floor of the portal before Selene had brought the secret door crashing down again? If so, then perhaps the door had not been able to close entirely.

His claws dove beneath the water, probing for a crack along the bottom of the door.

Yes! There it was!

At last, the deafening roar of the avalanche died down enough that Selene could actually hear herself think. Stray stones and chunks of ice clattered down from above, but the worst of the collapse seemed to be over. A cloud of raised powder reduced her visibility as she cautiously ventured out of the relative safety of the tunnel.

An eerie silence, broken only by the occasional falling rock, descended over the dungeons in the wake of the explosions and their cataclysmic aftermath. Selene listened in vain for the growl of an approaching werewolf. Peering up through the snowy haze, she saw that the exit by the ledge had been completely buried beneath a mountain of snow and ice.

She wandered beneath what was left of the bridge. Samuel's body was tangled in the heavy cables hanging underneath the wooden span. His eyes stared blankly into hers. Blood dripped from his mangled throat onto the snow several yards below.

To her slight surprise, she wasn't even remotely tempted by the mortal's blood. Her mouth failed to water at the sight of the crimson fluid. Her fangs remained snugly inside her gums. Corvinus's blood, it seemed, had satisfied her thirst for the time being. She wondered briefly how long it would sustain her.

The snowy whirlwind began to settle, clearing the air before her eyes. High overhead, the dense clouds parted to let the full moon shine through. Selene instinctively noted that the moon was sinking behind the mountains in preparation for the coming dawn. The night was almost over. Soon she would need shelter from the sun.

That shouldn't be a problem, she thought. Looking up at the sky, she saw the helicopter soar above the castle. Even if the chopper didn't come back for her, now that the other Cleaners were dead, there were certainly any number of gloomy catacombs in which she could wait out the day if necessary. *First, though, I need to determine whether William is still on the prowl.*

The silver moonlight filtered down through the icy haze. At last, Selene was able to truly appreciate the vast scope of the dungeons. She found herself standing at the bottom of a cavernous space surrounded on all sides by rubble both new and old. A timeworn set of steps led up to the demolished landings on the upper level. Amazingly, the bridge had remained more or less intact, aside from the snarl of ropy cables hanging beneath the wooden planks. Snow-covered debris was scattered all around her, along with the bodies of both Greenway and Levin. A gaping crater had opened in the floor before her.

Feeling only slightly like a grave robber, she claimed an Uzi and ammo from Levin's body. She locked and loaded, just in case either William or Marcus came after her. She felt bad about leading the Cleaners to their deaths, but, ultimately, that had been more Corvinus's doing than hers. They had merely been fulfilling his final commands. She could only hope that their deaths had not been in vain, that both William and Marcus had been neutralized for good.

The moon's cold radiance crept across the floors of the dungeons, spilling into the shadowy nooks and crannies while falling upon the scattered bodies of the Cleaners. Selene failed to appreciate the significance of this development . . . until she heard the ropes rustling over her head.

What the fuck? She looked up to discover that she was standing directly beneath Samuel's corpse, which abruptly jerked back to life. His eyes peeled open, revealing evil cobalt orbs. Enmeshed within the dangling ropes, he thrashed and squirmed against his bonds. His jaws snapped spastically, revealing elongated canines that were already starting to resemble fangs. The bones and muscles of his face shifted painfully, contorting themselves into a more beastly countenance. His feral eyes locked on her. He hissed like an animal, groping for her with clawlike nails. He twisted himself into a frenzy, doing everything in his power to break free and tear her apart.

Selene remembered the infected peasants in those old woodcuts. Tanis's words echoed in her brain: *"These weren't the lycans we know. . . . These were raging monsters, never able to take human form again."*

Apparently, the historian had not been exaggerating.

Selene knew what she had to do. Steely-eyed, without remorse, she raised the submachine gun and unleashed a fully automatic burst of silver ammo, chewing Samuel to shreds. She kept firing until the revived corpse stopped moving once more. She felt certain that was what the Cleaner would have wanted. His bullet-riddled body slumped limply into the tangled cables.

Once again, there was no time to mourn his death. The bridge creaked loudly, as though someone was running across it. Selene looked up in time to see a blurry form drop down behind her. She spun around to confront the resurrected corpse of Greenway, the young Cleaner who had died upon the bridge. If he recognized her, or remembered how she had saved his life, his crazed animal eyes gave no sign of it.

Like Samuel, the infected Cleaner was caught in the throes of a grotesque and painful transformation. His body was changing in fits and starts, some parts morphing faster than others, so that he presented a horrifying spectacle: part man, part beast, part shambling zombie. His ravaged throat still hung in tatters, despite the claws jutting from his fingertips and the fangs protruding from his gums. Patches of thick black bristles sprouted at random over his face and hands. Foam dribbled down his chin.

Some part of him must have recognized the Uzi in her grip, because he turned and fled instead of attacking her. Selene fired off the last of the submachine gun's ammo, then snatched a fresh rifle from Samuel's corpse.

Greenway ran below the length of the bridge. Selene whipped up the rifle and fired nonstop as she chased after him. The bullets slammed into his back, eventually bringing him down. He collapsed face-first onto the rubble. Selene squeezed a few more rounds into his skull just to make sure he stayed down this time.

A bestial snarl heralded the attack of yet another newborn lycan. Selene recognized Levin, whose body had nearly dropped onto her head before, as he came charging at her from the shadows. She opened fire, but Samuel's gun ran out of ammo almost immediately.

Shit!

Levin's own Uzi still dangled from a strap around his shoulder, but the infected Cleaner ignored his gun, intent on using his fangs and claws instead.

Tossing her empty gun aside, she grabbed on to the lunging lycan and flipped him over her shoulder, so that he landed flat on his back on the ice behind her. A sideways kick to his skull took the fight out of him, but only for a moment. Selene drew her silver-plated hunting knife from its sheath, just as two more lycans appeared on the scene.

She recognized the two Cleaners who had been killed near the water. They were further along in their transformations, looking more like werewolves and less like zombies. Bones cracked loudly as their wolfen snouts pushed outward from their faces. Their shredded black uniforms began to burst at their seams as their inner wolves swelled within them. Low growls emerged from their throats. Foam speckled their lips.

The third lycan, recovering from her kick, scrambled back onto his feet. Selene found herself outnumbered and armed only with a single knife. She could probably bring one of the lycans down by throwing the knife at his skull, but that would leave her completely empty-handed. The lycans circled her warily, slowly closing in on her. Selene twisted from side to side, trying to keep her eyes on all three lycans.

Things weren't looking good. . . .

The helicopter made another pass over the castle. Now that the clouds had blown away from the moon, the pilot could see all the way down into the open pit the ruined fortress had become. He saw the vampire woman, Selene, cornered by three nasty-looking lycans who seemed to be well on their way to transforming completely into werewolves. He couldn't help wondering what had happened to Samuel and the others.

Death Dealer or not, the woman was only moments away from being ripped to pieces by the hungry pack. According to

Samuel, the Old Man had been quite emphatic about doing whatever it took to help the vampire complete her mission.

"What are you waiting for?" he shouted at the gunner. "Shoot 'em."

The gunner peered down the sights of his fifty-caliber machine gun. "I can't!" he yelled back. "Not without taking her out, too! I can't get a shot!"

Damn! the pilot thought. Something fluttered at the corner of his vision, and he looked around to see the American's body bag blowing around the cockpit. His eyes widened as he realized that the unzipped bag was empty.

The gunner spotted the loose bag as well. Both soldiers spun around in their seats to see Michael Corvin, alive and well, standing behind them.

The fugitive doctor no longer looked human. His eyes were pools of molten blackness. His skin shone like silver in the moonlight. Powerful muscles bulged atop his bare chest. Claws jutted from his hands and feet.

"Holy shit!" the gunner gasped. His jaw was practically on the floor.

The pilot knew how he felt.

Ignoring the two humans, Corvin threw open the side door and stared intently down into the exposed dungeon. He growled savagely at the lycans converging on Selene. Without hesitation, he snatched up one of the coiled rappelling ropes piled up inside the copter and hurled himself out of the chopper into the empty air.

He plunged toward the ruined castle, clutching the rappelling line with one hand.

Selene slowly backed into a corner. The three proto-lycans closed in on her. Her eyes shifted from one to another, trying to anticipate which of the beasts would make the first move. As their transformations progressed, it was getting harder and harder to tell them apart. Not that it mattered. Their human identities were no longer relevant. They were nothing but bloodthirsty beasts now.

She waved her silver blade back and forth in front of them. *Come and get me,* she dared them. In her heart, she had always intended to go down fighting against one lycan or another. That was how a Death Dealer died.

The lycan on the right—she thought it used to be Levin—gave away its intentions by peeling his lips back away from his fangs. Tapered ears tilted forward, another sure sign that he was about ready to attack. Selene watched him carefully, while still trying to keep track of the other two lycans. That pair had evolved completely into werewolves by now. The shredded remnants of their uniforms lay discarded upon the snow, replaced by the shaggy black fur covering them from head to toe. Wolfen snouts drooled and snapped at her.

With a hostile growl, the third lycan lunged at her, but Selene was ready for him. She feinted with the silver blade, then punched the monster square in the face, nearly breaking its jaw. The startled lycan yowled in pain, but did not retreat. Blood gushed from its nostrils as it came at her again, even as the other two werewolves joined in for the kill.

This is it, she thought. Even with Alexander Corvinus's blood flowing through her, she doubted that she could fight off three werewolves single-handedly. She would be dead before the sun rose. *Who knows? Perhaps it's better this way.* She had nothing to live for anymore. *Wait for me, Michael. I will be with you soon.*

Then, without warning, an unexpected figure crashed to earth right behind the advancing beasts. Claws extended, he pounced on the werewolf in the rear, slashing away at him before he ripped out the beast's spine with his bare hands. The monster crumpled to the ground in a bloody heap.

That still left two lycans for Selene to deal with. Barely aware of what was happening a few yards away, she ducked beneath Levin's flailing claws and drove her silver knife into her assailant's shoulder. The lycan howled in pain. Smoke rose from where the toxic silver came in contact with his flesh and bone. Taking advantage of his agony and confusion, she slipped behind him and grabbed on to the Uzi dangling from his shoulder. She took aim at the second werewolf and squeezed the trigger. Red-hot silver brought down the advancing beast even as she slashed her knife across Levin's throat. A death rattle escaped his muzzle, and Selene callously shoved the dead body away from her, so that it smacked down onto the floor.

Only then did she look up to see who had come to her rescue. Her stoic expression melted instantly, like an ice castle in the sun.

"Michael?"

She couldn't believe her eyes. It was impossible, and yet there he was, standing before her in all his hybrid glory. She ran forward and smothered him in a tight embrace, all but dissolving him into her arms. Tears of joy streamed down her face. She couldn't remember the last time she had been so happy.

He was alive!

A furious roar shattered the moment. William lunged out of the snowy haze, snapping at them like a rabid dog. Selene dived out of the way of the monster's flashing claws, then watched in astonishment as Michael moved to defend her. One of them growled angrily, but she couldn't tell who.

The original, primal werewolf confronted his hybrid nephew. William reared back on his hind legs and slashed out at Michael's throat. Michael grabbed William's arm in midswing, and the two combatants went spinning across the floor, locked in a battle to the death. They slammed into the ancient stone staircase, which crumbled beneath the impact. Centuries-old steps broke apart in a matter of seconds.

Michael and William barely noticed. They grappled with each other like wolves competing for control of the pack. In a sense, William was the established alpha wolf, confident in his power and dominance, while Michael was the upstart challenger only recently come into his full strength. The past battled the future . . . with the safety of the entire world at stake.

In the flooded crypt, Marcus could hear the battles raging outside. His claws were thrust deeply into the freezing water as they dug into the narrow crack left behind when the hidden door had closed on top of the granite debris. His wings flapped impatiently as, grunting in exertion, he strained with all his might to lift the door back open. He cursed Selene's name with every breath.

William needed him! He could not tarry here any longer. Slowly, the door began to give way.

Chapter Twenty-four

*A*voiding the stairs, Selene sprang up onto the second level and sprinted over to the bridge. As she'd hoped, Greenway's gun was still lying on the wooden planks, not far from where he had died the first time. She ran out onto the bridge and scooped up the gun. *Please let it still have some ammo in it,* she prayed. *We're going to need plenty of fire-power before this is over.*

She was in luck. Not only was the Uzi not empty, but it was loaded with ultraviolet rounds. Not quite as good as silver nitrate when it came to killing werewolves, but beggars couldn't be choosers. She hefted the weapon and took aim at William, being careful not to catch Michael in her sights. She waited for her shot, then fired down at William from the bridge.

Blam! William took a hit to his chest. A bloody wound blossomed beneath his snowy pelt. He roared furiously, and Selene squeezed hard on the trigger. Michael wisely backed off as she blasted away at the freakish albino werewolf.

Die already! she thought. *Why don't you just die?*

A thumping noise came from above. Selene looked up to see the Lynx helicopter hovering over the breach. She remembered the gunner posted aboard the chopper and realized that this was their chance to exterminate William once and for all. "Stand clear!" she shouted to Michael, hoping that she and the helicopter crew were on the same wavelength. "Get back!"

The airborne Cleaners came through for them. With Michael and Selene both safely clear of the frothing werewolf, the gunship opened fire on William with its heavy artillery. Fifty-caliber shells strafed the ruins as they zeroed in on the monstrous lycanthrope.

Selene glanced nervously up at the sky, which was starting to lighten. Dawn was not far away, but she wasn't ready to panic just yet. With the advent of the helicopter, the battle seemed to be turning in their favor. She had every reason to hope that it was William who would be dead by sunrise.

Unless something went terribly wrong.

Marcus came rushing out into the open dungeon. Water dripped from his wings and satin trousers. The battered overcoat had been left behind in the deserted crypt. He no longer felt any need to conceal his hybrid nature.

He glared up at the helicopter attacking his brother. Although he had never laid eyes on such a craft before, the blood memories of Kraven and his other victims allowed him to recognize the threat posed by the armed chopper. He looked around for a weapon he could use against the gunship and its arrogant mortal crew, and his gaze fell upon the rappelling line still dangling from the copter. His black eyes narrowed in thought.

Aboard the Lynx, the gunner kept firing at the huge white beast below.

"Keep it up!" the pilot urged him. He recognized the albino monster from their mission briefing; that had to be the infamous William. He wondered what had become of the werewolf's hybrid brother. Marcus was the one who had attacked the *Sancta Helena* and killed Macaro and the others. The pilot wouldn't be happy until they had nailed the renegade Elder as well. *That's the bastard I really want,* he thought vengefully.

Suddenly, the chopper rocked violently. "What the hell?" the pilot blurted. He fought with the controls, trying to stabilize their flight. He worked the pedals and pulled back on the stick, while frantically scanning the monitors on the control panel. All systems were in order, so why did it feel as if they were being tossed around by a hurricane?

"What's happening?" the gunner hollered at him.

"You tell me!"

Down on the ground, Marcus held on to the rappelling line with both fists. He gritted his fangs as he physically dragged the copter down toward the gutted castle. Struggling against the lift generated by the chopper's spinning blades, he laboriously pulled on the cable, hand over fist, in a frightening display of superhuman strength.

Marcus knew he had his new hybrid nature to thank for the power he now possessed. Even as an Elder, and the primordial ancestor of the entire vampire race, he doubted that he could ever have performed such a feat before. Could Viktor have pulled down a military helicopter with his bare hands?

I think not, he thought smugly.

Already he had succeeded in disrupting the gunship's presumptuous assault upon his brother. The foolish mortals aboard the aircraft could hardly aim their weapons while being yanked out of the sky, but that was just the beginning. He wasn't finished with the copter yet.

The sky belongs to those with wings, he mused. It was time to teach this noisy, graceless vessel the folly of defying that obvious truism. *Down you come!*

The captured line snapped taut against the side of the bridge. Marcus gave the rope another tug and the Lynx crashed through the breach in the ground floor of the castle. Sparks ignited, and shards of broken debris turned into deadly shrapnel as the spinning rotor blades were sheared in half by the jagged stone edges of the gap.

The bridge was right below it.

Upon the bridge, Selene looked up in horror, barely able to believe what she was seeing. The Lynx was coming down straight at her!

She somersaulted out of the way with only a second to spare. The plunging helicopter crashed to a stop only a few inches away from her, caught upon one of the sturdy stone ledges supporting the bridge. Scrambling to her feet, she gaped in amazement at the mangled wreckage of the copter right before her eyes. Blood painted the inside of the windshield red, and she severely doubted that either the pilot or the gunner had survived the earthshaking crash. To her surprise, however, she saw that the turboshaft engine had somehow remained intact, so that the truncated rotor blades continued to spin like mad, tearing up the wormy timber planks nearest the crash site. Selene backed away warily as slivers of shredded wood went flying like dozens of miniature wooden stakes.

I don't understand, she thought, shaking her head in confusion. One minute the gunship had been leading the fight against William; the next, it had come plummeting out of the sky like a piece of space debris. *How could this happen?*

The answer came winging out of the night. Marcus swooped down and rammed her with his fists. The blow knocked the breath from her and sent the carbine rifle clattering onto what remained of the bridge.

The Elder didn't give her a second to catch her breath. Grabbing her arm, his sharpened claws digging into her flesh even through the skintight leather, he hurled her across the length of the bridge. She staggered backward upon the creaking wooden planks, coming perilously close to the spinning blades. The wash from the blades blew against her back and caused her dark hair to whip about wildly.

Marcus was in the hybrid form she recognized from their previous battles. She glared at him in disgust. Where she found Michael's hybrid guise strangely attractive, the Elder's batlike countenance was nothing but repulsive. He advanced toward her, forcing her back toward the spinning blades. Greenway's rifle lay on the bridge between them, frustratingly out of reach. There was no way she could go for the rifle and its lethal UV cartridges, not without Marcus descending on her first.

Michael! she thought desperately. Although she wasn't sure how he had done so, she knew that the demented Elder must have brought the helicopter down. His unwanted return filled her with dread. She was terrified that Marcus would murder Michael all over again. *Watch out! He's free!*

Down on the floor, Michael and William had resumed their epic clash. Michael wasn't entirely sure what had happened to the gunship, and at the moment he was too busy to care. Instinct had taken over and all that mattered was the enemy right in front of him. A bloodred haze descended over his

270

vision as he fought tooth and nail against the fearsome werewolf. William's claws raked his skin, digging deep gouges in his flesh, but the pain only increased the atavistic fury raging inside him. He gave as good as he got, ripping into the leathery hide beneath the werewolf's furry coat with his own bloody talons. His Hippocratic oath had vanished completely from his fevered brain. He wasn't a doctor right now. He was a killer.

William had the weight advantage, though, which he pressed by knocking Michael onto his back. The werewolf pounced on top of Michael, pinning him to the floor as his jaws zoomed in on the younger monster's throat.

Michael saw William's fangs coming at him. For a split second, he flashed back to Lucian taking a bite out of him a few nights ago. That was when his life had changed irrevocably, beginning the process that had turned him into this unnatural thing he had become. Now, it seemed, William intended to destroy what Lucian had created.

Like hell! Michael thought. His anger over what had been done to him boiled over, fueling his determination to stay alive. He had already lost his humanity. He wasn't about to lose his life, too. And his future with Selene.

He tucked his chin in to protect his throat. With an explosive movement powered by sheer determination, he rotated sharply to the right, throwing William off him. Before the werewolf could regain his footing, Michael leaped on top of him. He stared furiously into the monster's scarlet eyes, seeing in William's bestial face Lucian, Kraven, Viktor, Marcus, and every other heartless monster that had brutalized him and Selene over the past few nights. He pounded the werewolf's snout with his fists, taking out his fury on the subhuman creature beneath him

No more! he raged. *I'm ending this . . . now!*

Sinking his claws into William's muzzle, he ripped off the werewolf's snout.

"No!" Marcus reacted in shock. He turned to go to his brother's defense, and Selene saw her opportunity. She surged forward and drove her fingers into his throat, then followed up with a vicious knee to his groin. He dropped to his knees, doubled over in pain, just in time to see Michael tear out William's snout.

Blood spouted like a fountain from the werewolf's ruined face. He clutched at mangled flesh with his huge misshapen paws, but there was no recovering from such a wound. He tried to roar, but all that emerged from his gaping maw was a wet gurgle. He toppled over onto the snow and debris. His arms and limbs twitched convulsively as he drowned in his own blood. Finally, he fell still and silent.

After sixteen centuries, William, the father of all werewolves, was dead.

An anguished cry erupted from his brother's throat. The sight of William's death threw Marcus into a murderous rage that easily overcame the pain Selene had just inflicted on him. He sprang to his feet like a demon freshly released from hell. He attacked Selene with renewed fury, forcing her back toward the whirring helicopter blades until they were right behind her shoulders. She fought back as best she could, parrying his blows with every last bit of strength she could extract from his father's blood, but quickly found herself on the defensive. His right hand closed about her throat, drawing blood with his claws, and she gasped for breath. His hybrid flesh felt slick and clammy against her skin, even as he crushed her windpipe with killing force. The spinning blades roared in her ears.

"I knew Viktor made a mistake keeping you as a pet!" he

ranted. Even his voice sounded different in its hybrid form. Harsh and guttural as opposed to cultured and urbane. "He should have killed you with the rest of your family!"

His words stung like sunlight, reopening old wounds, but she was determined not to let her pain show. She faced the mutated Elder with the same icy mask she had presented to the world for more than six hundred years, until Michael had come along. Marcus was hardly the only soul ever to lose a loved one. . . .

Using everything she had, she pried his hand from her throat and thrust it up toward the blades spinning behind her.

Thwack-thwack! Marcus's hand was removed in the blink of an eye. He screamed in torment, blood spurting from his severed wrist, and his fearsome wings unfurled behind him. The right wing struck like lightning, spearing her right through the chest.

She gasped out loud. The shock and pain were even worse than when he had stabbed her hand and hip back at the pier. Letting go of the Elder's arm, she clutched at the deadly talon with both hands. She tried to tug it loose, give her body a chance to heal, but the wing was too strong. The talon refused to budge. Marcus gave the claw a sadistic twist, forcing another gasp from her lips. She felt her life force ebbing away, beyond even the power of Corvinus's blood to keep her alive.

A thin smile came to the hybrid's hideous face. He may have lost a hand, but Selene was only moments away from losing her life, along with everything she had fought for these past few nights. He drew back his second wing, preparing to impale her with the other talon.

No! Selene thought. She wasn't going to die tonight. For the first time in ages, she had too much to live for. Digging deep, she twisted the talon with all her strength. The rigid claw scraped against bone, and she let out an ear-piercing scream, but at last the talon snapped off at the knuckle and she yanked it out of her bleeding chest. The searing pain eased just a little.

"Bitch!" Marcus snarled. He grabbed her throat with his remaining hand and squeezed even harder than before.

Selene drove his own broken talon up through his throat and out the top of his skull. He stared at her with absolute shock, his black eyes filling with blood, before she spun him around and shoved him into the spinning helicopter blades. His body came apart, wings and all, in a tornado of blood and carnage that chopped him up and scattered the pieces all over. Selene scrambled backward to avoid being sprayed with hybrid gore.

Sparks flew from the rotor assembly, and the blades finally slammed to a stop. The clipped steel blades were now slick with blood. The remains of Marcus, the last of the Elders, were splattered all over the dungeon. Selene wiped a single smear of blood from her face.

Now she had killed two Elders.

The morning sun began to glide over the Carpathians, shafts of daylight slowly penetrating the breach in the dungeon. Selene heard footsteps upon the stairs and knew it had to be Michael. As far as she knew, they were the only people left alive in the castle. He emerged from an archway and stepped out onto the bridge behind her. She could tell by his scent, which was now almost as familiar to her as her own, that he had shifted back into his human form. He gasped out loud, stunned by what he now saw.

Frozen in place, almost afraid to move, she stared in wonder at the sight of her own hand lying directly in a sunbeam, completely unharmed. The morning's radiance warmed her chilled flesh, nothing more.

"Selene!" he said softly. Awe filled his voice.

She turned toward him slowly, her brown eyes filled with emotion. Holding her breath, she stepped entirely into the sunlight, exposing her entire body to the golden rays.

Nothing happened. She was completely immune.

Corvinus's blood, she recalled. She recalled the transcendent look on the old man's dying face, as well as his answer when she had nervously asked him what she would become.

"The Future."

Michael joined her in the daylight. She knew she didn't have to explain how much this meant to her. He was obviously just as moved as she was. They kissed passionately, the kiss evolving into an immortal embrace that seemed to last forever.

Together, side by side, they watched the most glorious sunrise she could ever imagine. Her moist eyes reflected the first light of a whole new day. Selene felt as though her old life, which had come to a brutal end one night in a blood-splattered barn, had finally been restored to her.

She still had questions, of course. The unknown was now her new reality, for she did not fully comprehend what she had become. The future would bring many new mysteries, maybe even new dangers and fears, but the first step, the first new day, had arrived at last.

Six hundred summers, she reflected. *Six hundred snowy winters. Thirty-five generations of mortal humanity. And finally, again . . . the sun.*

About the Author

GREG COX is the *New York Times* best-selling author of numerous novels and nonfiction works. He wrote the novelization of the first *Underworld* movie, as well as an original prequel titled *Underworld: Blood Enemy*. He also coedited two anthologies of science fiction vampire and werewolf stories, titled *Tomorrow Sucks* and *Tomorrow Bites*.

In addition, he has written books and short stories based on such popular series as *Alias, Batman, Buffy the Vampire Slayer, Daredevil, Fantastic Four, Farscape, Iron Man, Roswell, Star Trek, Xena,* and *X-Men*. His official website can be found at www.gregcox-author.com.

He lives in Oxford, Pennsylvania.